BEFORE
SHE WAS MINE

Praise for *Aurora*

"McGeown debuts with an emotional, character-driven take on the soapy romance trope of amnesia…McGeown's off to a strong start."—*Publishers Weekly*

"I don't know what it is about the amnesia trope, but I can always get into it no matter how cheesy it is. Only this one wasn't silly at all. It was very realistic and completely convincing…Overall, this was a very emotional story worthy of your time. Read this when you are feeling like you need something that that will make your heart ache."—*Bookvark*

"A very good debut by a promising author. I'm looking forward to reading her next book."—*LezReviewBooks*

By the Author

Aurora

Sugar Girl

Before She Was Mine

Visit us at www.boldstrokesbooks.com

BEFORE
SHE WAS MINE

by

Emma L McGeown

2023

BEFORE SHE WAS MINE
© 2023 By Emma L McGeown. All Rights Reserved.

ISBN 13: 978-1-63679-315-3

This Trade Paperback Original Is Published By
Bold Strokes Books, Inc.
P.O. Box 249
Valley Falls, NY 12185

First Edition: February 2023

CREDITS
EDITOR: BARBARA ANN WRIGHT
PRODUCTION DESIGN: STACIA SEAMAN
COVER DESIGN BY TAMMY SEIDICK

Acknowledgments

To my family and friends, thank you for your support over the years. Thank you to my editor, Barbara Ann Wright, for the continuous guidance. To my wife, Laura, thank you for always supporting me and my love for writing. You make every day better. Avery, keep being the best daughter in the world, but maybe let us sleep a little. If you don't mind. Welcome to the family, Rua, already family member of the month.

CHAPTER ONE

Dani Raye

I didn't usually have road rage. In fact, I had been referred to as quite a calm driver. I didn't get wound up about being stuck behind pensioner drivers, and I didn't even waste time with shortcuts to avoid long lines at traffic lights. That always seemed too tedious a thing to waste mental energy on. I relished the red light. It gave me time to take a breather, people watch, or just stare out into oblivion.

But not today.

My hands couldn't sit still. I tapped my thighs and the dashboard and fiddled with the radio. The red light had been taunting me for what seemed like an eternity. I wouldn't have minded so much if it weren't for its close proximity to Jonah's primary school. The light was my last hurdle before the finish line to meet with the school principal. I hated being late, especially when it came to anything involving my son.

He was in Primary Two, barely six, and already getting into fights.

We really picked a winner with his donor.

But that was one of the perks of using a donor. Any of Jonah's undesirable characteristics could quickly be blamed on the anonymous gene pool. It also meant I could blame my ex-wife a little too, considering she'd insisted on that donor. Though I had to say, Jonah was pretty flawless. That was why the phone call this afternoon was so out of the blue. I had to get the receptionist to confirm twice that the squabble in question involved Jonah Raye-Lewis, but with a name like that, it was hard to get him mixed up with anyone else.

My ex-wife, Catriona Lewis, had insisted on the double-barrelled surname, even though I thought it would be too much of a mouthful. It was just a shame that so many people assumed Raye was his middle name and absentmindedly dropped it. I wished I'd fought harder for Lewis-Raye, but the time for that argument had long passed. Along with everything else we could have possibly argued about. Back when we were still trying to make our marriage work. Catriona and I worked much better as co-parents, and our relationship had truly blossomed when we were no longer obligated to live together. Or sleep together, for that matter.

After I'd received the call from the principal, I'd called Catriona to see if she could collect him from school. She worked on this side of town and was supposed to have him after school today, but she had back-to-back patients.

When the light turned from red to amber, I was already accelerating. The green light was a distant memory as I sped through the front gates of Hillside Primary School. I'd barely pulled the hand brake before I was abandoning my car.

Once through the main doors, I could hear children singing from the assembly hall down the corridor. I tried to keep my voice low as I spoke to the person on reception. There wasn't time to catch my breath before she was pointing to the door on the left where the principal would be waiting. Impatiently, no doubt. After all, I was almost fifteen minutes late.

I rapped on the door and heard him ring out for me to enter. Mr. Simmons stood from behind his desk and waved at an empty seat beside another woman. Mr. Simmons was tall, lean, and had a stern expression. I'd never really gelled well with this pasty older man, but after Jonah had enrolled, I'd assumed our dealings would be minimal. Wishful thinking.

Mr. Simmons sat back down and straightened his tie once I'd taken a seat. I glanced at the woman next to me. She looked young, very young, actually, maybe in her early twenties. However, it was hard to find her figure underneath an oversized coat that seemed out of place on a mild day like today. It also aged her way beyond her youthful looks. The designer handbag on her lap, which she clutched nervously, also seemed like something my mother would use. Her odd ensemble made me a little curious about who she was. When she caught my eye, she offered a slight smile, but it was fleeting. I barely saw her eyes before she lowered them to the floor again. Her light brown fringe fell forward, covering most of her face.

Mr. Simmons pulled my eyes up front. "Thank you for joining us, Mrs. Raye."

"It's Ms., but please call me Dani."

My correction seemed to fluster him before he cleared his throat. "Dani," he said uncomfortably, making me chuckle inside. He was clearly very old-school in his approach, but considering that Mrs. Raye was my mother's title, I didn't feel comfortable being addressed as such. He gestured to the woman next to me. "This is Mrs. Lucy Matthews. Ryan's mother."

I turned to her to shake her hand or wave or offer any form of introduction, but she barely looked up. It would have seemed rude if I couldn't see just how terrified she was. As if she was the one in trouble and not our children.

"Oh, you're Ryan's mum?" I tried to get some form of engagement. "Jonah talks about him all the time." I was surprised Ryan was the other boy in the fight. I'd thought they were best friends the way Jonah talked about him.

"It would seem the boys got into an argument over football," Mr. Simmons interjected, pulling my eyes away from the shell of a woman. "The teacher on yard duty at lunchtime said she saw Ryan push Jonah."

Lucy sighed in what could only be described as desperation,

something that seemed like an overreaction, but perhaps there was more I didn't know.

"Jonah pushed him back, and there was some back and forth between them until the teacher could break it up."

I waited for him to add more details, but nothing followed. In fact, he finished with a dramatic pause as he looked between us disappointedly. Though I was left feeling considerably underwhelmed.

"Wait, let me get this straight," I said, leaning forward in my chair. "I left a meeting because two friends pushed each other?"

Mr. Simmons gasped in horror. He looked positively offended that I could make light of something so clearly serious. "We do not tolerate violence on school property."

"Violence?" I repeated, baffled.

"Yes." His face red grew, and he was practically flapping his arms in alarm, resulting in me giving up and leaning back in surrender, too annoyed at the overreaction to come up with an argument. He started a lecture on the parameters of violence, but I tuned him out.

I shook my head in confusion and looked to Lucy for support. I half expected to find her just as flabbergasted, but she looked devastated and embarrassed. "Please accept my apologies, Mr. Simmons, I just don't know what's gotten into Ryan." She rubbed her forehead tiredly, and I couldn't help but notice there was no wedding band.

"It seems there is a bit of a pattern here, Mrs. Matthews." He turned to her accusingly, and I looked between the two, feeling as if I was watching a tennis match. "This is the second fight your son has been involved in. We do not tolerate violent tendencies."

I would have loved to know what the other fight looked like, but this wasn't the time. She nodded frantically, her glassy eyes, on the verge of tears.

"I don't know what is going on at home, but Ryan cannot be taking it out on innocent pupils." There was an authoritarian edge to his tone, coupled with an angry brow that was borderline over-the-top. As if it was somehow Lucy's fault that her son was supposedly acting out. Though even referring to a push as acting out seemed like an overexaggeration.

"I'm sorry, Mr. Simmons, I will talk with him and explain—"

"See to it that you do." He stared down at her despite them being on the same level. "One more incident like this and we will have to discuss Ryan's place at this school."

I wanted to intervene. His tone and accusing features were nothing short of bullying. Lucy was young and perhaps intimidated by an older man on what appeared to be some kind of strange power trip. It wasn't my place. I didn't know all the facts, and even though I didn't like his tone, there was no reason for me to be someone's saviour. Reluctantly, I bit my tongue.

He rose and looked between us one more time. "I will go get your sons. As per school policy, they are suspended for the rest of the day."

I bit my tongue even harder to stop myself from voicing my frustrations. I was still shaking my head in bewilderment at the dramatics. I got my phone from my blazer pocket and composed an email to my boss, Harry, informing him that I would be working from home the rest of the afternoon. And all over a bit of pushing. I was about to voice as much to Lucy when I spotted her defeated posture. She was bent forward in the chair, her elbows resting on her knees, and her head buried in her hands.

"Hey, don't worry about it," I said.

"My son started a fight with yours," she said in a voice that sounded fragile, as though she was suppressing tears. "Aren't you annoyed at me?"

"Hell no. Jonah is an only child. He probably deserved it."

My response seemed to break through her troubled state. She shifted in her chair. "Ryan is too." Her tone already seemed lighter, and I finally saw her face. Her green eyes stood out behind that heavy fringe, but when I looked a little closer, I realised they were almost yellow around the edges, large eyes that searched my face and were not unlike a cat's and framed perfectly by dark eyebrows. She had light freckles on her cheeks, but by the makeup, it was clearly something she tried to hide. "I'm Lucy, and I'm a Ms. too, but I was too nervous to say anything before." She extended her hand. "I know he already introduced us but…"

"Dani." I took her soft hand and noticed it was a little on the cold side. Most likely due to her nerves and slight frame. She seemed to hold my hand for just a second longer than necessary, and my gaydar pinged in anticipation. She let go soon after, though, making me doubt those alarm bells. They'd been wrong in the past.

"Ryan talks about Jonah a lot too." She scooped some hair behind her ear. "I just don't understand why he would have pushed him."

"Ah, it was probably over nothing. You know what kids are like."

"I guess, it's just…Ryan has been acting up a little—" She stopped herself hesitantly, perhaps realising I was a perfect stranger. "Never mind." She stood and lifted her bag over her shoulder. "I shouldn't be keeping you. I'm sure you have work."

"Not anymore," I said teasingly. "I've had to cancel my meetings."

"I'm sorry."

"Don't be. Just means I get to spend the afternoon with Jonah."

She looked in my eyes, and something within me tweaked. I couldn't understand what it was, but something about Lucy Matthews intrigued me. There was a sadness to her that told me something was tearing her apart inside. I could have been wrong, but my gut instinct persuaded me to take a leap of faith in the hope that I could help.

"Why don't you and Ryan come back to our house?" She looked surprised. To be honest, I was too. "It would be a good excuse for Ryan and Jonah to make up. Besides, I think I'm glamourising the idea of being stuck in the house all day with him."

She laughed wholeheartedly, and her smile seemed to light up the whole room. It was infectious, and though it was fleeting, I was unable to look away.

"Yeah, it always sounds more fun than it is." She thought for a moment. "Are you sure you don't mind us coming over?" I shook my head, causing her smile to return. "Thank you. Do you live far?"

"No, not at all. Just off Ormeau Road."

"Okay," she agreed as the principal's door reopened.

Mr. Simmons stepped to the side as Jonah ran to me. He launched into me with a thud. It would bruise tomorrow, but he looked so relieved to see me. Every hair on his head was in place, not a scratch in sight.

Ryan moved to Lucy, and I could see her whispering to him in disapproval.

"I'm sorry, Mum," Jonah said. His dark curls fell to his shoulders as his blue eyes met mine. I didn't have blue eyes, so I could only assume they were a gift from his donor. He readjusted the little backpack uncomfortably, and I relieved him of it, slinging it over my shoulder.

"We'll talk about it in the car," I whispered before looking back at the principal. "Thank you, Mr. Simmons."

Jonah's hand found mine. I waited for a moment when we emerged outside. I gave Lucy my address and phone number in case she got lost on the way over. While she and I were speaking, Jonah's body language toward Ryan seemed quite hostile. He had his back turned and seemed to be inching closer to our car and as far away from Lucy and Ryan as possible. I waited until we made it into the car to find out the details.

I'd barely put my seatbelt on when Jonah snapped at me from the back seat. "Why is *he* coming over?"

"Never mind that. What was this fight over?" I asked sternly. "I thought you and Ryan were friends."

"We used to be," he said angrily. "And then he just went crazy at me when it was time for me to score. He didn't want to be the goalie, but it was my turn."

"And you didn't say anything that might have upset him?"

"No, Mum, I swear. Ryan just got really mad for no reason."

I nodded before regret seeped in, making me question the invitation. Perhaps Ryan wasn't the kind of boy I wanted Jonah to be around. Next, they'd be selling cigarettes on the side of the train tracks. It was a joke, but I was still dubious of this Ryan kid. What did I really know about him or his mother?

"I don't want to be friends with him anymore."

"Okay, love. I understand, but you know, you can't just push people when you don't like them."

"But he pushed me first," he said in outrage.

"Okay. I know he pushed you first, but his mummy is going to be telling him off for that." That seemed to ease him somewhat. "Friends fight, and then they make up again. It can make you even better friends sometimes. But if you decide you don't want to be around Ryan anymore, then that's okay too." I paused as he seemed to be contemplating what I'd said. "You used to be friends, and maybe Ryan is just having a hard time right now."

"Maybe," he said softly as silence fell over us. "He was crying a few days ago."

"What about?"

"He thinks his mummy and daddy are gonna break up."

"Why?"

"Because his daddy sleeps in the guest room, and they fight all the time."

I used that information to piece together a story in my mind. That would explain why Lucy didn't feel comfortable sharing in the principal's office. Her despair and the way she was on the verge of tears when the principal pointed out Ryan's behaviour was turning into a pattern. Part of me was glad I'd trusted my gut in inviting Lucy over. Perhaps my impartiality might help her come to terms with the end of her relationship. After all, I'd been there myself. Maybe I could help.

Or maybe it would be a complete disaster.

CHAPTER TWO

Dani Raye

As soon as I opened the front door, Jonah raced into the house and upstairs to his room. His assignment was to clean his room while I made a beeline for the kitchen. The house wasn't a complete mess, but with Jonah having stayed over for the last few days, I'd let the chores build up a little. Jonah would be going to stay the next couple of nights at Catriona's, so I was planning on cleaning more thoroughly then. Now I wished I'd gotten up off my ass last night instead of binge-watching *The Office*. Again.

Anything resembling a dirty dish or cup was thrown into the dishwasher. The clothes that had been hanging on the clotheshorse for several days were scooped up and thrown into the back room. I stuffed some of Jonah's toys into the back room as well, along with garden equipment and the pile of reusable shopping bags that had been living on my kitchen table for some time now. The door to the back room, where junk was destined to live forever, was slammed shut.

The doorbell rang.

I could feel my heartrate accelerating as I quickly swiped the kitchen countertops one last time. It wasn't pristine, but it would have to do. I never normally cared too much about the state of the house, but this was someone new. I knew very little about Lucy, and I was surprised to find myself caring about what she thought.

I avoided the other mums at school for this very reason.

Given that Hillside Primary School was part-private, it

attracted an air of privilege. It was the main drawback for me, but of course, Catriona had strong-armed me into it. The school itself was great, aside from its definition of what a fight actually looked like. The snootiness was what really irritated me. Especially when it came to the stay-at-home mums and their expectations. I always seemed to fall short in that department, or at least, that was how it felt. I was confident enough in myself to know I was a good mum, but I worked a full-time job with long hours. That always seemed to be "less than" when it came to the other mums. My store-bought baked goods were never good enough when it came to the bake sale, and my inability to volunteer on school trips because of work seemed like a cop-out to them. Perhaps they relied more heavily on their husbands' or partners' income, but Hillside was not cheap. Neither Catriona nor myself could afford its fees alone.

A part of me worried about what Lucy might think of my semidetached home. Her designer handbag touted that she came from money. I was also cynical as to what she and I might have in common. It didn't look like she had come from the office, and I feared she was just like the other intense stay-at-home mums at Hillside. Not to mention, there was definitely a bit of an age gap, maybe as much as ten years, so what would we even have to talk about?

I didn't really have the time to get bogged down about it because I was already at the front door, with Lucy and Ryan waiting on the other side. Jonah came bounding down the stairs but stopped a few steps from the bottom. Perhaps the elevation gave him more control on this forced playdate I'd landed us in.

"Hi, did you find the place okay?" I said, welcoming them into the hallway.

"Yes, thank you." Lucy smiled brightly as she ushered Ryan in first.

Standing face-to-face with her revealed she was just a little shorter than me, but I was thrilled to see she'd ditched her designer coat and posh handbag in the car. Her slender arms were exposed, and I was certainly very surprised to spot a tattoo on her forearm. It was really pretty, but I knew better than to ask about it, given how some people could be private about tattoos. She wore a fitted stripey T-shirt with a pair of low-rise jeans. How very '90s. Then again, perhaps that just showed my age as an outdated older millennial still clinging to my skinny jeans.

"Ryan," Lucy's tone dropped as she nudged her son in Jonah's direction. "Is there something you'd like to say to Jonah?"

Ryan's head was dipped as he took a brave step. It appeared that Lucy had reprimanded him on the car ride over. Jonah watched Ryan apprehensively and glanced at me for help. I tried to offer my best "be nice" face in return, and that seemed to encourage Jonah to take the three final steps downstairs.

"I'm sorry I pushed you," Ryan said in a small voice.

I saw the remorse written across his face, and my gut instinct told me Ryan wasn't a bully or a bad kid. He was a little taller than Jonah with short, light brown hair. It matched Lucy's hair colour, and his green eyes resembled hers, but that was where the similarities ended. While Lucy was pale, Ryan had a sun-kissed glow to make any sun worshipper jealous.

When Jonah rudely said nothing in return, I interjected. "Jonah?"

"Sorry," he said, but it wasn't as heartfelt. I grimaced at his disingenuous apology and caught Lucy offering a smile.

"Is everyone friends again?" Lucy asked them both.

"Yes," they returned in unison, but it couldn't have been any less enthusiastic.

"All right, no more fighting, then." Both boys nodded, and the atmosphere in the hallway seemed to lift. "Okay, off you go and play in the living room," I said as Jonah gestured for Ryan to follow him down the hallway ahead of us.

Then it was just me and Lucy.

"You have a beautiful home," she said politely but tensely folded her arms.

If my therapist ex-wife were there, she would have

immediately picked up on Lucy's awkwardness and closed off body language. It was a trait of Catriona's that I had never been fond of, her inability to switch off the constant analysing of body language. Though, after the years we were together, I found myself unable to miss body language cues.

"Thank you. Do you want tea or coffee?" I asked as I led her toward the kitchen.

"Coffee, please."

As we passed the living room, we lingered in the doorway and spotted the boys on the couch, huddled around an iPad.

"Sorry, I should have hidden that," I said to Lucy, preempting her judgement. I tried to limit Jonah's screen time, but sometimes, I needed a break too. I understood that I should have been better. Perhaps more engaged in arts and crafts and outdoor activities, and in my defence, at the weekends, we were very good at limiting screen time. But during the week, it was just easier. Not that I could admit that to another mum. I was sure that Lucy disapproved, but she ended up voicing something I wasn't brave enough to say:

"Oh, don't worry, I'm sure it was Ryan who suggested it." She shook her head in amusement as her bangs danced along her forehead. "It doesn't matter where I hide our tablet, he just seems to sniff it out."

"Really?" She nodded knowingly. "Oh, I'm so relieved. Jonah is the exact same."

"Yeah, but I'm sure Jonah didn't rack up one hundred and fifty pounds in credit card charges."

"No!" I spun to face her as we reached the kitchen island.

Her eyes widened in amazement, likely mirroring my expression. "I could have killed him. He was playing *Candy Crush* or one of those games and just kept on levelling up." I couldn't contain my laughter as she went on with wild hand gestures. "I was thinking, he must be some kind of *Candy Crush* prodigy, and it turns out, he was buying his way to the top."

"Fake it until you make it."

"He must get that from his dad," she joked, but I picked up on the sour expression that passed over her features. She hid it quickly, though, and it made me think back on what Jonah had said in the car about them separating, but I didn't have the courage to bring it up. It felt insensitive. "We had to remove all credit card details from the tablet just to protect our finances. Kids." She shrugged before glancing around the kitchen.

Her eyes seemed to light up, perhaps approving of my decorating skills; at least, that was what I told myself. I popped on the kettle and leaned against the countertop, glancing around the modern space myself.

Catriona and I had bought the house together before Jonah was born. It was a little rough around the edges, but the house was located in a very sought-after area that we loved. In terms of house prices, South Belfast was wide-ranging. One street could be affordable, and then, across the road, prices could be through the roof.

The only reason we could afford this house on Parkview was because it was neglected. An old woman had lived in the house for years, and she'd let it go to shit. She'd passed away, and it was her son who'd sold it. Catriona and I had put a bid in before we'd even finished the tour. There was so much character with its original fixtures still present. I couldn't bring myself to gut all of its originality, though I did make sure to put in an entirely new kitchen.

Looking back, it had taken almost a year to get the house renovated and up to code. My entire pregnancy, we were focused on getting the house ready. It was the perfect distraction from all our problems. We didn't get two good years here until the cracks in our marriage had become inescapable. We'd tried to stick it out and work through our problems, but it was useless. Soon after, Catriona had left me. Jonah was just a toddler. I'd now been in the house longer alone than I was married.

The pop of the kettle pulled me out of my daze and back to preparing the hot drinks. "Was it coffee or tea?" I asked over my shoulder.

"Coffee, please, with some milk," she replied, and I went about making the coffee. "What a back garden," she said in awe. When I glanced back around, she was seated at the kitchen island, staring out the floor-to-ceiling windows.

"I know. It was the main selling point for me."

"I bet. I didn't think houses around here had that kind of outdoor space."

"They don't," I said as she reached across the island and took the coffee from me. "We're on a corner, so for some reason, it stretches out a little farther. In the summer, we spent most of our evenings out there."

"I'd say it would be lovely and romantic." She smiled, cupping the mug in her hands. "What does your partner do?"

It was clear she'd mistaken the *we* in my sentence to mean me and a partner. "Oh, I'm not seeing anyone. It's just me and Jonah." I smiled, and she seemed to take a beat. I couldn't tell if she was awkward or just embarrassed, and I found myself elaborating. "Well, half the time. I share custody with my ex-wife."

"Oh."

I could practically see the cogs turning in her head at the word. "Two mummies" seemed to cause some people to slow up momentarily. It wasn't usually in a negative way. In fact, they didn't seem to realise that their facial expressions had shifted to bewilderment. It was as if they were trying to figure out a mathematical problem. It would have been comical if it didn't normally annoy the shit out of me, but I was pleased to see Lucy's bewilderment pass quickly. In fact, it transitioned into a knowing smirk. As if a light bulb had just gone off in her head, and then, she started laughing. It was definitely not the usual reaction.

"I knew we'd never met before," she said euphorically and

proceeded to palm her forehead. I could feel my face scrunching up, and it only made Lucy laugh even more. "I'm a stupid dumbass."

"What are you on about?"

"I thought I'd met you before." My bewildered silence seemed to prompt her to provide an explanation. "It was last year. I was collecting Ryan after school, and we were waiting with Jonah because his mum was running late. I must have met your ex-wife that day." I joined up the dots as she continued with an adorable grin. "So when *you* came into Mr. Simmons's room, I was so confused. You looked so different, and I thought you didn't remember me because you reintroduced yourself. I felt completely unmemorable."

"No, that wasn't me." I stopped her nervous laughter. "Trust me, I'd remember you." The room plunged into silence, and I almost regretted what I'd said until Lucy tilted her head. Then I could swear I saw a blush appear on her cheeks.

"I think I'd remember you too," she replied. It caused my heart rate to pick up and the temperature to spike in the room.

I needed some kind of distraction from those eyes. "I should probably check on the boys," I said, already moving to the living room. "See if they want a snack or anything."

Once out of the kitchen, I was shaking my head in frustration. I was annoyed at myself for leaving the conversation. She was probably just being friendly. But my gaydar was usually quite good. Maybe she was into women. Just because she was with Ryan's dad didn't mean she was straight. I guess I'd just assumed because she was a mum that she was straight, but how heteronormative of me. I was annoyed at myself for the assumption alone. However, there was still the small question of her actual availability. Ryan's dad appeared to still be in the picture. I would have to dig a little deeper before I got carried away.

After bringing the boys some juice and fruit slices, I made my way back into the kitchen again. I took a seat at the island beside Lucy, unable to escape her perfume. It smelt subtle but sweet, like honey or cinnamon. I swivelled on the stool slightly so I was facing her.

"Thank you for inviting us over." She met my eyes from behind her fringe. "I don't really know many of the mums at Hillside."

"I don't think you're missing out on much," I teased, and she returned a knowing smirk. "Some of them are a little intense."

"I know. I made the mistake of volunteering at last year's sports day." She puffed out a breath of what looked like contention. Her eyes widened as if she was reliving the day in her mind.

"Please, tell me everything." I rested my chin on my palm in anticipation.

"Oh my God," she started with animated gestures. "First, it was a really mild, overcast day, and one of the mums insisted that all the kids had to have a sunhat and sunscreen. I literally had to take off Ryan's hoodie to put sunscreen on. It was ridiculous. And half of the event was indoors." I was already shaking my head at the over-the-top precautions. "Then, they were worried the kids were having *too much* fun," she said with air quotes. "Everyone had to sit down for quiet time. And don't get me started on the snacks."

"Sugar-free?" I asked.

"Sugar-free, fat-free, gluten-free. More like fun-free."

"Yeah, sometimes there are perks to having a full-time job. I get out of volunteering."

Lucy watched me in amazement. "How do you do it?" She leaned forward, and the intensity of her catlike eyes had me drawing a blank.

"Do what?"

"Have a career with a six-year-old?"

I thought carefully for a moment, but being under her gaze made me nervous. She was just so pretty. I took a sip of coffee, needing the diversion from those entrancing eyes.

"I don't know. I mean, it's hard sometimes."

She listened intently, almost as if she was taking mental notes.

"I'm lucky because Catriona doesn't live far from here, so she takes him half the week, and I have him the other half. Usually, I can move things around to make sure I'm here for him on my days too." She nodded but looked deep in thought. "And then, my parents aren't far, so they chip in if I'm really stuck. What's that phrase? Raising a child takes a village."

"Yeah." She sighed almost sadly.

"Is it just you and Ryan?" I broached the topic delicately.

"No," she said slowly. I scrutinised her expression more intently as I watched it move to a place of uncertainty. "We live with Ryan's father. My boyfriend." It was a strange introduction. Surely, boyfriend would come first. Unless his relationship with her was in limbo. Her eyes fell to the ground as she slumped. "Well, I don't know if we're still together anymore."

I didn't say anything, though I wanted to know more. I could feel my fingertips twitching to know what had happened between them that could have caused her features to grow so small and lost. She had a carefree energy when she was joking around, but the mere mention of her long-term relationship seemed to engulf her in sadness. A moment passed, and she glanced up at me, perhaps deliberating whether or not she could trust me. "We're…" she started, and I could see the tears welling up. "Kind of separating. I'm not even sure. It's a little bit tough at home. He still lives there, but we barely talk anymore."

"I'm sorry," I said and resisted the urge to reach out. I had to remind myself we'd only known each other an hour or two.

A personal conversation like this seemed almost inappropriate. We barely knew each other. Heck, I'd had longer conversations with my postman, and yet, there was a familiarity with Lucy. As if I could tell her anything, and I wondered if maybe she felt it too.

"I think it's why Ryan is acting out," she said in a meek voice full of disappointment.

"Kids have a way of picking up on these things. I know Jonah did." Her eyes collided with mine, almost hopeful. I decided to share more with her in the hope that it would ease some of her guilt. I remembered that feeling of failure when Catriona and I were separating. That worry and fear that the breakdown in our relationship would adversely affect Jonah. "When me and my ex-wife were separating, I worried about Jonah. We tried to make it work for a long time." She hung on my every word. "He was only two or three, so things were already tough at that age. But we were just at each other's throats more and more. Anything I did seemed to irritate her…" I trailed off, remembering the fights and tension in our home. It was unbearable and horrible for everyone, even Jonah. "And then, she confessed to cheating."

Lucy's eyes widened before fleetingly jumping around the room. Her eyes seemed to well up even more, and her breathing turned shallow. Watching such a raw and undiluted reaction told me something similar was likely happening in her own relationship.

Her energy turned to empathy. "How could you be amicable with her after she cheated on you?" It was almost like she was asking for a step-by-step guide.

"I wasn't," I replied honestly. "I was devasted when she told me. Broken. I took it out on her the only way I knew how." I could feel my chest tightening as I remembered those harsh emotions. "I wouldn't let her see Jonah."

I thought Lucy might have shown more judgement at my horrible actions, but she reassured me of her character by silently waiting for me to continue in this safe space we'd created.

"I used Jonah as a pawn to get back at her. She begged to see him. And I kept him from his mother. It's not something I'm proud of." I still carried a lot of shame about my actions. The things I did were cruel but had come from a place of unbearable pain. "It doesn't matter what you feel for your partner, you should never keep your child away from their other parent. It's not fair." My voice was full of regret, I could hear it loud and clear, and I think Lucy got it too. "No matter how broken I was, I promised to never use my son to get back at my ex again. Catriona is a lot of things..." My voice dipped. "But she's a great mother. It took a long time for us to get to this place. We don't bad-mouth the other in front of Jonah. Fuck, Catriona still gets me flowers on Mother's Day and signs it as Jonah. And I do the same."

"Wow," Lucy breathed out. She sat in deliberation for a moment, digesting my words. "It's amazing that you both could get to that place. I can't imagine ever being there with Matt," she said, deep in thought before seeming to check herself. "That is, if we even separate. Which, maybe we won't, you know." There was optimism in her voice, though it was weak. "Maybe he will get this thing out of his system, and we can move past it."

I nodded, not fully understanding what the problem was. I tried to stop my brain from hypothesising what Matt needed to get out of his system. It sounded like another person, but Lucy didn't divulge any more and instead sipped her coffee.

"I know I've already said this but," she said, biting her lip and meeting my eyes, "thank you for inviting us over." I was a little speechless when I caught the look on her face. She seemed filled with appreciation and relief. I could feel my lips tugging upward. "I don't really get out much. My folks live in Enniskillen, so it's just kind of me, all day, alone. It was really nice to speak to someone. Especially about Matt. I haven't been brave enough to tell anyone else what's going on."

"I get it." I sighed, remembering the feeling. "But you know, there's nothing to be ashamed of." She met my eyes, and I could see the tears forming again. "I didn't tell anyone what was going on with Catriona, either, but it eats you alive." That revelation caused her entire face to contort. Perhaps her secret was already eating her up inside. "If you're not ready to talk to your friends and family, you can talk to me." A small smile slid onto her face, breaking through the clouds of heartache. "It gets lonely going through that."

"Thanks, Dani." She touched my arm.

It felt intimate, and I knew in that moment that she really appreciated my company. I felt humbled and privileged that I could help out a new friend. At least, that was how it felt initially. But then, her eyes dropped to my lips, and her thumb caressed my arm. The air stilled around us, and I wondered what that gesture might have felt like on my bare skin.

"Mum?" Jonah called before darting into the kitchen.

Lucy quickly dropped her hand.

"Yes, love." I stood to meet him and also create a little space for Lucy.

"Can I go to Ryan's birthday?"

Ryan appeared out of nowhere. "Yeah, can he come, Mum?"

"Yes," Lucy said to Ryan and turned back to me. "Of course Jonah is invited." The boys talked excitedly. They began giggling as Lucy said to me, "Only if you both can make it."

"Where? And when?" I was already mentally running through my calendar.

"It's not for a couple of weeks. Saturday, the sixth. At my house," she said matter-of-factly. "There will be a bouncy castle and games and food. You should come."

The intensity of her eyes had my knees turning unsteady. I wondered if she was aware of the effect she was having on me. "Well," I tried, but when it came out as a bizarre squeak, I had to clear my throat. "It's just...he's with Catriona that weekend." Her face fell. "But I'm sure she'll take him."

"Okay." Her voice sounded upbeat, but I could see what looked like disappointment. "That's great." She nodded a few times, and I felt myself crumble.

"But I might be able to take him myself." That hope returned to her eyes. I relished evoking that excitement from her. "You know, if you need help with the party."

"I could never subject you to that," she said, and a look of detachment made its way onto her features. "Even Matt is clearing off to go golfing."

"I don't mind helping you," I said honestly, and she seemed to give me a double take.

"Yeah? You really don't mind?"

"No, of course not. What are friends for?"

Her eyes locked me in, and I felt my breathing turn uneasy. A small smile appeared, and she held my gaze for just a moment longer than what I would class as straight. "Amazing, thank you." She touched my arm, again, igniting a wave of butterflies in my stomach. "Well, we should probably get going. I'm sure you have work," she said, and I begrudgingly had to agree. I was supposed to be working from home. She glanced in Ryan's direction. "Say good-bye to Jonah, honey." She moved out of the kitchen to leave before checking over her shoulder to find me. Perhaps to make sure I was following her out. I almost tripped over myself to ensure I was.

"What's your address?" I asked and then remembered to play it cool. "That way, I'll know it for the party."

"I'll text it to you." She reached into her pocket and pulled out her phone. I had given her my number already, but she must not have saved it yet. "Is Dani with a *y*?" she asked, but her eyes remained on her phone.

"No, an *i*."

"That's so cool," she said and then, daringly, she bit her lip. It lasted no more than a second, but it was probably one of the sexiest things I'd ever seen. I felt my face heat up, but I tried to hide it with a wave good-bye.

"See you tomorrow," Jonah called to Ryan as we watched them move down the cobbled pathway and close the wooden gate behind them.

I was consumed with thoughts of Lucy for the rest of the evening. While initially, I was only interested in helping out someone who was clearly going through a hard time, perhaps it was turning into something else. Her heartbreak had been written across her face at Hillside, and yet, a cup of coffee later and she was a new woman. Funny, kind, and with so much compassion. She had done a one-eighty on the sad and hopeless young mum I'd been introduced to and had transformed into someone I could be friends with. The age difference didn't seem to even come into play, though I was still aware of it. I never normally went for younger women. After all, Catriona was nearing forty, eight years older than me. Getting excited about the possibilities and the what-ifs of Lucy Matthews was so uncharacteristic of me. Especially when I still had no idea how she identified. I didn't want to be a cliché chasing a straight woman. Not to mention the fact that she wasn't exactly single.

I needed to get a better handle on my emotions around her. She needed a friend right now, and anything more seemed a little too complicated. Besides, I'd sworn off complicated long ago. That was why I stuck to friends with benefits on the weekends Jonah was with Catriona. Though, even those types of friends had dried up in recent months. Perhaps that was why I was imagining sparks with Lucy. It had been a while since I'd met someone new. Maybe it was time to dust off the cobwebs on my dating profiles again.

CHAPTER THREE

Dani Raye

Catriona opened the front door, and Jonah went happily into her arms. "Hi, baby."

I watched their embrace, feeling a tug on my heartstrings. His connection to both of us never seemed to falter, even though our relationship had evolved.

She spotted me over his shoulder and offered a warm smile. There were greys peppering her fair roots, touting her age. She wasn't a natural blond, but her frequent visits to the hairdresser fooled most. She pulled back but remained at his level. Her face hardened, and a brow arched. Though I couldn't see his face, his tense shoulders told me he knew he was in trouble.

"Now, what's this I hear about a fight at school?" she asked in a low tone before she seemed to crumble. "Is someone picking on you?" She was the softer one.

I shook my head and rolled my eyes at the same time, causing Catriona to relax.

"No, it was just a mister-inning," he stammered.

Catriona's face crunched up in confusion, and she looked to me for help.

"A misunderstanding."

He tried again to say the word but failed. Catriona cut in, saving him. "Are you friends again?"

"Yes," he said. "I'm going to Ryan's birthday party."

"You are?" She phrased it as a question to me.

"In a couple of weeks," I said. "Two weeks, to be exact." My face must have shown my guilt.

It was a sacred rule that we didn't make plans on the weekends that Jonah was with the other one. It was something we'd agreed upon in our custody arrangement. Although, over the years, there had been exceptions. It was still something we usually ran past the other before committing.

She stood again and gestured for him to go on inside. "You best come in too," she said in a tone that wasn't angry but in need of answers. I apprehensively pottered in behind her and closed the door.

Catriona's home was stylish and modern, though it still made me feel a little uncomfortable. After all, it was the home she'd bought after we split, and the one she shared with her new fiancée. She'd always had a great eye for interior design, but in a big old house like this, she'd made sure to keep upgrades simple so as not to destroy the aesthetic. I remembered her saying that she'd bought this home after our breakup. Of course, I'd gone online straightaway to find out how much she'd paid for it, and I'd almost choked on my tea. I guessed a five-bedroom home in a sought-after area such as this one was going to be priced at the top end of the housing market.

I'd always thought it was too big a house for her and Maeve. She was the woman Catriona had cheated on me with. I could never determine my feelings around her. She was perfectly civil, but that didn't mean I had to like her. I'd always wondered if it would have been easier to digest if Catriona had just had a one-night stand when she'd cheated, or was it better that she had found her soulmate? The fact that they were due to get married in a couple of months and had been happily together for the last three years would indicate that they were set for life. I guess that made me happy for her, even if I hated the way it had started.

"No snacks before dinner," Catriona warned as she caught Jonah with his head in the cupboard.

"Please?" he whined, his eyes enlarged, making him look even cuter.

"Okay, but just one."

I shook my head dismissively, catching Catriona's eye in the process. "Still bending to his will, I see." I poked fun of her, but she knew there was no malice.

"He's my little man, and he's obviously been through a tough day." Catriona gestured for me to join her at the kitchen table. Once I was seated, she got on topic again. "What happened?"

"Just Hillside being overdramatic. As usual." Jonah had already left the room, so I felt no need to hold back. "I don't know why you insisted we send him there—"

"Because it's the best, Dani," she returned, seeming irritated already.

"Bunch of snobs. The principal was whinging over nothing."

"If it was nothing, Mr. Simmons wouldn't have called us to come and collect him. What happened?" Her tone was low and showed her urgency. It was clear she wasn't messing around, and the creases across her forehead revealed that Jonah's fight had worried her.

"Another boy in his class pushed him. That's it."

"Why? What's that little shit's problem?"

"He's not a little shit." I defended Ryan for reasons I didn't understand. "I think there is some stuff going on at home..." I trailed off, not wanting to divulge what Lucy had told me in confidence. "Besides, they made up this afternoon. The fight was all over nothing."

"When?" she asked, a little baffled. I tilted my head, hoping my obliviousness would cause her to leave it, but she pushed ahead. "When did they make up?"

I was hesitant to reveal Jonah's playdate, especially after he'd just been suspended. It wasn't exactly ethical parenting, and she probably would have preferred I'd scolded him, not rewarded him. But by Catriona's quirked eyebrows, I knew I had to give

her something. She was like a dog with a bone. Being evasive
would only lead to more excruciating questions.

"Well, I invited Ryan, the little boy who'd pushed Jonah,
over to the house—"

"What? Why?" she interrupted. "So he could beat on our son
some more?"

"No." I cut her off, my frustrations rising. "They're friends.
Best friends, according to Lucy."

"Who's Lucy?"

"She's Ryan's mum. She came over too."

"Oh, did she? Huh." Catriona's tone heightened in intrigue,
and now I was most definitely regretting going down this rabbit
hole. But I didn't give her the satisfaction of addressing her
suggestion.

"Look, it was actually really productive having Ryan over.
They played, and they're friends again."

"Sounds like he's not the only one who made a new *friend*."
The insinuation was glaringly obvious. To avoid the bait would
be a declaration that I was into Lucy.

Which I might not be, I told myself half-heartedly. It was
best to deflect. "Give me a break. She's clearly straight."

"Lucy," she mused, "Lucy? Why does that ring a bell?"

"She said she met you before."

"Describe her," Catriona said, scratching her head. "I can't
remember her. I have to make small talk with a lot of boring
housewives."

I had to bite my tongue from defending Lucy. I wasn't sure
why I wanted to defend her. We'd just met, but that was precisely
why it was all the more worrying. "Uh, well, she's a little smaller
than me. Light brown hair." Catriona didn't seem to be recalling
her, so I continued. "She's quite slim and has a fringe—"

"Oh, I know her! The teen mum with the bangs?" Catriona
looked horrified and amused at the same time.

"She's not that young," I said, trying to keep the annoyance
from my voice. "She's in her mid-twenties."

"But she looks about sixteen, right?" She was exaggerating. "Oh, I know *Lucy*." The way Catriona said her name filled me with annoyance. "I've seen her a couple of times at pickup. I tried talking to her once, but she is just horribly quiet and dull." She laughed to herself, and all I could see was red. "I'm sure having to make chat-chat with her was a complete nightmare. There's obviously nothing going on behind those eyes. What on earth did you manage to talk about?"

"You know, the usual. Small talk." I batted her off, finding myself getting far too wound up to hide it anymore.

"And that's the birthday party that Jonah wants to go to?" She sighed in dread once I'd nodded. "Oh God, no. The birthday party is on my weekend, isn't it? I have to go to that girl's house? It will be dull as anything."

"Well, if you don't want to take him…" This was my opportunity without revealing my ulterior motive. "I can."

"Really?" She seemed to be holding her breath in anticipation. "You don't mind going?"

"No, it's cool. I have something on next weekend anyway. It works for me to swap."

The delight that passed across her face had me relaxing in my chair. "Brilliant. It's settled. I have him for the next two weekends, and you can take him on my scheduled weekend?"

"Yes, that's no problem."

Catriona looked smug, and I was already feeling thankful that I didn't have to explain my real reasons for wanting to go to a six-year-old's birthday party. Perhaps I did want another opportunity to spend time with Lucy.

A comfortable silence fell over us as the TV show Jonah was watching travelled from the living room and into the kitchen. I was about to say my good-byes and show myself out when she changed the line of conversation.

"How are you keeping?" she asked, but there was an angle to it. There always was.

"I'm fine," I said. "How's the clinic?"

"Busy, busy." Her eyes lit up, and I breathed a sigh of relief that the spotlight was off me. "We're thinking of opening another clinic in Newry. Mental health services are all the rage right now, and we can't keep up with demand."

"That's great. I mean, not the mental health crisis but for your business."

"It's very exciting for us."

With the mention of the word *us*, the conversation came to a screeching halt.

Catriona couldn't really hide her discomfort when talking about Maeve around me. Maybe it was because she knew how I felt about her. Maybe it stemmed from her shame about cheating on me with her. The last time she'd mentioned her, it was to tell me that they were engaged, and that hadn't gone down so well. I would have been lying if I'd said it didn't still hurt. But at the same time, I couldn't deny their compatibility.

Though I didn't spend a lot of time with Maeve, it was clear they were a much better fit than me and Catriona had ever been. Catriona had always wanted to open her own clinic. But she'd never had the confidence to run it herself. Until she'd met Maeve. They'd met in her last job and as she put it, had quickly fallen in love with each other. When our divorce was finalised, and they became an official item, they'd decided to go out on their own. Their clinic was a roaring success, and now it would seem they were ready to expand. I was happy that the clinic was thriving. Their livelihood ultimately filtered down to Jonah, and his future was all I really cared about.

"I'm happy for you, Catriona."

"Thanks, Dani." She patted my hand, though she didn't linger. "I just wish..." She trailed off thoughtfully, and my gut instinct told me where this was going. "I just want you to find happiness too."

"I am happy." I patted her hand just as condescendingly.

She seemed to recognise her own patronising action and backpedalled. "I know. I know you're happy being single."

"Yes, I am."

"I'm sorry." She tilted her head apologetically. "But you know, if you change your mind, Maeve has some friends—"

"I'm never taking you up on that offer," I cut in playfully. "We're good." I gestured between us. "But that's a little too incestuous for me. Getting your partner to hook up your ex-wife. No, thank you." Catriona laughed as if realising the absurdity. "I can find my own women, thanks."

"I know you can. Offer revoked," she joked as the front door opened.

"Baby?" Maeve called, making me tense.

Catriona didn't miss it. "I'm in here with Dani," she called, and Maeve emerged into the kitchen.

Her jet-black hair was tied back in a ponytail. She had minimal makeup on, but it did nothing to detract from her natural beauty. She was dressed in a Gaelic jersey, and her cleated football boots clip-clopped along the tiled floors. It annoyed me, along with a lot of things about her, that she could still look good after playing a match. She moved cautiously toward us at the far end of the kitchen and plastered on a polite smile. "Hi, Dani."

"Hi," I said, though there wasn't much volume in my voice. I really couldn't be bothered talking to Maeve, not today. It had been a really long week, and I just wanted to go home.

"How was your game?" Catriona asked over her shoulder.

"We beat them so bad. It wasn't even a challenge, to be honest." She reached for a glass and filled it up at the sink. It took everything in me not to roll my eyes. Her presence was draining me, and it made me want to leave their home as fast as I could.

"Amazing, well done, babe."

I was almost on my feet when...

"How'd the principal's meeting go, Dani?" she asked.

Tension crept into the room. It was always like this when she tried to discuss Jonah with me. It felt as if she was overstepping, even though I knew deep down it was concern for his well-being. Over time, I'd gotten better at making small talk with Maeve, but above all else, I still held resentment for her. She'd known Catriona was a married woman when she'd slept with her, and I would never forgive her for that.

"He's okay."

"Good," she returned pleasantly. "You know, I could have gone today if you had meetings." That seemed to plunge the entire room into hot tension. I locked eyes with Catriona, unable to hide my annoyance, but she stared at the table, avoiding me. "I don't mind chipping in with him."

Chipping in? My son was not some sort of chore that she could "help out" with whenever she felt like it. We were his parents, not her. It bothered me because while I had to be civil to Catriona for Jonah's sake, Maeve was not someone I had to put up with. Especially when it came to my son. I was not about to add "the other woman" into this co-parenting routine.

Maeve cleared her throat when I didn't say anything. She'd obviously picked up on my mood shift. "Or not." She laughed it off. "I just wanted to be helpful."

"It's none of your concern," I said with an edge that caused Catriona to throw me a pleading look.

"Right," Maeve said curtly. "Okay. I'm going to grab a shower," she announced before retreating from the kitchen and leaving us alone again.

"Dani," Catriona started calmly.

"No way." I knew the sternness in my voice was likely on my face as well. Catriona gave me a confused look, as if not seeing the big deal with Maeve offering to meet with Jonah's principal. "You'd better tell your girlfriend to know her place."

"Fiancée. Maeve is my fiancée." Yeah, I used to hold that title too, I thought, but bit my tongue as Catriona turned fiery. "Dani, come on. She was just trying to be helpful."

"She's not his fucking parent, Catriona."

"She's going to be his stepmother. There will be certain roles that she—"

"Not yet." I slammed my hand on the table. My voice had

risen, and I couldn't contain my frustration. "There are certain things in Jonah's life she can't be involved in. School meetings, doctor's appointments, and other important things." I couldn't think of anything else in my state of panic. "She might be your new wife, but she's not his mother."

"And she never will be," Catriona said calmly. I didn't realise how erratic my breathing had turned. "Maeve will never be his mother, okay?" She repeated herself, perhaps as a way of calming my fears. "Dani, we're his parents. That will never change. I will talk to Maeve and explain there are certain things that are just for us."

Her voice dropped an octave, and it lifted that weight off my chest. That feeling of being pushed out of Jonah's life began to dissipate. The loss of control that had caused my emotions to escalate simmered. It was as if she knew exactly what I needed to hear. As a therapist, she was well used to calming a tense situation.

I realised just how unreasonable I was being. "Okay. I'm sorry." I exhaled, and she smiled back at me warmly.

"Let's keep our cool, all right?"

"Deal. Well, I should really get going."

"Are you sure? You could stay for dinner."

"No, I have plans, but thank you." It was a lie. I was too embarrassed to face Maeve after how I'd snapped at her.

I wanted to appear cool and confident around Maeve, but naturally, when it came to Jonah, there were some responsibilities I wasn't willing to forfeit. I was just pleased Catriona and I were on the same page about it. She walked me to the door and waved me off into the night.

CHAPTER FOUR

Lucy Matthews

He was late. Again.

Tuesdays were supposed to be his late night at work. That was the arrangement. But it was Friday. He was supposed to be home with his family. Matt knew I was meeting with Ryan's principal today. The least he could have done was make it home in time for dinner. I would have liked him to speak to Ryan about his actions. But I guessed we were less of a priority to him now. My irritation was spiking as the minutes rolled on. I must have cleaned the kitchen three times as a distraction.

It was almost ten when I heard his key in the front door. I was waiting for him in the kitchen. He usually came looking for food before he went upstairs and took a shower. Why he needed a shower immediately after work used to bother me. It used to leave me reeling with speculation. I reckoned it was because he didn't want me to smell her perfume. But that was when we used to share a bed. It would be unlikely that I would get close enough nowadays to actually smell it.

We'd stopped sleeping in the same bed a little over a month ago. He'd moved into the guest bedroom and hadn't even bothered to put up a fight. At the time, I didn't realise that sleeping next to one another was our last real couple activity. Now, it was like we were roommates. I often wondered how he could possibly be happy with the arrangement. Perhaps he wasn't, but like me, he was too proud to admit defeat.

When I'd gotten pregnant, the odds had been stacked against us. Everyone had said it. Even I'd thought it at times but not Matt. I was only nineteen. When I went into labour, Matt was taking one of his last exams for university. We were just kids. But no matter how hard things were back then, I'd always had Matt. He'd always been there. We'd been best friends since we were six. He knew me like no other. Even when I didn't believe in myself, it was okay because Matt did. He loved me with such fierceness, my mum had said once. It was something I'd taken for granted until one day, I'd woken up, and he didn't love me like that anymore.

I listened to his every move from the kitchen like some kind of deranged predator. He removed his coat and shoes, leaving them in the closet under the staircase. I sat at the kitchen table, still and silent. I could feel my rigid limbs and my shallow breathing that was filled with rage. I hated the person I'd become. Angry, calculated, and resentful. But what I hated more was that it was Matt who'd led me to this dark place.

His relationship with *her* had reduced me to this powerless, anxious shadow of a woman.

"Oh, hey." He spotted me in the darkening kitchen. I might have startled him. "I didn't think you'd still be up." He flicked on one of the lights and made his way past me.

"You're late." The calmness in my voice even set me on edge. But the eery stillness had to be better than shouting. I didn't have the strength to scream and shout at him anymore.

"Sorry, work's crazy right now. It's year-end."

Year-end. Was that what he was calling her these days? The bitterness in my mouth could easily seep into my tone if I let it. Instead, I swallowed what I actually wanted to say. "Your dinner is in the microwave."

"Thanks, I'll have it for lunch tomorrow," he said, grabbing a beer from the fridge. "I bought takeout for a few of us at the office. I figured it was the least I could do for keeping them so late." There was a lightness to his voice, but I still had too much irritation coursing through my veins to care about his day.

"I wish you'd told me you were going to be late. You were supposed to talk to Ryan tonight."

"Shit." He rubbed his forehead. "Was that today?"

"Yes." The calmness in my voice surprised me again, especially considering that on the inside, I was practically pulsating with anger. "Mr. Simmons said Ryan has a pattern of bad behaviour." I wondered where he'd gotten that from.

It was the third time I'd met with the principal. At first, it was because Ryan had talked back to his teacher. I was no angel in school, either. I hadn't worried too much about his spirited ways, but then, it got more frequent. It was the violence toward another student that confirmed my suspicions. Ryan was picking up on what was happening between me and Matt. I'd spoken to Matt about it weeks ago, and we'd made a conscious effort to be affectionate around Ryan. A smile here and there, a peck on the cheek, etc. It had helped for a while, but his fight today with Jonah had reaffirmed that our charade was fooling no one.

"I'll talk to him tomorrow," Matt said, but his eyes didn't stay on me long.

"Fine." My voice sounded tired and old. I barely recognised it, and by the look on Matt's face, it looked like he didn't recognise me either.

"Hey, are you okay?" he asked with worried eyes.

"I don't know. Are you still fucking *her*?"

The shock was written across his face. I wasn't expecting what came out of my mouth; it was just another part of myself that I hated. My anger and betrayal had made me unpredictable around him. He struggled to say anything resembling sense.

"I guess I'm still not okay."

"Lucy," he tried desperately, but I'd heard it all before.

"I'm going to bed," I said, standing and moving out of the kitchen without another glance in his direction.

I used to be unable to hide my frustration at what he'd done to us. I used to be so pent-up with anger and devastation that the second he walked through the door at night, I would be waiting. Hoping he would step out of line so I could go through him. I couldn't exactly yell at him for what I really wanted to scream about, and therefore, I would settle for him forgetting to take out the rubbish or leaving dirty dishes in the sink. Then a row would erupt. It almost always led back to *her*. She was the crux of our problems. The reason our family was falling apart. The reason I was meeting with the school principal, the reason I cried in the shower every day, and the reason Matt no longer touched me. The reason I felt more alone than I had in my entire life.

I couldn't exactly tell anyone what I was going through. What would they think of me for *allowing* Matt to sleep with someone else? Because the truth was, I'd allowed it to happen. I'd granted him permission to cheat. I had only myself to blame, but what else could I have done? He'd asked me outright if he could explore his feelings. He was ashamed and crying when he'd admitted that he had developed feelings for someone else. Initially, I was so caught off guard and devastated that I'd shut it down. Absolutely not. What would people say if they knew we were in some kind of open relationship? This was Northern Ireland, after all, nothing was ever swept under the carpet for long.

It was his mood that had worn me down. His borderline depression and disinterest in our family had meant that I didn't have a choice. It was either let him see *her* or wait for the day he left me. He began seeing her, and as if overnight, his mood was restored. Matt was himself again, and Ryan had his dad again. There was no way I could have foreseen just how much his new relationship would destroy me.

I used to be fun. I used to have fun, but it had been months. Each day, a part of me seemed to slip away and with that, my love for him. The love I had for him and our life together had shrivelled like an old bouquet of roses. I wondered if that love could ever be nurtured back to life again. I held on to the hope that one day, it could. And though I'd thought frequently about ending a relationship that had filled me with such despair, my pride wouldn't allow it and neither would Matt's.

We had made it this far against all odds. From renting a one-bedroom flat with a baby to owning our own family home off the Malone Road. Ryan attended private school, we drove nice cars, and had family holidays abroad. We were the couple who'd surprised everyone, who had made it through everything and seemed to always come out stronger on the other side. Maybe we were just going through one of those hard times. Maybe we would come out the other side stronger. He just had to get it out of his system. Get *her* out of his system.

Until then, I would be alone and grappling with his decisions. I felt like I was at his mercy. Powerless in my own life. It left me terrified that one day, he might turn around and say he wanted to be with her. Throw me and Ryan out on the streets, and then, where would we be? Of course, Matt would never do something like that. My rational mind knew that, but my fears still existed. I was reliant on him. I had allowed myself to become domesticated and financially reliant on a man. If my teenage self could see me, she would be disgusted.

But my dreams had to be put on hold. For Ryan. I loved being his mother, but I wished someone had prepared me for what I would have to give up by taking that role. It was a full-time job being a mother, and while I loved every moment with him, there were times that, when I thought about my future, it filled me with such hollowness. Ryan and Matt were my whole world. I'd devoted myself to them. And now that one of them didn't seem to want me anymore, it had rendered me useless and empty.

Until today.

Today had been a break in the monotonous hollowness. Thinking about it as I lay in bed filled my insides with excitement and dared I say, hope. Just thinking about Dani had me smiling.

I had felt invisible when I'd left the house this morning. It was the only reason I'd worn that ridiculously overpriced coat my mother-in-law had bought me for Christmas. I had hoped the coat's expense, along with my designer handbag, gifted to me by my cheating boyfriend, would give me more authority when talking to Mr. Simmons. I'd deluded myself into thinking that the pretentious accessories would provide me with some confidence. In fact, Mr. Simmons had seen right through it, and while I was sure that the other mother would too, Dani had ended up surprising me.

The invitation to her home was kind and genuine. I had never been invited to one of Ryan's friend's homes unless I'd volunteered to bake something. I was nervous Dani might be like the other mums at Ryan's school, who were only interested in gossip and petty scandal. I was so relieved when she turned out to be nothing like that. She was ambitious, kind, and funny. And in those rare moments when she'd looked the other way, I got to sneak a glance at her, and the only way I could describe Dani Raye would be: strikingly beautiful. Full ruby lips and dark curls I could just imagine running my fingers through.

That flutter returned in the pit of my stomach just thinking about her. It had been years since I'd felt that type of *flutter* about someone other than Matt. And while that offered excitement, it also left me concerned about what an attraction for Dani would mean for my relationship with Matt. That thought seemed to plague me long after I'd heard Matt lock up downstairs and go to bed.

The clock on my bedside table revealed it was almost midnight, and yet, I felt like it was six a.m. For the first time in so long, I felt wide awake and not just sleepwalking through my life. I didn't feel powerless and weak. It was as if Dani had unknowingly injected me with life again. Hearing her personal journey and her revealing such a heartbreaking, yet similar story to my own gave me hope. Her co-parenting relationship with her ex-wife was proof that Matt and I weren't stuck together. That we could separate amicably and still raise a well-rounded child.

It also put an excited bounce in my toes and a tingling sensation that left me inspired. A desire to be creative. So much so that I climbed out of bed and put on my old dungarees, which were only ever worn when I wanted to work with clay. It had been months since I'd felt creative, and I wasn't going to let it stew until the morning. Just in case it vanished. I crept downstairs and retrieved my sneakers from the closet. I grabbed the garage key en route through the kitchen and slid out the back door and into the garden.

It was a mild evening, and with each step toward the garage, I felt my excitement growing. I couldn't remember the last time I'd felt this motivated and creative enough to do pottery. It was long before Matt's request to see *her*. I flicked on the light, and my work space seemed to come to life before my eyes. The clay I had left over had dried slightly, but I'd stored it well, and after adding some water, it was workable again. My mum's potter's wheel was exactly where I'd left it, and I got to work. Shaping and moulding the clay allowed some of my worries to melt away.

It was therapeutic being out in my work space again, and oddly, it felt like I'd never left. Without meaning to, I got lost in my creativity and revelled in the hours that passed where I actually felt like my old self. Being in my safe space seemed to ground me, and I wondered if working again was what had been missing in my life lately. But then again, the creativity to be out here at all had only emerged when I was thinking about Dani. What was even more mysterious was that being in my work space again made thinking about anything other than Dani Raye damn near impossible.

CHAPTER FIVE

Dani Raye

The weekend had passed in the blink of an eye. Though it was fairly lowkey, given that Catriona had Jonah, I still wished for more time off. Like most weekends. I was pulling up to the school gates to collect Jonah on Tuesday afternoon. I was a little early for a change. Working from home today had given me a sense of freedom, and I'd decided to take my time driving over to his school, and then I saw her. Lucy was standing on the playground waiting on the bell to ring.

I got out and made my way toward her. She was wearing a pair of ripped baggy jeans with an oversized plaid shirt tucked in. It was probably the gayest outfit in the yard. She looked good, really good. I wondered if I'd looked this cool when I was young like her. It made me wish I'd changed out of my yoga leggings before leaving the house. She was immersed in something on her phone to the point that when I reached her, she almost had a startle.

"Dani," she said, gripping her chest, "I didn't see you there."

"Sorry, I'm stealthy that way."

She laughed as her free hand scooped some strands behind her ear. Something caught my eye on her arm. It was combination of beige smears mixed with navy strokes of paint lazily painted across her arm and even across her tattoo.

"Oh." I pointed at her arm "You have something there."

"Shit," she said, contorting her arm to get a better look, "I thought I got it all." She rubbed a little, removing some of the smears. The same specks were all over her jeans too. "That's what I get for throwing clay before pickup."

I nodded, but I had disappeared into my thoughts, trying to figure out what throwing clay was.

She was observant, though, and must have decided to have a little fun at my expense. "You don't know what throwing clay is, do you?"

"Of course I know what throwing clay is," I said sarcastically, and I was extremely pleased to see she was playing along. "I'd have to be an idiot to not know what throwing clay is."

"Hmm." She watched me with amusement. "What is it, then?"

"It's…" I started off confidently, though it ended after one word. "It's when you…throw clay."

"Throw clay at what?"

"At…" I trailed off and said the first thing that came into my head. "Pigeons."

"What?" She burst out laughing, and I had to laugh at my own absurdity. When she had composed herself again, she said, "No, not even a little bit close. Throwing clay at pigeons? What the fuck?"

"I thought maybe it had to do with clay pigeons. As in, clay pigeon shooting?"

"No." She was still laughing as she shook her head. Then, something thoughtful seemed to cloud over in her eyes. A softness that seemed more intimate. I didn't know what she was thinking, but I had to admit, I really liked seeing her smile. "Throwing clay is a term used in pottery," she explained, and I found myself rolling my eyes at my own grossly inaccurate assumption. "As in, throwing clay at the potter's wheel. Then, you mould it into ceramics. Bowls, cups, that kind of thing."

"Ah." I nodded, joining up the dots, feeling like an idiot for not knowing. "That's clever."

"That's why it's called throwing clay."

"Do you make a lot of ceramics?" I asked as she looked into the distance.

"Sometimes. I kind of take notions." Her brow furrowed. "I've felt really blocked recently."

"Blocked?"

"Creatively blocked, I mean."

"Oh." The quirk of her lips said she took amusement at me being out of my depth. "How do you get unblocked?"

She blushed and pursed her lips. It was almost sexy. "There are ways," she alluded and finally, I caught on.

"*Oh.*" I had to redirect my eyes out of embarrassment. "I get it now."

"Yeah." She shrugged unashamedly. "And with things between me and Matt being a little strained, I'm not...you know." Her eyes locked with mine for a second too long.

Holding Lucy's gaze was sensual if not seductive. I couldn't be sure if she knew what she was doing to me, or perhaps she was this candid with everyone. Regardless, it made my head dizzy.

"I understand." I decided to bring the conversation back into the realms of acceptable topics for the playground. "That's really cool about your pottery. What kind of stuff do you make?"

"Everything," she said. "Mugs, saucers, bowls, serving dishes, plant pots."

"Wow, that's amazing," I said, and she watched me a little suspiciously. But I was impressed. In fact, she looked a little touched that I was even showing an interest. "Can I see some of your work?"

"Really?" She frowned, but something in my expression must have been all the encouragement she needed. "I have some pictures. I'm not very good, though. My mum taught me everything I know." She swiped through her phone. "I just do it for fun, and I'm sure there are better techniques. I know there are, and if I'd made it to final year of college, I would be better but..." She trailed off as she passed me the phone.

"Why didn't you make it to final year?"

"Ryan," she said with a weak smile as she folded her arms tightly. She mustn't have been very old when Ryan was born, but I thought I'd better not dig too deep. Her body language told me she didn't want to dwell, and therefore, I focused on the phone.

The picture revealed a tall mug painted in burnt orange that faded into a pale grey toward the rim. It looked sturdy, beautifully shaped, and with a unique handmade feel to it, though it was the vibrant colours that sold it for me. So precise, with a delicate and even fade.

"You made this?" I asked. It came out as a whisper, and she nodded shyly. "This is incredible. Have you ever thought about selling your work?"

She didn't think on it at all. "It's not good enough." She moved closer and looked at the picture. "See, look at the rim, it's not perfectly even." She pinched the screen, zooming in on it. "And when you set it down on a flat surface, it's a little—"

"Stop. Don't rip apart your work. This is beautiful." I met her eyes, and she seemed to hesitantly listen to what I had to say. I hadn't realised just how close we were. "Seriously, I've seen ceramics not as well-finished as this in craft markets. You could sell your work."

"I don't know," she mumbled, but I could see the cogs turning in her head. She took the phone again and stared at the picture. I could actually see her starting to believe me. Believe in her craft. "Do you really think so?"

"Yes," I replied, and her enlarged eyes kept me in a trance.

The air stilled around us, and I felt this invisible tug toward her. I wondered if she felt the energy shift beneath us as well. I couldn't put my finger on what was happening; it felt like it was happening on another plane, too delicate and magical for either of us to see in plain sight.

The ringing of the school bell severed the connection. Her eyes dropped, and I found myself letting go of the breath I was holding.

"I wouldn't even know how to start selling my work."

"I'd start with Instagram or TikTok." She glanced at me, but I kept my line of vision straight ahead in an effort to make me sound less invested. "Create a business page, get a few followers, maybe contact some influencers to promote your products, and get yourself trending."

"Trending?"

"Hashtags. Such as local pottery, handmade, Northern Ireland, small businesses. That sort of thing." I turned back to her and witnessed her lost in thought. Perhaps I was getting through to her. "Locality is huge right now, especially for small businesses. If you present your brand properly, you can strategically embed your business into the niche of locally produced products."

"You're speaking another language," she teased. "Is this what you do for a living?"

"Basically," I replied and, she seemed beyond impressed.

"Do you think you could help me?" she asked hesitantly, as if the request for my help was completely unreasonable.

"Of course." My failure to stop and think about it resulted in the most adorable and infectious smile from Lucy.

"Really? Well, how much are your fees?"

"Give me one of those cool-ass mugs, and we're even."

Her eyes widened excitedly. "I'll give you the whole damn set if you help me." She launched herself at me and pulled me into a hug I most definitely wasn't expecting. "Thank you," she murmured. I felt her words drift through her chest and into my own. It was warm, and my insides felt like they were swirling around.

"No problem," I replied once she'd pulled back.

She didn't have time to say any more when she spotted the boys in the distance, Jonah walking next to Ryan. They were chatting, and it was clear they weren't ready to say good-bye just yet. I wasn't ready to say good-bye either. Lucy jumped at the suggestion that we go to the park. I didn't really have much going on this afternoon in work anyway.

While our sons played on the swings, we got to work

establishing her social media presence and with any luck, a long and successful business. Lucy's Ceramics. We ended up spending almost an hour on a park bench, getting her Instagram set up. Everything from the brand name to the pictures we posted were in an effort to entice new followers. She reached out to farmers' markets and craft pop-up events as a way of gauging interest.

She was already gaining followers by the time we were leaving the park. It only seemed to fuel her confidence. "I can't believe I have over one hundred new followers. I only started the account an hour ago," she said in amazement as we walked back to the cars with the boys trailing behind.

"I told you, you're really good. Just keep up the posts, and you'll do great."

"I think it's more to do with your marketing skills."

"I'm only as good as my material."

Her head dipped, and that heavy fringe blocked her eyes again. I found myself itching to reach out and sweep it away.

We moved in the direction of the car in comfortable silence. A twinge appeared in the pit of my belly with each step closer to the car. I still wasn't really ready to say good-bye, and that was worrying. It concerned me how much I enjoyed her company.

"Thank you for your help," she said. "You've been so nice to me, and honestly, I don't know why."

I struggled to contain my racing thoughts. Why was I being so nice to her? I tried to pawn it off as friendship, but I knew something else was brewing, even if it was just one-sided. I didn't want her to think I was being too affectionate, either.

As I internally analysed my actions, Lucy perked up again. "I'm kinda glad Ryan pushed Jonah now. Otherwise, we would have never become friends. Is that bad?" She clicked the button to unlock her car.

"No, not at all. We should start a fight club next."

She giggled, and a glint appeared in her eyes. I was so mesmerised that I hadn't realised my phone was ringing.

"Aren't you going to get that?" She gestured to my pocket.

"Shit." I grabbed the phone and saw it was work. "I gotta take this. Hey, Heather, what's up?"

"Hey, are you working from home today?" Heather, my friend and Finance Director, asked.

"Yes."

"You didn't respond to my email." I'd forgotten. "Why do I hear birds? Are you skiving?"

"No, I'm at my kitchen table. Working," I lied and badly at that.

But Heather chuckled, telling me she wasn't going to rat me out. "Whatever. I sent through that budget report for last quarter. The one in deficit. Did you look over it yet?"

"Yes, this morning," I replied confidently, having actually looked at it. "There was an error in Cali-tech's budget allocation. The hours are incorrect, it was supposed to be one hundred and thirty rather than one-fifty," I explained, pacing slightly in the carpark as Lucy kept throwing me glances. "Harry must have typed it in wrong."

"Well, that wouldn't be like Harry, would it?" she said sarcastically, throwing a jab at the CEO.

"Tell me about it. He also increased his consultation fee by about fourteen percent." I could hear Heather typing the information. "I double-checked the contract, and it was crystal clear. You can tell him he inflated beyond what was agreed. I know the MD at Cali-tech, and there's no way she's taking that lying down."

"Fuck's sake." Heather sighed. "Why does he keep doing this?"

"Because he's an idiot. A greedy idiot."

"An idiot who pays our salaries," she pointed out, and I found myself having to ease my temper. I loved Harry, we had a great boss, but he was rather cheeky when it came to expenses and billing that on to the client. "Can you talk to him?" she pleaded. "You have a way of standing up to him, whereas he will make me crumble and bill the client anyway."

"Do not bill Cali-tech anything out of contract," I said firmly. "I'll give Harry a call."

"You're the best," she said, and I could hear the smile in her voice. "I got to go, but let me know how you get on."

"Bye, Heather." I hung up the phone and turned back to Lucy.

Ryan was already in the car with his seatbelt on while Jonah spoke to him through the lowered window. Lucy moved next to me, and I couldn't quite read the look on her face. It almost looked like she was impressed.

"Everything okay?"

"Yeah." I rubbed the back of my neck. "Just my stupid boss trying to steal from our clients."

"Wow." She struggled to hide her concern. "Is that legal?"

"It is, and it isn't." I shrugged before adding, "But I'm not going to let him get away with it. Clients don't typically like their invoices being higher than quoted." She watched me carefully for a moment, and then a curious smile tugged at her lips. "What?"

"You're different." She tilted her head cutely. "You're all business-y on the phone." Her comments caused a heat in my cheeks, and though I tried to suppress it, she didn't miss it. "It's not a bad thing." Her eyes danced around my face, and I could swear they darkened when they landed on my lips.

"Kind of sounds like a bad thing. What does business-y even mean?"

"I don't know." She shrugged, but the look on her face told me she knew exactly what she'd meant. "Confident," she said in a low voice. "Kinda hot." Speechless. There were no words.

She thought I was hot. My breathing turned shallow, and I couldn't tear my eyes away from her. It was confusing and alluring all at once, and I wondered if she was panicking as much as me.

"Anyway." She shook her head, almost pulling herself out of the conversation. "I should let you get back to work." She moved back to her car at a remarkable speed, perhaps doubting her wording.

"Yeah," was the best I could muster. "Jonah, come on." He made his way back to the car. "I'll see you later," I got out before her car door slammed shut. I didn't even look to see if she'd waved us off. Her car was speeding out of the carpark before Jonah had made it into the car.

I gripped the steering wheel, still unable to control my breathing and sieve through my muddled and frantic thoughts. That was definitely flirting. She had to be flirting. Friends didn't describe each other as hot. Or at least, if they did, they said it in an empowering way, not in an "I want to see you naked" way.

"Why aren't we moving?" Jonah asked, pulling me out of it.

"Sorry, love," I returned a little breathlessly as I started up the car.

CHAPTER SIX

Dani Raye

I didn't run into Lucy for the rest of that week, though she played on my mind often. And I didn't see her this week, either. Catriona had Jonah so I had no excuse to "bump into" Lucy at school pickup. I wanted to text her, but we'd never done that before, and I felt that could be a little weird after how we'd left it last time.

My only interaction with her was via social media. It felt unpersonal and lacking. She had invited me to follow her Lucy's Ceramics business page, and I'd been liking and sharing a few posts for her. She hadn't asked me, but I figured it could help grow her following, which it had. She was now close to five hundred followers. And in just over a week. Every time I shared anything, she showed her appreciation with a comment underneath the post. It always had a couple of emojis, and one time, she even added the heart emoji. I was getting beyond excited over a fucking emoji. It was pathetic.

I was at least glad that I was in the office today, as it meant the endless social media stalking was limited. The afternoon had passed nicely. I found myself comfortably on track in terms of preparing for my next pitch.

Skylar Marketing was one of the most prestigious digital marketing firms in Northern Ireland. We had produced and instigated a number of successful campaigns in recent years, including the launch of the new public transport system, the new hotel opening on Bryson Street, and we'd even managed to clean up some of the PSNI's latest bad press.

I'd worked in marketing for three years after university before taking the leap into digital marketing, where I'd devoted the last eight years to pioneering businesses' online presence. It was always interesting meeting a new client because if they were going to the effort of outsourcing, then they must have been really desperate. In this day and age, any Gen Z with an iPhone could run a business's social media. Probably not as successful as Skylar Marketing, or more specifically, me, but they'd have a decent stab at it.

I'd been with Skylar Marketing since it was just a start-up, and as it had grown to become one of the key players in the industry, so had I. Dani Raye was a household name, and that wasn't me being overly confident, considering I'd been headhunted countless times over the years. But Harry Skylar had always looked after me. Ample annual leave, working-from-home flexibility, a private office with a view of Victoria Square, and of course, my own Mercedes company car. Furthermore, none of the bonus offers thrown at me over the years could possibly compete with my current margins.

A knock at my office door interrupted my workflow, but it was opened without waiting for invitation. It was Harry Skylar, of course. He never waited for approval. Not because he was arrogant, but his excited and motivated temperament meant that anything he needed to share had to be right away. He moved into the room like a tornado. His suit was tidy, as always, but his red face indicated a little stress. New grey hairs used to be my gauge for how stressed-out Harry was, but lately, there was no dark hair left.

"Dani, how's your morning?" He stopped at the back of an armchair facing my desk, seemingly not ready to take a seat.

"Good, just prepping for our Turlough pitch in a couple of weeks."

"Oh great, that's why I'm here." He grinned and took a seat. "What have you got in store for them?"

I began to run through the campaign. Of course, he was glazing over. Harry was a lot of things, but for someone in charge of running a marketing consulting firm, he was seriously lacking creative vision. He was a smart salesman, though, and surrounded himself with the best. That way, no one could look too closely at his shortcomings. Harry was just evidence that actual knowledge in a specialty was not a requirement.

"Excellent work, Dani," he said after my thirty-second pitch. I had a lot more up my sleeve, but I knew he didn't care for the details. Harry would accompany me to the meeting with Turlough Enterprises next week, and he would have to sit still long enough to hear me out, but for now, Harry didn't seem inclined to waste his precious golfing time on this nonsense. "That's why I pay you the big bucks."

I tilted my head in acknowledgement of my own worth before his face turned serious. He rubbed his cheek, and I could hear the roughness of his early stubble from across the desk.

He looked off uncomfortably and seemed to lower his voice delicately. "Have you, uh…spoken to Heather today?" His eyes were wide and borderline scared.

It made me concerned. "No, is everything okay?"

"Apparently, she was crying in the kitchen this morning."

"Again?" It slipped out, my concern replaced with disappointment.

He nodded aggressively. "That's the third time this month. I know she's going through a breakup but…" He trailed off as his hands flew up in outrage. "This is a place of work."

"Okay." I used my calm voice and tried to soothe him a little. Emotional women were something Harry couldn't cope with, even though I would hardly class a few tears as hysterical. "I will have a word with her."

"Thank you." He sighed in relief before standing. "Well, I'll let you get back to work. I have a meeting to get to anyway."

I smiled, even though I knew the golf course was the only meeting pencilled into his diary.

I went in search of Heather as soon as he was gone. She was one of the only colleagues I had any time for. Digital marketing was a young persons' field, so we tended to get a lot of graduates who eventually moved on. Usually because the pay wasn't great at entry level. It was like a revolving door of new faces in Skylar Marketing. Heather was around my age too, so she didn't make me feel as ancient as the rest of the team. She had also been here for an extended period of time.

I spotted her across the office floor. On my route to her desk, a couple of the younger staff members smiled and asked about my day. I rarely retained anyone's name until they were in the business for at least a year. But being a senior associate, I typically received this kind of attention when I came downstairs to the main floor. Executive members were upstairs with the nice views and good coffee.

"Hey," I said offhandedly, leaning against Heather's desk.

She glanced at me tiredly and sighed a long, drawn out, "Hi."

"All right, what's going on?" I had little patience. We had reached that stage in our relationship where I didn't need to pussyfoot about.

"Daryl is seeing someone." Her face scrunched up, and soon enough, she let out a sob.

"It's okay." I tried to calm her as a few of the junior consultants stared over at us. "Let's go upstairs."

"Why?" she asked, seeming a little confused when I was pulling her up and dragging her with me.

"No reason." I was supposed to be stopping the crying, not starting it.

A part of me felt sorry for her heartbreak, and I wanted to comfort her away from prying eyes. This wasn't Heather's first time breaking down in the middle of the office; therefore, I wanted to save her dignity. If there was any left. I knew she didn't care what others thought, but the idea of having my dirty laundry aired for my colleagues to see made me feel physically sick. As a senior associate, it was my job to set an example of professionalism, and as the Finance Director, Heather should have really been doing the same.

We climbed the stairs two at a time to avoid Harry. I didn't slow or let go of her arm until we made it into my office again. With my arm around her shoulder, I closed the door and led her toward the couch. We sat next to each other, and I heard her sob again.

I nudged the box of tissues closer. "Are you okay?" I kept my tone soft, not having seen her nearly this upset throughout their breakup.

They had been dating for a few months, possibly a year. Heather had a habit of going through men quickly and seemed to dive straight into a relationship. She was the personification of the term "wearing your heart on your sleeve." I couldn't tell if it was her poor choice in men or just her eccentric nature that seemed to always result in heartache. She looked distraught, and the words got trapped in her sobs. I felt bad for her because she really was a fantastic person who didn't deserve this much heartbreak.

"My neighbour said her sister saw Daryl with another woman. Can you believe it? That's how I find out he's seeing someone else."

"Well, you did kick him out." I tried to reason with her, but I was pretty sure she didn't even hear me.

"What a miserable excuse for a man. That's it, Dani. I'm done with men." It definitely wasn't the first time she'd said that. "Show me your ways."

"It doesn't really work like that, Heather."

She was an attractive woman. She had short blond hair with a very pretty face, but I didn't see her that way. Not that I thought she was being serious. She was more like a sister. Or at least, what I imagined a sister was like. I had a brother who lived in America with his family, so I hardly ever saw him.

"I just feel so hurt and ashamed. Another failed relationship. It's pathetic. I'm pathetic."

"No, you're not. You're just having a run of bad luck."

"I've had bad luck my entire life." Her head rested in her palm as she stared at nothing. I continued to offer what I hoped would be soothing circular motions on her back. "I need a drink," she said out of nowhere. I gave her a double take, and she nodded, more convinced than ever. "Let's go to the bar."

She was already moving out of my office before I could stop her. I had no other choice but to lift my bag and follow her out of the building. It was just after five p.m., so the day was practically over, but still, I didn't usually like to go out on the town on a whim. But to be honest, a drink didn't sound half-bad after a long week. Especially after all of my speculative thoughts about Lucy.

We landed at a bar near work and stayed for a couple of cocktails. They went from fruity, syrup-based cocktails to the harder stuff as the evening ticked by. We moved on to the next place, moving farther into the Cathedral quarter. It was a Thursday evening, so not quite the weekend, but there was still a lively buzz about the city. The warm autumn temperatures were helping as well, with many patrons drinking out in beer gardens or on terraces. After a few drinks and a bite to eat, Heather had mellowed and relaxed considerably. The alcohol was also giving me the perfect buzz. That was, until everything turned a little south when Heather mentioned dancing. I wasn't keen on the idea, especially on a school night, but she was persistent. There weren't many places in Belfast city centre that offered music during the week, and that was almost our saving grace until the bartender recommended Basement.

Heather was adamant that we had to go. Her excitement was off the charts because she hadn't been to a gay bar in ages. I hit a major downer at the prospect of going. For one, I was far too dressed up, and I was only wearing a blazer. And secondly, Thursdays were notoriously students' night at Basement. I would be the oldest person there by about ten years. I tried to redirect

Heather on our walk, suggesting other bars or a taxi ride home, but it was getting me nowhere.

"What is wrong with Basement? I used to love that place back in the day," she said as we staggered across the junction in the direction of Union Street.

"Exactly." I couldn't hold back the bite in my voice. "When we were young enough to go."

"We are young."

"I'm a mum, Heather."

"And? You're only as old as you feel," she said, dismissing my arguments. "I'm not too old."

"You're a year older than me." She wasn't listening anymore. "Do you want to dance that bad that you're going to gate-crash students' night?" I tried from another angle.

"That just means cheap drinks. And I love Dua Lipa. We're going to fit in just fine." She batted me off as we approached the door. The two large bouncers eyed us suspiciously, but it was Heather who took the lead. Her confidence was unwavering after a few drinks. "Hi, ladies," she flirted, despite my pleas not to. "Looks like a busy night." She peered behind their heads. "Room for two more?" She batted her eyes furiously, causing me to cringe.

"Always," one of them flirted back before they granted us access to the club.

Heather was giddy like a child as she grabbed my hand and dragged me in. The lights were dimmed to the point of disorientation, but I might have been able to cope better if it wasn't for the thumping music destroying my eardrums. It was sensory overload, and the many drinks I'd consumed this evening weren't exactly helping.

Basement was bizarrely laid out. I remembered a lot of nights getting lost and aimlessly searching for the toilets. It was because the lights were so dim in the hallways that led to different bars and other sitting areas. It was a bit of a maze, but that was all part of Basement's traditional charm. It was likely so that gay people could come and go in the shadows without being recognised. Of course, being decreet was less of a necessity today than it was thirty or forty years ago, but Belfast was still a small place. Some people still weren't out.

When we emerged from the corridor and into the heart of the club and dance floor, the memories came rushing back. I had spent many weekends in Basement, more than I could count. I'd met Catriona here. Back in my twenties, before Jonah, I was here two to three nights a week. Drinking, dancing, and having fun. It was the place to be, and by the crowded dance floors, I could tell that was still the case. Basement was the oldest gay club in Belfast, and so it always had that feeling of exclusivity. A safe haven for people to be themselves. I looked back fondly on how much it had helped me discover who I was.

Heather must have caught the nostalgic glee on my face. She winked before pulling me onto the dance floor. We danced to a couple of the old classics as I shook off my worries. Turns out, I didn't need to dread the thought of being here. I was too drunk to care that everyone was half my age. It was freeing, and by Heather's hollering, I could tell she was having just as much fun. A group of gay men joined us soon enough, and that seemed to only spur Heather on to ramp up her so-called slutty dance moves. The DJ played ABBA, Spice Girls, and Cher until the tempo increased, and newer music started playing. I think the change in tunes was indicative of the fuller crowd now trickling through the doors. It was after eleven p.m., which was around the time that Basement picked up to full capacity.

I excused myself to grab a drink while Heather continued her provocative dance moves with everyone in sight. There was some queuing at the bar, but given that it was still early, I didn't have to wait long. The bartender was making up two gin and tonics when I felt a tap on my shoulder.

I spun around, expecting it to be Heather, but I was faced with a gorgeous brunette. She was dressed in a tight-fitting black dress that left very little to the imagination and heels that made her legs stretch on for days.

"Hi," I flirted but watched as she frowned back at me.

"Dani?" The words fell from her red lips, and I vaguely recognised the voice. Eventually, my brain started to work. "It's me. Lucy."

CHAPTER SEVEN

Lucy Matthews

"Who's up for a Jager bomb?" Nathan, my younger brother, said to the table. It wasn't actually an offer, considering he was carrying a full tray of it. The table all yelled in glee, and it was just a reminder that I was clearly at the wrong table. What had I gotten myself into?

Nathan had invited me to his twenty-first birthday party a few days ago. I was having a pretty rough week with Matt, and I wasn't exactly in a good mental space. If Nathan hadn't shown up on my doorstep unannounced, I don't think I would have divulged what was happening between us. He'd just showed up on the wrong day, when I couldn't hide my tears. He'd been furious. He'd wanted to drive straight to Matt's work and sort him out. There was barely an ounce of muscle on Nathan, and he wouldn't stand a chance, but it was still sweet that my little brother would get his ass kicked for me. He'd sat with me all afternoon and had offered his undivided attention. He'd helped me feel less alone, and though he couldn't offer any advice, I'd just needed someone. When it had been time to leave, he'd insisted I come along to his birthday party. He'd claimed it would be good for me.

I hadn't realised I'd be the only one not in their early twenties. Or not a gay man. I was glad that I had come along, though. Matt was at home with Ryan, and so Nathan made sure that I could enjoy myself fully. Which of course, meant plying me with lots and lots of alcohol.

When I refrained from taking one of the drinks off the tray, it was Nathan's boyfriend, Alec, who wouldn't let me get away with it. "Nathan," he called and nodded in my direction, "she's slowing down again."

"Lucy, what the fuck?" He tutted in disapproval. "I only turn twenty-one once. Don't you remember what it was like turning twenty-one?"

"Yes, I do. But I had a screaming one-year-old. I wasn't out drinking my liver to death."

"Oh, honey." One of Nathan's friends leaned over to me with sympathetic eyes. "Are you telling me you didn't go wild on your twenty-first birthday?" When I didn't say anything, the entire table gasped dramatically. "That's so sad."

"Okay, fine," I yelled and reached for the Jager bomb. I gulped the entire drink to the sound of clapping and cheering.

"That's more like it." Nathan grinned with excitement.

We stayed in the Union Street bar for a little longer. Mainly, it was so that Nathan could take about a thousand selfies with all his friends. When he was satisfied with the photo shoot, he led us out of the bar and into the cool air. The fresh air hit me hard, and that was when I realised just how drunk I was. I wasn't stumbling, but I wasn't exactly mastering walking in a straight line either. Nathan and Alec slung their arms over my shoulders, clearly enjoying my more carefree demeanour.

"Where to?" I asked Nathan.

He grinned as if it was obvious. "Basement, of course." A sea of cheers surrounded us, and it was clear Nathan's friends agreed.

"I haven't been in Basement since I was about your age." I pointed at Alec, knowing he was a year younger than Nathan.

"Back in the '90s?" Alec teased and bumped his hip into mine. Nothing like partying with a bunch of students to make me feel old.

"Shut up. I will have you know, I was in here a lot when I was your age."

"Why do you think I'm dragging you back here?" Nathan pecked my cheek. "I'm trying to reawaken your gayness!" He shouted the last part before he laughed mischievously.

Alec turned to me in surprise. "Wait, you were gay?"

A couple of the other boys turned in delight. It was clearly something Nathan hadn't told them. They were so eager for some gossip.

"I'm not into labels," I explained.

"You've really went down on a girl?" Alec asked in outrage, resulting in the group of boys shouting, "Ew!" They laughed and continued walking as the club appeared a few doors down.

"It's better than going down on a guy," I said, just to get another rise out of them. I didn't actually have a preference.

"Should you be admitting that when you're basically married to a dude?" Alec giggled with a drunken glint in his eye.

"Fuck Matt," Nathan spat out of nowhere, showing his rage.

"Nathan," I warned, alarmed by his change in mood.

"I don't want to hear that wanker's name tonight."

"Hey, stop," I said, latching on to his arm to get him to stop walking. Alec rubbed Nathan's back, and that seemed to calm him a bit as the rest of the boys walked on ahead. "He's still your nephew's father."

"And that's something I can't change." Nathan turned to me disappointedly. "He can still be Ryan's dad and *not* your boyfriend." He stared deep into my soul, and it stirred a heartache. "You deserve better, Luce." Nathan looked at me with so much compassion that it was hard to hold eye contact. I could feel a stinging in my eyes, but I wouldn't let my fucked-up relationship ruin my brother's birthday.

"I know," I said heartfeltly. "I'll figure it out, okay. I promise." He smiled at that. "But for now, let's just enjoy ourselves, okay?"

"Let's go dance." Alec beamed at Nathan before he pecked his lips in excitement.

I tried not to dwell on what Nathan had said, his outburst and anger at me for staying in a relationship that was not what I wanted. It was easy for him to judge. He was young. He didn't realise what was at risk. He didn't know how badly it could go or how it might affect Ryan. But despite all that, my unhappiness couldn't be ignored forever, and eventually, I was going to have to do something about it.

By the time we got to the club, the rest of the boys had bought a round of drinks. They were seated at a table waiting for us. I was chatting with one of Nathan's friends when someone on the dance floor caught my eye. I wasn't even sure when she'd arrived, but once I spotted Dani, it was impossible to look elsewhere.

She hadn't seen me yet. I was thankful of that because it meant I got to enjoy watching for a little while longer. The way her body moved to the beat of the bass was hypnotic and sensual. She was still in her work clothes, which made her dancing all the sexier. The only thing I didn't like was the other woman she was dancing with. I watched her closely, as well. Her hands were sometimes on Dani, and it irked me in ways I couldn't explain. She was really pretty and blond. Perhaps blondes were Dani's type. Catriona was blond, and that thought caused disappointment, considering my dark hair couldn't compete.

"She's hot," Nathan whispered beside me. I jumped to attention. I hadn't even realised he'd sat next to me. His friend who I was talking to was long gone.

"Who?" I played dumb and instead took a few large gulps of my drink. I hadn't realised how thirsty I'd gotten.

"The woman you've been staring at for the last hour."

"I have not." At least, I hoped it hadn't been an hour.

"Why don't you go dance with her?"

"I'm not interested in anyone." My stuttering made that sound like a very weak argument. "I know her is all."

Nathan looked surprised. "You know her?" He pointed into the dance floor just as Dani turned in our direction.

I grabbed his arm and pulled it down. "Jesus, could you be

any more obvious." I couldn't hide the panic in my voice, and it only caused Nathan to laugh hysterically.

"You *like* her."

"No, I don't. She's a friend. Ryan and her son are friends. We're sort of friends," I rambled aimlessly before sneaking a glance back at the dance floor. But she was gone. "Just shut up, Nathan." I could still hear his sniggering, but I was too busy searching for her, afraid that perhaps she'd seen me leering. Or worse, that she had left.

"She's at the bar, dickhead," Nathan teased.

I saw her and knew I had to say something or risk it being completely awkward next time I saw her at school pickup. I got up and didn't miss the shakiness in my limbs as I moved in the direction of the bar. Nathan watching me from the table also didn't help.

Chapter Eight

Dani Raye

"Lucy," I practically yelled at the poor girl, and the look on her face showed her startle. "Sorry. Hi, oh my God. I'm so sorry," I rambled. "I just didn't recognise you, you look so, so..." I glanced down her front, which was the worst thing I could have done because staring at the body of a supermodel meant that the only descriptive words in my mind were most definitely not friend-appropriate. "Neat." Her forehead creased in confusion. "I mean, nice," I corrected, not that it was much better. Why was I suddenly a blubbering idiot? "You look very nice," I added awkwardly, but she seemed to be enjoying my stuttering.

"Thanks." She tilted her head the cute way that she did. "I actually brushed my hair today."

"That must be it."

"I'm wearing lipstick too."

"I can see that," I said as the bartender placed my drinks down. "Do you want a drink?" I asked, but she shook her head.

"I have one over at my table."

I passed the bartender some cash as Lucy thumbed to the far corner, and I saw a large group of men. I wondered if Matt was there for a moment, but I doubted it, considering the way they were dancing and grinding on each other while others were taking selfies.

She pulled my eyes back to her again. "I wasn't expecting to see you here," she said, seemingly with double meaning, then clarified, "just with it being a weeknight. Don't you have work tomorrow?"

"Yeah, I do. I'm sure I'll regret it in the morning but—"

"Me too." She smiled knowingly. "Especially when I'm having to get Ryan ready for school. But it's a special occasion. My little brother turned twenty-one, so I figured I had to be here, regardless of the hangover."

"Wait until you hit my age. The hangovers are much worse," I teased, taking a sip of the drink.

"You know, you're not that much older than me," she said in a sultry tone that caused me to choke slightly on my drink. "Besides, the way you were dancing out there, you looked pretty limber to me." I felt my face heat up at the thought of her having seen me make a fool out of myself. I had no idea she was here; otherwise, I would have never gotten up to dance. "But I'm sure your date is missing you out there," she finished with what could only have been described as a raspy, indifferent edge to her voice.

I followed her line of vision to Heather. When I snuck a glance at Lucy, I saw a hardening of her expression that I wasn't expecting. She'd been drinking. I could tell by her inability to hide what could be mistaken for jealousy. "Heather?"

"She looks...nice," Lucy commented, but it lacked any real sincerity. Her apparent jealousy filled me with confidence.

"She's not my date. Heather's straight." Lucy's eyes colliding hard with mine told me it was what she wanted to hear. I didn't miss the excited glint that appeared in her eyes either, and it resulted in me pushing the boundaries. "I can see why you thought that, though. It can be hard to tell these days. Who's straight and who's..." I glanced at her lips. "Not."

The air stilled around us, and I couldn't stop myself from being completely entranced by her. The way her eyes held mine and the way she showed a knowing smile revealing she understood my suggestion loud and clear. This woman showed nothing but a sexy confidence that I'd only seen a glimmer of at the park last week. It was like a completely different person.

"And sometimes," she said and took a daring step toward me, "it's obvious." The intensity in her eyes caused my throat to dry up. She leaned in as if about to kiss me.

"There you are," Heather said, standing right in front of us.

Lucy took a step back, and I probably looked positively flustered. I drank half the drink just to distract myself from how good Lucy looked. I wondered if this was how she looked when she was turned on. But that wasn't helpful, either.

"Hi, I'm Heather." She waved to Lucy, but given the suggestive look she was throwing me, I'd say she'd picked up on the chemistry between us.

"Right." I switched into pleasantries, "Heather, this is Lucy. Her son is friends with Jonah. And Lucy, this is my colleague, Heather."

"Lovely to meet you, Heather."

"And you."

"I'd be interested to know what Dani's like at work." She side-eyed me sexily, and once again, my throat dried up. She was confident, alluring, and I could barely keep a handle on my attraction.

"She's a real hardass at work." Heather's country accent had intensified with alcohol. "It's all business with her." She shimmied behind me to get her drink from the bar.

In her momentary absence, Lucy murmured just loud enough for me to hear, "What do you do for pleasure?"

"I can show you." It slipped out before I had a chance to check myself. I was glad it did because the look on Lucy's face solidified my theory that she was into women. And more specifically, me.

Heather manoeuvred back with her drink again.

"I should get back," Lucy stammered before glancing fleetingly, almost in panic, between us. "I'll see you later."

She left, and my mind went into overdrive, analysing the interaction. Was I too predatory? Had she even leaned in, or had I imagined that? Shit. Perhaps she was just being flirtatious. Hell, maybe she was just being friendly. Fuck. Did I just completely mess up a friendship? Regret settled in my chest, and I couldn't help but feel I'd overstepped a boundary.

Lucy didn't come back over again, and that only added fuel to my fire of insecurity. It was a little while later, and Heather and I were seated at a table near the dance floor, talking. Heather had somehow moved on to the topic of her ex, Daryl, which I already knew was dangerous. It wouldn't be long before it led to sloppy tears, and that wasn't going to help anyone. Besides, it was past midnight and time we were making tracks.

I was trying to reassure Heather when I looked up at the dance floor, and there she was. Lucy was dancing with her brother and his friends. I tried to focus on Heather and what she was saying, but my eyes were pulled to Lucy like a moth to a flame.

Her arms were looped around the neck of one of the boys. By their almost sensual dancing, I knew it wasn't her brother. Her shoulders swayed as their hips moved in unison. His exaggerated hip thrusts and head whips proved he wasn't getting off on Lucy's moves, but I couldn't say the same for myself. My line of vision was unwavering. Like a car crash but a really fucking hot car crash. With flames and destruction.

She spun around so her back was to his front. The other boys in the group hyped the two of them up, knowing that it was all very innocent. Though there was no need to feel threatened by him, I was envious. I wished it was me she was pressed up against. That thought caused a wave of arousal that I tried desperately to ignore. Her body slid down his front, and when I finally met her eyes, I realised she had been staring back at me.

A seductive smile played on her lips as her hips rocked from side to side. Her hands slid down her thighs, and I imagined what it would feel like to be between them. In that moment, there was nothing more that I wanted to do than walk right over to her, take her hand, and take her home with me.

"I don't feel so good," Heather said, pulling me from Lucy.

I woke from whatever fucked-up fantasy I was living in and turned to my friend. She was beyond drunk, her head slumped into her palms on the table.

"Okay, let's get you home." I helped her to her feet. I made sure we had everything before we left the club and made it out into the cool night. The breeze seemed to bring Heather around a little. She was no longer feeling sick as we waited for the taxi outside, though she plonked down on the curb to wait.

"Hey." Lucy appeared next to me, and it made me jump. "Sorry," she said with a sweet smile. The previous raw sex appeal had disappeared now that she was standing next to me in the sobering air. "Are you two leaving?"

"Yeah, it's late, and I've work tomorrow."

"Plus, I'm pretty fucked," Heather added from her position on the curb.

"Cool." Lucy nodded a few times. "I'm actually going home myself."

"Why don't you share our taxi?" Heather suggested. "We're going to South Belfast."

"Me too," she said, but of course, I already knew that. She'd texted me her address for Ryan's party a couple of weeks back. She lived on Myrtle Drive, not far from me. Not that I'd memorised that information or anything.

"Then it's settled," I said as the taxi I'd ordered pulled up.

The ride home was quiet but eventful. Though I was sure Heather felt nothing, the electricity in the back seat was enough to power an entire city. Heather had dozed off to my right while Lucy was on my left. Her bare thigh was touching my leg, and I could feel the heat through my trousers. As we turned onto the Ormeau Road, her hand slid off her thigh and landed in the slither of space between us. Then, I felt it. Her index finger caressed my outer thigh. I couldn't control my breathing. Her touch was intimate and delicate and yet was sending my body into overdrive. My fingers begged to touch her, and I could tell she was watching my every move. I could hear her shallow breaths, and it turned me on. The unspoken energy swirling between us was enough to set my body alight.

The taxi pulled onto Heather's street. I cleared my throat and moved my leg out of Lucy's reach before rousing Heather awake. "You're home, Heather." She cocked her head in an unconscious daze. "Do you have your key?"

"Yep." She jiggled them in my face before she went searching in her purse for something.

"Do you have everything?" Lucy piped up from beside me.

"Yep. Here." She passed me a twenty to pay for the taxi, and though I tried to protest, she launched herself out the door, slamming it shut.

"Can you just wait for a minute until she gets in?" Lucy asked the driver.

It was thoughtful and sincere, and I couldn't help a smile. She saw it and mirrored it. Her eyes pulled me in again, and my breathing turned uneasy. She was so beautiful, and every time I looked into her eyes, I felt myself become more and more attracted to her.

"Where to next?" the driver asked, resulting in a tension to surround us in the back seat.

I didn't say anything and neither did she. I could feel her eyes on me. Begging me to make the decision for her. Or at least, that was how it felt. Her reluctance to say her own address made me think she wanted to go to my place. Maybe it was innocent. Maybe she just wanted to drop me off first. But given her seductive actions all night, I couldn't be sure that it would be innocent. The possibilities were running through my head, but it all felt too sudden. And aside from anything else, I had to remind myself of the number-one roadblock in this plan. She had a partner. And I was most definitely not a cheater.

"Myrtle Drive, please," I said, her street, and then slid over to where Heather had previously sat.

I needed the space. I could feel her disappointment, and it

lingered in the air around us. Part of me regretted not inviting her back to mine, but at the same time, this was already complicated. This wasn't just a woman I'd met at a bar; this was my son's best friend's mum. How could we look each other in the eye afterward? Our magnetic chemistry tonight meant that we probably would have had amazing sex. Earth-shattering, perhaps. But I couldn't go through with it. She wasn't available. She had a boyfriend, I had to remind myself again. And I refused to be anything like Maeve. It was a tough decision but the right one.

Lucy failed to look me in the eyes again. When she got out of the taxi, she said good night, but it sounded like it came from a place of embarrassment.

That was the last thing she said to me until the day of her son's birthday.

CHAPTER NINE

Dani Raye

I could feel myself wound up tighter than a new coil. The two-day hangover hadn't helped. I'd never gotten this nervous going to any other six-year-old's birthday, but it was his mother I was worried about seeing. Especially after how I'd rejected her explicit suggestion the night before last.

"Do you think Ryan will have a birthday cake?" Jonah asked from the back seat.

"I don't see why not," I returned but focused on the road. "Why do you ask?"

"I really like cake."

"I know you do." I smiled to myself. "But one slice only."

"Do you think he will have a Spider-Man cake?" he asked, and I could see him smoothing out his Spider-Man costume in the rear-view mirror.

It was sweet and adorable how excited he was. He didn't get many invites, mainly due to his shyness; therefore, a birthday party of someone his own age was huge. We got his costume last week, and even though it was a size too big, he was insistent. I was pleased to see him so excited and not at all nervous, perhaps because I would be sticking around to help chaperone.

"Well, it's a superhero party," I replied. "But that doesn't mean he will get a Spider-Man cake. He might have something else on it."

"Like Batman?"

"Or anything," I said in an effort to broaden his scope of suggestions.

"Like Superman? Or Captain America or Iron Man…" And that was the rest of the car journey spent discussing superheroes.

When we pulled up outside the house, I found myself thinking back to the night I was last parked outside. In a taxi, late at night, the cold shoulder I'd faced from Lucy, and in an instant, my dread returned. It weighed me down as I got Jonah out of the car, and we moved toward the front door. With each step, I felt the pit in my stomach growing. Jonah had insisted on carrying Ryan's present the entire way to the door, which was a relief because I was sure it would have slipped out of my sweaty palms.

He pressed the doorbell, and I could hear it ringing. When the door swung open, we were greeted by an unknown man. He was tall and handsome, with light facial hair grazing his chin.

"Hi, are you here for the party?" he asked, most likely noting Jonah's costume.

"Yes."

"Great, I'm Matt." His hand shot out as I tried desperately to ignore the panic coursing through me. His handshake was firm but warm.

"Dani. And this is Jonah."

By his pleasant smile, it seemed unlikely that he knew about Thursday night, but I also couldn't deny my disappointment. Lucy had said Matt wouldn't be here. If I'd known her boyfriend was going to be chaperoning too, I would have sent Catriona.

"Jonah." Matt grinned at him. "I've heard a lot about you, buddy. It's great to meet you, and what a very cool costume."

Matt seemed perfectly lovely, but Jonah was a little standoffish when it came to men in general, mainly because he wasn't around many. Fortunately, Matt didn't look offended and stood back and welcomed us inside.

"The party is mainly outside," he explained as he walked us through the house. "But not everyone is here yet, so it could get pretty hectic. Do you want a drink?" he asked me. "A coffee, glass of wine?"

His welcoming nature made eye contact all the more difficult. I felt like a sleazeball in his company. He had the same smile as Ryan, and that made him look as innocent as it did charming. My stomach churned as I entered the kitchen and saw her. She locked eyes with me from across the room, then looked at Matt. Her gaze jumped between us as he made idle chitchat. Perhaps she feared what I might say to him.

"Jonah, do you like bouncy castles?" Matt asked, pulling me back into the conversation. Jonah's eyes expanded excitedly, though he held on tight to my hand. "Look out there." He pointed toward the garden, and I caught sight of the inflatable castle. Jonah's hand went limp as he stared out, hypnotised. "You can go on out."

Jonah glanced to me for approval, and after I nodded, he disappeared outside without a look back. It didn't take long for him to find Ryan. I could see them interacting with some other children. The costumes were fantastic and very well put-together. There was Thor, Wonder Woman, and others. There were a couple of adults too, but they all seemed a little older, closer to my parents' age.

Matt ushered me to the drinks table. "Red or white wine?" he asked, lifting a wineglass.

"I shouldn't really."

"I can make it into a spritzer." He grinned, revealing a perfect smile to break any woman's heart.

I gave in, feeling Lucy's eyes piercing my skin from across the kitchen. "Okay."

"So, Dani, what is it you do?" Matt asked, but I struggled to focus on him. To focus on anything with her eyes on me.

"I work in marketing." I knew I was being curt, but I could see her approaching, and it made my breathing erratic.

"Hey, Dani." Lucy breezed effortlessly alongside Matt. "I'm

so glad you and Jonah could make it." His arm slid around her shoulders, and the gesture caused a clenching on my insides.

I watched for any signs of discomfort, but she seemed at ease with his touch. It amplified the churning in my stomach. I was furious. She'd led me to believe they were separated or on track for some kind of separation, but this was hardly the display of a couple in trouble. I could feel my blood boiling and the saliva turning sour in my mouth. What kind of game was she playing?

The mood shift must have been obvious to Lucy because she piped up, breaking Matt from whatever he was saying. "Hey, can you check on the barbeque?"

"I think your dad is looking after it," he said but glanced over his shoulder at the back garden. "But maybe you're right. He might be on his third beer," he teased before turning back to me. "Make yourself at home, Dani."

If he wasn't so nice, this would have been a lot easier. Before leaving, he pecked Lucy on the lips, and I couldn't even stomach to look at her. We plunged into deafening silence, and I knew anyone would be able to see the tension from a mile off. My lungs felt hot with rage. I didn't think Lucy was the kind of woman who wanted to have an affair, and seeing her playing happy families with her boyfriend after our flirting the other night made me really uncomfortable. Whatever I thought was going on between the two of them was a lie, and that made being in her home beyond unsettling. I felt like a criminal, no, worse, I felt no better than Maeve, and I was annoyed at myself for even engaging in her advances the other night.

"So much for separating," I muttered. "What the hell was that the other night?"

"I could ask you the same thing," she said with an angry brow.

What had I done?

She checked over her shoulder and gestured for me to follow her into the living room. I left my wine on the table and followed, making sure we weren't being watched. We moved into the spacious, tastefully decorated living space, and finally, we were alone. She didn't bother to close the door. Perhaps that would raise an alarm; besides, I didn't think I could cope with being locked in a room with her. She moved away from the door, perhaps as a way of keeping our conversation private.

"It's a show." She spun to face me before I could speak. Her voice sounded desperate, and when I didn't say anything, she waved in the direction of the kitchen. "Our families don't know we're separating."

I crossed my arms, unconvinced. "Well, it's certainly an Oscar-worthy performance." It was nasty, and I regretted it when I saw the hurt on her face. It made me feel terrible. "I'm sorry," I whispered, and she seemed to accept it. "But can you see where I'm coming from?" My tone softened; even having this conversation felt inappropriate. Like it shouldn't be above a whisper. "He's all over you."

"He's always *appeared* affectionate." She stepped closer, keeping her voice low. "Only in public. If he were to stop now, it would be glaringly obvious something was wrong."

I still couldn't look at her. Glancing around their family room also poked holes in her story. There were pictures of the three of them everywhere. The guilt swirled around in my stomach, and it made our conversation feel seedy and dishonest. "It just doesn't feel right." I shook my head. "I don't know what's going on between us but—"

"Same," she launched back, agitated. It felt like her emotions had flipped almost instantly, and I was at a loss for the reasoning. "What was that yesterday? Why did you blank me at school?"

I hadn't thought it was that blatant, and it caused the regret to seep in. I couldn't face her yesterday. When I was collecting Jonah, I'd deliberately sat in my car until the last possible second. It was to avoid getting out and standing anywhere near Lucy. It was petty, but I couldn't face her after the night at Basement.

As soon as I'd spotted Jonah, I'd gotten out of the car and had practically rushed him out of sight. Looking back, it was pretty immature, but I'd panicked.

"I don't know." I tried desperately to siphon through my racing thoughts, but it felt like a blur. Her watching my every move didn't help. It was as if my mind was out of its depth, and my heart was forced to lead my explanation. "I felt awkward, and I didn't know what to say to you. What was I supposed to say to you after…" I trailed off, thinking about that night, and by the look on her face, it was clear that she was also replaying it. "On Thursday night, I thought we were going to…" I couldn't say it; my guilt wouldn't allow it. "I just don't understand what's going on here."

"Neither do I." She breathed out, showing her frustration. "Sometimes, you act like you're into me, but the next minute, you go cold again."

I didn't have a defence. I knew I had been sending mixed messages.

But she barely stopped long enough to take a breath. "I like you, Dani." Her vulnerability had my heart fluttering, and I couldn't help but get carried away with being desired by her. "Sometimes, I feel this intense connection. Like, if you touched me, I'd burst into flames." She'd lowered her voice, and my entire body went rigid. Her honesty touched me on a deeper level. "Sometimes, when I think about you…" She bit her lip, and it caused my breathing to turn uneasy. "I can't think about anything else. I wanted to talk to you yesterday to figure out what the fuck is going on because honestly…" Her eyes widened in what looked like desperation. "I have never felt like…I mean, I practically threw myself at you on Thursday, and nothing. I can't keep overthinking everything like this, or I will go crazy. If you're not attracted to me, just say it, okay?"

Before I knew what I was doing, I kissed her. She inhaled sharply, though it was short-lived. I took a step back before I could even really savour the moment. But the short burst of bliss didn't seem lost on her either. She was heaving as she stared at me in shock.

"You're not crazy. I like you," I said as a lazy smile tugged at her lips. "And I really wanted to invite you back to my house on Thursday night."

She squeezed her eyes shut in what appeared to be relief. Maybe she had worried that she'd imagined our sexual chemistry.

But I forced myself to focus on my words. I needed to articulate where I was coming from. Her smile seemed to vanish when I hesitated. "But I don't want to do it like this." I took in their living room again as family photos created a wave of guilt. "I'm not going to be the other woman," I said firmly and watched her face contort in confusion. I wouldn't be the reason a relationship ended like my own. "I can't do this if you're still with him."

My words seemed hard for her to digest. "It's really complicated, Dani."

"I know." I nodded, even though the truth was, I had no idea how complicated it was. Her relationship with Matt was not something she'd gone into detail about.

"I like you too," she said, and I could see the truth. "A lot. But I understand where you're coming from. I don't want to lead you on." She sighed in frustration. "I want to tell you everything. You deserve that. And then we can decide…" She trailed off. "You decide what happens. If you decide it's too much or too—"

"Mummy," Ryan shouted from somewhere in the house.

Her gaze broke away. "Fuck," she whispered sadly. "I'm sorry."

"It's okay." I waved her off, and she moved past.

Music was pouring in from the party, and I knew this was not the right setting to talk. Sometimes, we had to put the kids first, even above our own happiness. This was a conversation we needed to have, but it could wait. Ryan needed his mum today.

She surprised me when she turned back to me at the door. "Will you stay? I don't want to make you uncomfortable but…"

She frowned as if she wasn't sure what she wanted to say. "I really like having you around." She seemed almost embarrassed to have admitted it, but I couldn't deny how her declaration made my insides dance.

"I'll stay."

"Are you sure?" Her head tilted, concern making its way onto her features.

"Yeah. I'm not going to rip Jonah away from the party of the century." She laughed as I walked toward her. "I'm also *so* glad that Ryan is Captain America. There would have been tears if he was also in a Spider-Man costume."

"Can you imagine?" She reached for my arm excitedly. "It would have been a full-blown civil war." She laughed genuinely, and I couldn't tear my eyes away. She looked so carefree and beautiful.

She watched me carefully for a second, and before I'd even registered what she was doing, she had pecked me on the cheek. No one had seen, but it left a flutter in my chest that would no doubt remain for the rest of the afternoon. "Come on."

I was pleased when Lucy stayed close for most of the party. Of course, there were certain hosting duties which she had to take care of, but she always appeared back with me. And true to her word, I saw minimal interaction between her and Matt. The closer I watched them, the more apparent the tension was. The photos no longer seemed genuine. If there was love at some stage, it looked more like a complacency now. Of course, I wasn't an expert on the ins and outs of their relationship after spending one afternoon with them, but if it was clear enough for me to see the cracks, I wondered why no one else had.

I spent a lot of time talking with Lucy's mother, Denise, a fascinating woman. She couldn't have been older than her early fifties, if her flawless skin was anything to go by. She ate her own vegan food that Lucy had prepared earlier. She had a similar frame to Lucy's, a slim build, but her attire made her stand out like a sore thumb. She was dressed in a baggy, oversized garment that could have been a dress or a T-shirt, that blended into a long skirt. It only added to her bohemian persona.

"And so there I was," Denise said in a thick New York accent with wild and expressive hands, "stranded in the middle of the Nevada desert in a pair of hot pants and a bikini top, hitchhiking to LA." She couldn't contain her own laughter, which made it difficult for me to control mine. "And that, my dear, was the last time I ever slept with a woman." She shouted the last part a little loud before she guzzled half her can of beer.

Denise Matthews was a character, but I would have never thought she could have birthed someone like Lucy. Lucy was sweet and shy, whereas Denise sounded like she smoked twenty cigarettes a day and lived out of the back of her van. I loved her flower-child vibe, and I was completely fascinated by her lifestyle.

Lucy's dad had made an appearance too. He was from Northern Ireland originally but seemed to have travelled a lot. He was a little hippie as well but not anywhere near the level of Denise. Nathan, Lucy's brother, who I vaguely remembered from Basement, was also there, but he and his boyfriend were outside most of the afternoon. They were the two biggest kids in the bouncy castle.

"Mum?" Lucy appeared out of nowhere with a stern expression. "Maybe leave Dani alone. And take it easy on the beers."

"I'm having a great time." I smiled and watched her stern expression crumble.

"Your friend is wonderful, Lu," Denise said while patting my shoulder. "I was just telling her about the time I was a lesbian—"

"Mum!" Lucy cut her off sharply and glanced over her shoulder at her in-laws. "Leave the 'free love' stories for another day, okay?" Denise frowned. "Please, Matt's parents are right there."

Denise turned back to me and threw me a defeated look. "They think I'm white trash."

I looked to Lucy in the hope she would reassure her mother, but she didn't. That was a surprise and a little disheartening. Lucy just looked away, seemingly a little ashamed. For someone who had so much compassion, she neglected to stand up for her own mother? It was clear she was incredibly embarrassed by her mum, perhaps both her parents.

I guessed it made sense. Matt's parents came from money. I'd barely spoken two words to them, and even I could tell that. Matt's dad, Patrick, wore a tweed jacket, and he'd already mentioned his Porsche twice. Matt's mother wore diamond earrings and flung her designer handbag onto the floor like it was nothing. Even Lucy and Matt's home reflected an expensive lifestyle. It looked new and was on a very nice street. And though Lucy hadn't given off a materialistic impression, perhaps around her in-laws, she felt the need to do so.

"Well, I think you're fabulous," I said to Denise and clinked my glass of spritzer with her can of beer.

"And I think you're pretty awesome too, Dani," Denise said as she picked over her food. She tapped the plate once or twice. "That's a great plate, Lu."

"Thanks, Mum."

I looked a little closer at the dinnerware. "Did you make that?"

Lucy smiled bashfully.

"She's got the gift." Denise pulled my attention back to her. "She took everything I taught her, and now, her technique is much better than mine ever was. My Lulu." Denise winked at her proudly.

"You used to throw clay too?" I glanced at Lucy smugly because I'd finally learned how to correctly use that phrase.

She rolled her eyes playfully.

"Yes, well, I was an art teacher for ten years," Denise explained. "I even took the kiln from the high school I used to work in, but my arthritis started playing up, and I had to give it up. But I passed it on to Lulu. Are you still spinning?"

"Yeah, I'm getting into it again."

"Good," Denise said excitedly. "I know you've been feeling blocked for a while. You must have found your inspiration."

I was taken aback when Lucy's eyes jumped to me. "Yeah, I think so." I gulped, hoping no one else noticed what that comment did to me. "I've a load of pieces in the garage, actually. That's where I work," she explained to me.

"I'd love to see it," I said, and Lucy once again seemed suspicious of my interest.

"Yeah?" I nodded frantically. "Okay, I'll show you." She got up and motioned for me to follow.

I extended the invite to Denise, but she said, "I'm dying for a piss."

I perked up as we moved outside and into the garden. "Your mum is…" I tried to find the correct word.

But Lucy wouldn't let me. "I know, she's so embarrassing."

"What are you talking about? She's so fucking cool."

"Yeah, not if she's your mum."

The children's laughter flowed out of the top of the bouncy castle. It was moving in all directions, perhaps struggling to keep up with the constant bouncing from the many children and grown men inside. I could see Jonah with Nathan, holding his hands for balance. He was having the time of his life. I waved, even if he didn't see it.

Lucy ran a hand through her hair, straightening her bangs. Even though her fringe tried to hide it, I spotted the hardening of her brow. She looked deep in thought, and it brought me back to how she'd interacted with Denise.

"Are you ashamed of her?" I asked.

"Only around certain people." She met my eyes as she came to a halt outside the garage door.

"What, like your stuffy old in-laws?"

Lucy cracked a smile, and I could tell I was hitting the mark. "They already think I'm classless." She joked, but there was truth there too. "And when you add in my hippie-dippy parents…"

"I happen to like your parents," I said and looked back toward the house. "And they're a lot more interesting than Patrick and *Audrey*." I said her mother-in-law's name in a posh accent, causing her to giggle.

"Stop making me laugh."

"Why?"

"It makes me want to kiss you." She said it so effortlessly, it took my breath away. She broke eye contact with me first. "And I can't do that." She focused on unlocking the garage door instead.

The door opened, and she flipped the switch. I stepped into the room and couldn't describe the rush of excitement that came over me. I wasn't overly spiritual, but seeing Lucy's work space felt like I was walking into the room where creativity was born. She had shelves of ceramics. I could see mugs, bowls, and plates in every colour imaginable.

"This is it," she said shyly and closed the door behind her.

The loss of music shielded us from the rest of the party. It felt like we were in our own little world. I wanted to go straight to the ceramics to see her artwork for myself, but my feet were taking me to the place where all the magic happened. The wheel was caked in clay in the middle of the room. Even the stool next to it was covered in the beige substance. I could imagine Lucy working here, and I enjoyed that image. At the other end of the garage, a metal sheet hung from the roof and seemed to quarantine the kiln from the rest of the room.

She spotted me staring at it. "It gets super-hot in here when it's on. You can't even be in the room."

I spotted a table in the corner that was covered in paint. I moved toward it and had to smile because it looked like a rainbow had thrown up on it. Every colour had made an appearance. Above the table was a shelf of at least twenty or thirty different bottles of paint and glazes.

"I'm not exactly the tidiest of painters." She shrugged, touching the dried paint blobs on the table.

"It's amazing. Seriously," I said breathlessly, "you're amazing." It just fell from my lips.

When I met her eyes again, it was like a magnet. She gazed at me with what I could only describe as want, and being on the receiving end of it was exhilarating. I knew it was inappropriate, but there was an invisible rope pulling me to her, and I couldn't break it even if I tried. She closed the gap, and her lips found mine. It was nothing like our first kiss, soft and timid. This was charged, and I could have done nothing to stop it. Her arms looped around my neck urgently, and she moaned into the kiss. Her hands moved frantically from the base of my neck and into my hair while mine moved to her hips. I felt the warmth of her skin through her dress, and it made me want to undress her there and then.

I was at the mercy of her urgency. Before I knew what was happening, she'd pushed me up against the wall. There was so much need in her movements, or maybe it was the desperation in her kiss. Perhaps it was both. Whatever it was, I was happily being led.

"Lucy?" A voice outside the garage caused us both to jump apart. It was Matt, and I felt horrible for getting carried away. And at their son's birthday party, of all places.

She straightened her dress and moved toward the door, looking panicked. I was fixing my hair and wiping my face in case our lipsticks had created a mess.

"Hey," she said from the door.

"Should we do the cake soon?" Matt said, and I had to turn my back to him. "It's getting late."

I knew he could see me in the back of the garage. I made out like I was perusing the shelf of ceramics. It was the only thing I could do to avoid the agony of having to look him in the eye. Especially after what I'd just been doing with his girlfriend.

"Yeah," she replied. "I didn't even realise the time. Okay, I'll be out in a minute. I'm just showing Dani my work."

"She's amazing, isn't she?" he said to me, and I was forced to see the proud smile on his face. It made me feel like complete shit. Worthless. The shame on Lucy's face wasn't helping either.

"Yeah," I just about got out through the internal turmoil threatening my voice.

Matt closed the door, and silence fell over us. I couldn't stand it, and so I tried to leave. I had my hand on the handle when she grabbed my other hand. I reluctantly faced her, ignoring the guilt disturbing the acid in my tummy.

"Can I come over tonight?"

Her request rendered me speechless. That she could be so brazen as to suggest a secret rendezvous when she knew how I felt about cheating. My face must have shown my outrage, and she seemed to panic.

"Not for that," she murmured. "To talk. I want us to be on the same page. You need to know what's going on between me and Matt." My gaze dropped. "If it's all too much, then I'll understand if you want nothing to do with me, but please don't write me off until I can explain."

I very reluctantly saw her desperation. My gut instinct told me to listen. "Okay." Her shoulders relaxed a little, but I still couldn't face her. My emotions were too conflicted.

I left the garage and moved into the back garden. Lucy made the walk alone to the kitchen. I stayed outside and watched Jonah play with his friends, finding it too difficult to be in their family home. Not after what had happened in the garage. Not understanding the situation surrounding Lucy and Matt's relationship had me feeling guilt, shame, and unbelievable discomfort. I wanted to leave the party as soon as I'd left the garage, but I forced myself to stick it out. For Jonah's sake alone.

Nathan appeared alongside me. "Hey, Dani, right?"

I wasn't sure how long I was staring into space, but I'd missed him completely. "Yeah, hi. You're Lucy's brother?"

"Nathan." He reached out his hand, scrutinising me a little. "Have we met before?"

"I don't think so. But I was talking to Lucy the other night at Basement—"

"That's it." He clicked his fingers and smiled knowingly. He was very tall, lean, and seemed to tower over me. He had similar features to Lucy's, but it was his smile that reminded me of her most. "That night was a bit of a blur for me."

"It was your twenty-first birthday, right?" I said, and his grin seemed to widen even further. "Well, happy birthday."

"Thank you. I nearly shared the same birthday as Ryan, but he was two days late." He shrugged. "It was still pretty cool becoming an uncle at fifteen."

I got a little lost in thought. It must have been quite a shock for the whole family when Lucy had told them she was pregnant. It would have been a scandal if it was mine. Perhaps it was. "That's young."

"Well, she was only nineteen when Matt knocked her up."

"Were they together long? Before she got pregnant." I tried to remain nonchalant. I didn't want Nathan knowing why I was so interested.

"No, they weren't even together." My head snapped up to him. "They were best friends, though. He was actually our next-door neighbour, but I guess they must have been hooking up at some point." He took a swig from his beer.

My mind felt like it was running away with itself. Matt and Lucy had only become a thing after she'd gotten pregnant. I wondered why Nathan was revealing so much. I was a stranger. Maybe he was drunk, but I got the vibe that he was up to something.

He quirked his brow mischievously. "Are you gay?" he asked out of the blue.

"Yeah."

"Thought so." He laughed, leaving me with no response. I couldn't figure out if I was offended or not. It must have been my silence that caused him to elaborate. "Lucy has a huge crush on you, but you didn't hear it from me."

"What?" I squeaked and quickly scanned around the garden to make sure no one was nearby. "What are you talking about?"

"Oh, girl, chill. I overheard you two in the living room." The blood drained from my face, and it felt like the oxygen in my lungs had evaporated. "By the way, next time you're going to kiss my sister, maybe don't do it at a family party with her boyfriend in the next room."

I was practically panting as the contents of my stomach felt like they could erupt. I wanted to lie and tell him he was mistaken, but he'd caught us red-handed, and now, I felt even worse for getting involved in anything with Lucy. I was so unhinged by what he was saying, I hadn't even clocked his calm demeanour. It seemed misplaced, considering what he'd revealed.

"I'm not going to say anything." His voice lowered. "Your secret is safe with me. Lucy was the first person I came out to. She had my back, and I'm going to have hers." I let out a breath of relief. "Besides, you're way cuter than Matt. And I hate him so—"

"Nathan," Ryan called from the bouncy castle.

"Coming," Nathan shouted back, but he turned to me one last time with a more serious expression. "Lucy has been through a lot. It's not been easy for her these last few months. Just don't hurt her. Okay?" He cracked a brief smile before leaving.

I was glad the cake followed shortly after because I didn't have the strength to be in that home of surprises any longer. Though, I was happy Jonah got to see his best friend blow out the candles. We even got to take a piece home with us, but I was more grateful that we got to sneak out with another family to avoid having to say good-bye to Matt. I managed to successfully dodge Lucy as well. I had such little control on my feelings that I worried I would say something out of anger or hurt or embarrassment. I wasn't really sure. I told myself whatever I had to say could wait until she came around tonight.

CHAPTER TEN

Dani Raye

Lucy texted me saying she would come by shortly after nine. I assumed it was after Ryan's bedtime. I'd gotten Jonah tucked in not too long before, though it proved to be a challenge with the amount of cake and sweets he'd had. He was practically vibrating from the sugar.

I'd poured a glass of wine with dinner but hadn't touched it. Usually, I wouldn't have any bother polishing off a glass or two at the weekend, but I could barely stomach dinner, let alone anything stronger. The glass was still on the coffee table as I channel hopped. I wasn't particularly invested in anything on TV. The game shows offered little distraction from my troubled thoughts.

After leaving Lucy's home, the guilt had eaten away at me slowly. I rationalised it by telling myself they were in an open relationship; at least, that was what I hoped. But regardless of their arrangement, the reality was that Matt wouldn't have been so hospitable if he'd known there was something going on between us. He'd been innocently hosting me and my son while I was secretly making out with his partner in the garage. Even the knowledge that Nathan knew was enough to send me running for the hills. That was one person too many for my liking. Despite my growing attraction for Lucy, it didn't sit right with me, and I'd vowed long ago to never break up a family. I knew firsthand of the devastation that infidelity caused.

A knock at the door caused my heart rate to spike. My body felt like lead on the couch, and I was nervous to see her face-to-face. I took a few deep inhales but couldn't seem to regulate the shaky exhales.

When I opened the front door, I was pleased to find her still wearing the summer dress from earlier. It was flattering on her, and she had seemed more carefree in the bright colours. However, now she seemed weighed down with worry. Probably a mirror image of myself. She offered a cautionary smile, but perhaps she could already detect my apprehension.

"Come in," I said, stepping back to give her some room.

She followed me quietly into the living room. The TV was still on, but I'd muted it before getting the door. She stood awkwardly in the entrance, perhaps not knowing where she should sit. Maybe she wanted to stand. It felt like we were both hovering above eggshells, afraid of cracking whatever it was growing between us.

"Is Jonah in bed?"

"Yeah," I said. "Can I get you a drink?"

"Sure."

"Do you drink wine?" I motioned to my own glass.

She nodded shyly, as if we barely knew each other.

I hated that her energy was so tense. We weren't normally like this around each other, but perhaps it was necessary to get through this conversation. I excused myself to fill a glass in the kitchen and tried to ready myself. I'd been preparing for this all day. I wanted to be firm yet reasonable. I needed to hear the full story in order to make up my mind about whether I could engage in this any longer. I just had to resist how good she looked in that dress.

When I arrived back in the living room, she was on the couch. I was thankful it was a large couch so we could be in our own corners. Though being on top of each other sounded good. *Damnit, focus, Dani.*

I took my seat and handed her the wineglass. She took a

modest sip before setting it on the coffee table. "I'm sorry about earlier," she started softly as I took a sip of wine, needing something to focus on.

"You'd said Matt wasn't going to be there." I heard the accusation in my tone despite trying my very best to sound neutral.

"He wasn't supposed to be," she said. "His parents had a trip planned, and at the last minute, it was cancelled, and that was the only reason he stayed. Because they were coming," she said, growing agitated. "I don't know if you've noticed, but I don't exactly get on with Matt's parents."

"Yeah, that was pretty obvious."

A defeated look passed over her features. "It was always like that. Even when we were in high school."

"You two met in high school?" I asked, even though Nathan had already provided that information.

She nodded and seemed to get lost in the memory. "He moved into the house next door. We were in the same class from first year. We were really good friends all the way up until sixth year. And then, he asked me to go to the formal with him. We started dating. On and off." She waved. "But it wasn't really serious."

I couldn't control my face, and it must have revealed my doubt.

"We would casually meet up once or twice a month. Jesus, I was seeing other people all the way through art college. Until final year."

I thought back to the conversation with Nathan. I thought about what Lucy had said on the playground about learning pottery techniques at college, even though she'd never graduated. Their relationship timeline started to make sense. "That's when you got pregnant."

"I don't regret Ryan," she said firmly, as if I could somehow think she might. "But would my life have been different without him? Yes." I admired her honesty. She squeezed her eyes shut as if searching for the strength to proceed. "If my teenage self saw me now…" She shook her head bitterly. "I never thought I'd become this person. I had things I wanted to achieve, but…I fell into a routine."

"How so?"

"Matt started working for his dad straight out of university, and he was earning good money. We agreed that…well, actually, I don't think it ever was my decision. That I would stay home and look after Ryan." Her posture showed defeat. She looked tired, as if she'd aged before my eyes. I felt sorry for her. "It made sense, you know? Matt made more money, and I had no degree, no experience, no skills—"

"That's not true. You're talented, Lucy. You could do something with your art. With your ceramics."

"I thought about it." A disappointed smile made its way onto her face. "Over the years, I thought about going out and trying to make something of myself." She sighed and fixated on a spot in the corner of the room. "But it's like…do you ever start folding clothes, and before you know it, you've folded all of it, and you don't know where the time has gone?"

"No, not really. I hate laundry."

She cracked a smile, and her shoulders seemed to relax a little.

I couldn't help but smile back at her. "But I know what you mean. You get comfortable."

"Almost as if you're sleepwalking," she whispered. "I guess I was. Sleepwalking through my life. It was easier than analysing my discontent. The unhappiness and unfulfilled aspirations." Something darker appeared on her face. "Sleepwalking for all those years. All of my friends from art college had moved abroad or were progressing with their careers, and there I was. Burying my dreams. For them." Her tone was dull and empty. I felt sorry for her but also a little bit privileged that she felt comfortable enough to be so honest. "Well, at least, it was. Up until a couple of months ago. Up until the bubble burst." She took a large gulp of wine, and I could tell she was on the verge of unleashing what lurked beneath the surface.

There was hesitancy, though. Maybe she'd never told anyone what had been troubling her. I wanted to create a space where she felt comfortable enough to be vulnerable. "You can tell me." I touched her arm briefly. "Only if you feel comfortable."

The gesture seemed to ease her. "I do." Her hand rested on top of mine, and it didn't move. "It was going on for a while. Matt started acting cold and being short. He had no interest in family time, and well, our sex life was never amazing to begin with, but it had nosedived into the ground." She tilted her head. "I thought about confronting him, but why rock the boat?" Her eyes narrowed with regret or disappointment or maybe both. "I guess, it wasn't really my decision. One day, he just blurts it out. He had feelings for someone else." She kept it together despite the pain in her voice.

I wondered if she was too proud to be upset, or maybe it was me she didn't want to break down in front of. I admired her for that but remembered how difficult it was to learn that heartbreaking truth. When Catriona had told me about Maeve, it had felt like my entire world had been knocked out of orbit. I hadn't seen it coming.

I could also resonate with what she had said about not wanting to rock the boat. It had been horrible because I'd known something was going on. I'd felt it in my gut every time I'd looked at Catriona, getting suspicious when she'd started to take calls in another room. Or when she'd panic if I lifted her phone or her short temper when I'd asked too many questions. It was like a war zone.

"Who was it?" I asked.

"Her name is Shannon. They work together." She looked pent-up with a mixture of sadness and disbelief. "What a fucking cliché."

"Catriona worked with Maeve too."

Her features softened, and she looked at me with empathy.

Perhaps it was a mirror of my own facial expression. It was as if, without needing to say so, we both knew what the other was going through. It made my chest heat up and my heart flutter.

Her look transformed into something more uplifting. "I was so glad when you told me about you and Catriona." Her eyes searched mine. "I felt so alone before. I was going out of my mind and then you"—she tilted her head thoughtfully—"you shared your story. I felt relieved someone else had been through it and had actually managed to come out the other side. Meeting you started to heal me."

That touched me on a level that felt deep. It made me nervous that she could have such a strong impact on me emotionally, especially if this was going nowhere good. I batted it off to protect myself. "I think you're giving me too much credit."

"No," she said wilfully. "Your co-parenting relationship with Catriona had a chain reaction in my head. If you could get to a place where you could be amicable with your ex-wife, then maybe I could…I was able to start imagining myself getting to that place with Matt." She took a deep breath as if readying herself to reveal a secret. "The truth is, Matt and I love each other, but we were never in love. Not the way you see in the movies. Fuck, we were just so young when Ryan was born. We wanted to give it a go, and it was working. For years, we didn't fight or argue, but now that I've had time to reflect, I wonder if that was even a good thing. We didn't fight because there was no passion. We were basically a friendship raising a child."

After she was done, something resembling a revelation washed over. A light bulb moment. It looked as though she'd never said that out loud. As if a ton of weight had been dissolved into the air. She seemed lighter, and I was just happy I had helped her get to that conclusion.

"So what is your situation now?" I asked, holding my breath in case my heart was about to be crushed into a million pieces. "With Matt?"

She took a beat to compose herself. "He wanted to explore things. He said he came to me before he acted on his feelings." She nodded. "And I believe him. Matt is a lot of things, but he would never lie to me. He would never cheat, either. I mean, even when we were kids, he couldn't keep anything from me. He always told me everything."

I was beginning to grasp the depth of her connection with him. He was someone who she'd grown up with. Someone who'd loved and cared about her throughout most of her life. The fact that he respected her enough to reveal his feelings for someone else before acting on them was a testament of their long-lasting relationship. It was a connection that few would ever experience. And I wondered what a strong friendship that transitioned into a romantic relationship would feel like. Being with someone who knew me so fully and unconditionally. But Lucy's story appeared to show more of a deep connection with a friend than any great love story. At least, that was from my perspective.

"I couldn't bring myself to even contemplate the idea of him sleeping with her. Not after us being committed for so long. In uni, it's fine to sleep around, but we had a kid." It seemed difficult for her to say it out loud. Her voice was small and uneven, perhaps exhausted from fighting off her demons. "But I saw how it was affecting him. He was so miserable and closed off. Even Ryan started noticing. That's when he started acting out too." She looked broken and fragile, her tone revealed a heartache I remembered all too well. "I just wanted it to stop and for us to be okay again. I just needed it to stop. And letting him explore was the only way I knew to make him happy. To do what he had to do. He's been seeing her for weeks now. Maybe months. I lost count of the time." She paused and took another sip of wine. "I told myself that once he got this thing with Shannon out of his system, he would come to his senses and come back to me."

Silence surrounded us as I contemplated what exactly her revelation meant for me. It was selfish to be thinking about myself after hearing her hardship, but I couldn't help my disappointment. Like I was some sort of a distraction while her boyfriend fooled around with someone else. And when he came to his senses, I would be kicked to the curb. A crushing force pulsated around my heart as the reality of her circumstances became clear. I was her entertainment until Matt was ready to be a family again.

"I get it." I broke the silence, and my disappointment must have been clear as day. Lucy watched me carefully. "It's okay. Maybe he will come to his senses, and you two can…" A lump in my throat made it too difficult to even finish that sentence. "I just want you to be happy."

Her eyes shifted back and forth in bewilderment before she seemed to follow my train of thought. "No, Dani." Her voice heightened in worry, but I couldn't be sure as my eyes were firmly planted on the ground. "That's not it. Look at me." She shimmied closer and pulled on my shoulder to face her again. She was so close, I could practically feel her breath on my lips.

"That *was* how I felt," she said, searching my face like I was the only person in the world who mattered. "And then I met you." My heart started to accelerate. "And I know that sounds crazy because we barely know each other but…" She sucked her lip between her teeth. "Me and Matt have a long history, yes, but there's no passion. He doesn't make my heart race." Her voice hitched, and her breathing turned shallow. "Or make my hands shake." Her hand crept onto my forearm, and it felt like the room intensified. The air turned thick around us as her breathing quickened. "I don't think about him when it's late and I'm alone." It felt like every nerve in my body was heightened and throbbing at the same time. I could barely focus on anything over my heartbeat booming in her ears. Having her this close sent an exhilarating rush from my head to my toes. "He doesn't look at me like that," she murmured.

"Like what?" It came out breathless and needy.

"Like you're about to rip my clothes off."

I made the mistake of catching her eyes and saw just how dark they were. Heat radiated off her as she inched closer. I couldn't take it any longer. The ache between my thighs propelled me toward her. She gasped as I kissed her deeply. Her hand cupped my face desperately while the other seemed to be struggling to keep herself upright. Before I knew what was happening, she had pulled me down on top of her.

The thin material of her dress rode up as we kissed. Her kiss was invigorating yet calming. I'd never felt this insatiable hunger for anyone in all my life. I slid my hand down her outer thigh as she arched into my front. She began grinding into my pelvis slowly at first, but when I kissed her neck, her hips seemed to lose control. I didn't know how long we were kissing or at what point my shirt had been removed and Lucy's dress had been unbuttoned at the front.

Time was irrelevant.

Until it wasn't.

I heard Jonah's faint voice calling my name. I pulled back as Lucy stared at me with confused eyes. "Did you hear that?"

"Hear what?" she asked as I raised up slightly and listened again.

"Mummy?" Jonah said, but this time his voice was louder. Closer.

The stairs creaked as he moved. I jumped off Lucy and quickly retrieved my top. She was buttoning her dress again and smoothing it out. I made it to the door in time to see him reach the last step of the staircase.

"Hey, love," I said, trying to keep my voice under control through the shortness of breath. "You okay?" I closed the door behind me to avoid him catching a glimpse of Lucy.

"I don't feel good," he said glumly. I moved to him and registered just how pale he was, borderline green.

"Do you think you're going to throw up?" I asked, and he nodded frantically. By the gulp and sickly look on his face, I knew we didn't have long. "Okay, let's go to the toilet."

I led him down the hall and into the kitchen, but sadly, we

didn't make it to the toilet. He retched violently, and his vomit splattered across the kitchen floor. I didn't even have time to look at the damage before he was heaving again. I knew more was to come, but thankfully, this time, we just about made it. Jonah regrettably misjudged the distance to the toilet bowl, but most of it ended up in the right place.

I rubbed his back soothingly in an effort to get everything up. "You all done?" I asked after his breathing returned to normal. He nodded tiredly, and I flushed.

I wiped his face with a damp cloth and spotted his heavy eyelids. I made sure his temperature wasn't high in case it was something more serious. But my best guess told me it was likely all the cake he had eaten at Ryan's party. Jonah didn't eat a lot of sugar, so when he got an opportunity to indulge, boy, did he.

We sat for a little while longer on the floor of the bathroom. I wanted to make sure he was fit to go back to bed. I cradled him in my arms just like I'd done when he was a baby. I was stroking his head as I rocked him back and forth. It didn't matter how big he grew, he still loved to have his head stroked. It was my only surefire way to get him to sleep when he was being cranky. His breathing evened out, and so I snuck a peek to find him fast asleep.

I carefully lifted him, and he nuzzled into the crook of my neck. His arms and legs wrapped around me, assisting me in carrying him. He was definitely getting too heavy to be carried, but he looked so weak and tired.

When I emerged into the kitchen, I was shocked to find Lucy on her hands and knees, scrubbing the floor. She looked up as I said, "Leave it." She shook her head, dismissing me, and went back to cleaning.

Jonah's weight was causing me to lose my grip, and I begrudgingly left her to it. I got upstairs as quickly as possible and settled him into bed again. I left the duvet down a little so he didn't overheat. He was passed out, and I didn't see the need to stick around. I came back downstairs into the kitchen as Lucy was finishing up.

"Lucy, you really didn't have to." I tried to apologise as she threw the dirty kitchen towels into the bin.

"I kind of think I did," she said a little guiltily as I closed the gap between us. "You see, at the party, Jonah asked me for another slice of cake when you were in the bathroom."

"You didn't," I said, narrowing my eyes.

"But in my defence, he's super hard to say no to."

"Uh-huh?"

"Yes, it's his cute little nose and missing front teeth."

I couldn't stop myself from smiling even if I wanted to, and her hands seemed to naturally loop around my neck. My hands found their place on her hips.

"It's not my fault your little boy is too perfect to resist. Bit like his mum."

I planted a soft kiss on her lips, and she settled nicely against my front. That kiss had passion, but it wasn't driven by pure lust like before. It was sweet and warming. "Thank you," I said when she pulled back. I gestured to the kitchen floor so she knew what I was referring to.

"Don't mention it," she returned, and a reluctance came over her. "But I should really be heading home soon. It's getting late." We slowly broke apart, but I was glad when she reached for my hand. "Is this," she said, gesturing at our intertwined hands, "okay?" She didn't make a move to the front door yet.

"Yes."

"And are *we* okay?"

"Yes."

"Am I gonna get more than one word from you?"

"Yes." I raised a brow teasingly before turning a little more serious. "I like this."

She smiled with a long, contented sigh, and I had to admit, I loved seeing it.

"And I want to see where this goes."

She nodded, appearing to be on the same page.

"But you have to be discreet, right?"

Hesitation appeared on her features, like perhaps she worried I might recant my interest if we couldn't be "out." But her concern was misplaced.

"It's okay. I don't…" I started but took a beat. I wanted to make sure I got it out right. "I'm not ready for people to know, either. I don't introduce people to Jonah unless they're sticking around."

"I have already met him, you know."

"I know." I deepened my tone seriously, and her teasing disappeared. "That's sort of part of the problem. If things didn't work out, the whole school would probably know." I could tell by the change in her expression that she agreed. "I just want us to figure it out on our own before we go including anyone else."

"I agree," she said and smiled at me sweetly before faltering. "Even Matt. I'm not ready to tell him, either."

I was glad for that too because if more people knew, it would only be a matter of time before it got back to Catriona or Jonah. "It's just a shame Nathan already knows."

Her eyes widened. "What?" she said a little loudly. "Nathan knows about us?"

"He said he overheard us in the living room."

"Nosy little shit!"

I couldn't contain my smile, but Lucy seemed beyond pissed.

"He's always spying on me, the little creep. I'm going to kill him."

"He said he wouldn't tell anyone."

"And he won't, I promise. Especially by the time I'm finished with him."

"Well, don't be too hard on him. He revealed some very vital information."

That interrupted her annoyance. She squinted curiously.

"He said you're totally crushing on me," I said smugly, and her face reddened.

"He's also a pathological liar." She shook her head in frustration, but amusement pulled at her lips.

"There's no truth in it?"

"There might be some truth in it. I guess I should have been a little more discreet at Basement. I kinda couldn't look at anything else when you were dancing with Heather." Indifference clouded her features. It was the same look I'd encountered in Basement. "I thought you two were together, and I...hated it."

"You were jealous." I wanted to have a little fun at her expense. "You were so jealous, weren't you?"

Her inability to admit it gave me unmeasurable enjoyment. But she stubbornly shook her head. It was adorable, and I couldn't resist leaning in and kissing her lips fleetingly. She melted against me, and I decided to let her in on a secret of my own:

"When Matt kissed you at Ryan's party..." I paused, recalling that crushing feeling in my chest.

Lucy's smile saddened. "I'm sorry." I heard the conviction in her voice, and her expression revealed just how much she meant it.

"It's okay." I caressed her cheek, and she moved into my touch. "I know there's nothing between you two anymore."

"There isn't," she stressed and proceeded to plant a soft kiss to the inside of my palm. "I promise. Even if this goes nowhere, Matt and I are done." I believed her. "But for the record, I hope this goes somewhere."

"Me too." I trusted her fully, and perhaps I would live to regret placing that much faith in someone who appeared to be in a monogamous relationship. But the truth was, I was in too deep. I couldn't see a way out of this now without getting hurt. And I wanted her. More than anything, I wanted to see where this was going, even if it ended up breaking my heart.

"I don't want to go but..." She sighed in disappointment.

"I know." I reluctantly took a step back and walked her toward the front door. We faced each other one last time as I pecked her on the lips. I opened the door for her, and she went out into the night.

Chapter Eleven

Dani Raye

"Why was Ryan's mum here?" Jonah asked. He was seated at the kitchen table eating a bowl of his favourite cereal.

I'd just started buttering my toast at the kitchen counter when the room stilled. I decided to play aloof. "What?" I said casually, failing to turn. I could hear the crunching coming from across the kitchen, and I waited until he had swallowed. It was taking too long, and so I took my toast and coffee to the table and sat opposite him.

"What was Ryan's mum doing here?"

Again, I played dumb. "When?"

"Last night," he said, putting another spoonful of cereal in his mouth. He had a prominent crinkle across his forehead that melted my insides, his confusion clearly written in his expression.

I tried to figure out when he'd seen her. Cleaning the kitchen floor? Perhaps he'd caught sight of her in the living room? I really thought we had gotten away with it. "Oh." I pretended like I'd just remembered something. "That's right. She called round to borrow a book." I took a bite of toast to cement my calm demeanour.

"Okay." He thought carefully. "Why'd you kiss her?"

The toast seemed to swell in my gullet, and I began coughing uncontrollably. He looked alarmed until I managed to swallow it thanks to my coffee. "What?" I bought myself some time while I thought of a solution. "Where did you see that?"

"At the front door." He scooped up another helping of cereal. "Before she left." He must have woken up again to go to the bathroom and had seen us from the top of the stairs.

I'd had no idea he was awake or that we were being watched. Though, I was somewhat grateful our tame good-bye kiss was the height of what he had seen. If it had been our make-out session on the couch, I would have had a much harder time glazing over it.

He watched me curiously as I tried to sound as blasé as possible. Any hint of nervousness and he would pick up on it. "Oh that." I shrugged. "That's just how good friends say good-bye."

"Oh." He nodded a few times. "Okay." He seemed to accept my reasoning, and I breathed a sigh of relief.

I didn't like the idea of lying to him, but I hoped that wouldn't become a pattern. Lucy and I would have to be much more careful. I honestly thought I was in the clear with my excuse that friends kiss until later that night. I had just dropped Jonah off at Catriona's house. It was a Sunday evening, and he would be spending the next few days at her home.

I hugged Jonah good-bye at the front door and gave him a kiss on the forehead. There was no reason for me to go inside, though Catriona had welcomed me in. He was still lingering in the doorway as I turned to her. "I've packed all his things," I said. "He still has to finish reading his book for school tomorrow. There're only a few pages left. It shouldn't take long to get through it at bedtime."

She ran a hand lazily through his hair and nodded.

"Don't forget, he has football after school on Tuesday. I packed his kit."

"No problem, we're going to have fun aren't we, little man?" She glanced at him as a smile spread on his face.

I loved how cooperative he was with our separation arrangement. It helped that Catriona and I lived barely ten minutes' drive from each other, so the upheaval was minimal. I guessed going between houses every few days was all that he had ever known, and therefore, he'd never seemed fazed by it. "Okay, well, I will see you next week," I said to him.

"Aren't you gonna kiss?" he said as he glanced suspiciously between Catriona and me.

I was already panicking while she looked completely bewildered by the suggestion. "No, honey," she said softly, leaning over to see him more fully. "Me and your mummy don't kiss anymore. We're just friends."

"But Mummy kisses her friends."

My brain was working at a hundred miles a minute, trying to pull together some kind of an explanation.

Catriona looked in my direction, and her eyes narrowed. A mischievous smile played on her lips, and I knew I would have some explaining to do. She looked positively victorious, as if she'd uncovered a dark secret. "Why don't you go play, Jonah?" she asked.

He waved me off before moving farther into the house and out of sight.

"Wow, look at the time. I should really be going," I said, trying to escape, but I knew it was a lousy attempt.

Catriona's curiosity was unwavering. "Not so fast." Her firm tone carried far enough to stop me in my tracks halfway down the driveway. She stepped beyond the threshold and followed me. "Who have you been kissing?" Her voice rose teasingly. "And in front of Jonah." That part wasn't quite as teasing but more in disapproval.

I rolled my eyes and let out an exaggerated sigh. "It was nothing."

She clearly didn't believe it.

"Jonah thinks he saw something but really—"

"Oh, come on, he's six. He's not stupid."

"I know he's not stupid—"

"Who is she?" She took a step closer. "This friend of yours who you have been kissing."

I knew I couldn't bluff her. Not Catriona. I hated to admit it, but she would see straight through a deflection, and so I had to fabricate something out of my ass. "It's new, okay? I'm not really ready to talk about it."

"But you have no problem letting her meet Jonah." The edge of disapproval returned.

"He was in bed. I thought he was asleep."

"She stayed over?" Her tone deepened in agitation.

"No—"

"Because I remember you giving me a very hard time when Maeve and I were first starting out."

I saw red. "That's completely different, Catriona, and you know it." My voice had risen, and Catriona didn't look happy about it. "We were still sleeping in the same bed when you started your little sleepovers."

She cut in just as angrily. "We filed divorce papers before Maeve ever met Jonah. I'm not the one inviting strange women over when my son is tucked up in bed."

"I've never done this before," I said and didn't mean to sound so lost.

By the look on her face, my outburst had revealed my disappointment at letting Jonah see me. She seemed to ease.

"I don't let him meet the people I'm dating. Ever. Last night was an accident, but I promise, she didn't stay overnight. She came round to talk, and it was when she was leaving that he saw us kiss."

Her brows rose as some scepticism lingered.

"Cat, it won't happen again."

It was as if the mention of her nickname seemed to smooth out her roused features. She let out an exhale, seeming to accept my explanation. "All right, as long as it doesn't happen again."

"It won't. Are we good?" I asked, and she nodded.

That was how we left it.

Catriona and I had a good co-parenting relationship, but there were certain rules we had for each other. All of which concerned

Jonah. Most of the rules were simple: limit screen time, don't teach him bad words, make sure he doesn't eat too much junk, get him to school on time, make sure he's happy, and the list went on. But one rule which had always caused contention was Jonah's exposure to our romantic partners.

In Catriona's case, I hadn't wanted Jonah meeting Maeve, full stop. But when it had become apparent that Maeve was sticking around, I had to give in. Our partners had to be serious before it warranted an introduction. Up until now, Jonah had yet to meet anyone I was dating. There were a couple of women who I'd been semi-serious with, but I'd always wanted to protect him. I couldn't bear him getting attached to someone I was dating just for it to all fall apart.

That was what made whatever this thing was with Lucy all the more difficult. Jonah knew Lucy, and in some ways, he was comfortable around her. There was a familiarity, and there was the added complication of how a potential relationship with Lucy would affect Ryan and Jonah's friendship. The truth was, I wasn't ready for any kind of commitment, especially not one that could carry repercussions for my son.

CHAPTER TWELVE

Lucy Matthews

It was Tuesday morning, but unlike most days of the week, I wasn't dragging myself out of the car at school drop-off. Even Ryan commented on my giddiness. I couldn't help it. I was excited to see Dani at drop-off, and with any luck, she would be dressed for work. Seeing her in a suit did things to me. Things I thought about a lot.

When we pulled up at school, I let out a sigh of disappointment when I spotted Jonah getting out of an unfamiliar car. His other mother got out and walked him in the direction of the entrance. Catriona. I'd only met her the once, but first impressions were lasting. I found her to be abrupt and not overly nice. Even when making small talk, she didn't seem to have the time to let me finish. It made me drag my heels a little when getting out of the car to avoid a run-in with her.

To my relief, she passed without stopping to chitchat. I was thankful because honestly, I didn't know how I would have been able to hold a conversation with the woman who'd hurt Dani. I needed to see a photo of Maeve because Catriona must have been fucking blind to trade Dani in for anyone else.

My thoughts were filled with her, and my good mood was reaching higher peaks. On my drive home, the radio was interrupted, and ringing came over the speakers. My Bluetooth had picked up on an incoming call from the very person who was occupying my thoughts. "Hello?"

"Hi, is this a good time?" Dani asked hesitantly, no doubt really asking if I was alone.

"It's great. I was just thinking about you." I heard a small laugh, and it melted my insides. "Are you in the office?"

"Yes, but let's go back to you thinking about me." I could hear the smile in her voice and couldn't resist my own grin. "What were you thinking about?"

"Oh, I couldn't possibly reveal that. Besides, it wouldn't be very work appropriate."

"Really?" Her tone dropped in what I took to be anticipation, and it gave me an excited tinge in my stomach. "Like what?"

"I could always show you. You have a private office, right?"

"What?" she breathed out. I was teasing, of course, but I loved the nervous quiver in her voice.

She seemed to present herself as confident, someone who didn't take shit, but I was noticing she got a little flustered around me, especially when I was being suggestive in *that way*. It was endearing, and I really enjoyed seeing her confidence dip, as if she was waiting for me to lead. Not that anything physical had happened. Besides, I wasn't exactly ready. Sure, I'd thought about it, probably more times than I'd ever admit, but things were too complicated to bring sex into it.

"I'm just messing with you," I said. "Besides, I wouldn't want to get you fired."

"Aw, I'm a little disappointed. I thought I might get to see you today." Her voice grew small.

"You can if you want." The words were out before I'd thought too much about them. "I could bring you lunch." It was my turn to feel nervous. Perhaps it was too forward; maybe I wasn't playing it cool like I should have, but I hated hearing disappointment in Dani's voice. It felt wrong on a cosmic level. I waited for a response at the traffic lights.

"Really? You want to meet for lunch." There was a nervous edge to her tone too, and it warmed my heart.

"Yes?"

"Okay."

We made arrangements to meet at one p.m. at her office block. I picked up some lunch on the way. I recalled her talking about a sandwich shop near her work that she loved, and of course, no lunch order was complete without two cups of tea. When I made it into her building and up to her company's floor, I had a nervous tingle. The businesslike layout and people in suits made it seem very professional, and that was always something that put me on edge. I wasn't the corporate type. I wouldn't have had the patience to sit at a desk, but in an art studio, I could work all day without batting an eyelid.

The person in reception gestured toward the stairs with some loose instructions on where to find Dani. I clocked the upgrade upstairs. The art deco furnishings and stylistic choices must have been in an effort to impress. I imagined their external meetings would be held here too. I especially liked the glass partitions separating offices, but they'd managed to maintain a frosted segment for privacy.

An older man approached me. "Excuse me, what's your name?" I wasn't sure which office he'd walked out of, but his flushed cheeks told me he was in a rush.

"Eh, Lucy?" I felt as though I was trespassing, and perhaps he was about to throw me out.

"Lucy, can you print six copies of this?" He handed me several documents, and for some fucking bizarre reason, I actually took them. "I need them for a meeting in twenty." He was already disappearing down the hallway before my mind could process his request.

"Sorry." I followed him. "I don't actually work here."

"What do you mean?" The confusion was clear on his expression. "What are you doing here?"

I was beyond relieved when a door opened to his left, and Dani poked her head out. She looked between us and must have caught my panic. "Harry," She pulled his eyes off me. "I see you've met my friend, Lucy."

"Oh, I'm sorry." He turned to me and laughed, allowing the accusation in the hallway to evaporate. "I thought you were one of the new starts." He turned back to Dani. "Doesn't she look like one of the graduates?"

"No." Dani shut him down and sent me a look of apology.

"Well, no matter." He shrugged it off and moved away. "Nice to meet you, Lucy."

Dani perked up after he was out of earshot. "I swear to God, he's losing it." A smile played on her lips until she looked at my hand. "What's that?"

In one hand was the paper bag of lunch and in the other hand were Harry's documents. "Yeah, he wants six copies of this."

"Fucking idiot." She rolled her eyes. "I'll sort it." She moved to the side and pushed open her office door a little farther. "Make yourself comfortable. I'll be back in a minute." I handed her the papers, and she threw me a wink. It generated excitement in my tummy. Seeing her walk away in a suit that seemed to hug every inch of her was only fuelling the fire in my belly.

I took her absence as an opportunity to look around. That fact that she had an office of her own was impressive, even if it was relevantly modest in size. It was neat and warm, just like her. She had two filing cabinets beside the window, with a small couch to the side. Her desk was in the centre of the room with quite a bit of paperwork scattered about. I didn't miss the frames on her desk either. One of Jonah, of course, alongside a picture of who I imagined were her family. I lifted the picture and took note of a vague similarity between them all, but I couldn't help but home in on how much older her parents were compared to mine. Mine were in their fifties, whereas Dani's siblings looked as though they might have been that old too. Maybe I was looking at her grandparents.

"Sorry about that." Dani arrived back and spotted me with the picture in hand. "That's my folks."

I was glad she volunteered an answer. I wouldn't have

BEFORE SHE WAS MINE

wanted to offend her by referring to them as grandparents. She came up alongside me and looked at it over my shoulder. "Is that your brother and sister?"

"My brother and sister-in-law, actually. They were visiting home last year with my two nieces." She smiled fondly. I took the nieces to be the two younger looking women in the picture. They looked to be in their early twenties.

"You and your brother kinda look alike."

"I find that hard to believe." She grinned. "Considering he's adopted."

"Oh," was all that came out through the embarrassment.

She just laughed. "You're grand. We do actually look a lot alike, even if we aren't blood related." She lifted the bag of food from my hands and moved to the couch, motioning for me to follow.

"He looks a lot older than you. No offence," I said, even though it was obvious from his thinning hair. Actually, he didn't really have much hair at all.

"No offence taken. They adopted him first. There's a sixteen-year gap between us," she said, as if it was something she'd had to explain frequently over the years. For that reason, I tried to control my expression. Sixteen years was pretty unusual, and I got the feeling that she was tired of the questions that arose because of it. "My parents struggled to conceive, so they decided to adopt instead."

"Are you adopted too?"

"No." She titled her head in amusement. "No, I'm the mistake." She nudged one of the sandwiches closer to me and took the other. My face must have revealed my shock. "I'm just joking, but I definitely wasn't expected. Mum was in her forties when she had me, and my dad was almost fifty. I think they only ever wanted one kid, and to be fair, John is the perfect son. He's a big shot lawyer in Boston, and his wife is in local government. Their kids went to private school, and one of them goes to Harvard now." There was nothing but pride when she spoke of them. Which I was glad to hear because family meant everything to me.

"Well, if it's any consolation, Ryan was most definitely unexpected, but he's a little miracle."

Dani watched me thoughtfully for a moment. "That's what mum used to say about me too." We shared a sweet smile, and it set my heart alight. She broke first, going back to her sandwich, and I did the same. We ate in comfortable silence for a moment or two while I thought about what it would be like to have such older parents. "I was only the miracle baby until I came out, though." There was still an element of teasing in her tone, but I could tell she was being serious. Her humour appeared to be hiding a sore point as well.

I took a few sips of tea to clear my throat. "Your parents aren't okay with you being gay?" It must have come out more accusatory than I meant it to because she moved quickly to reassure me.

"They are now. But when I came out, my parents were in their sixties. They're from a totally different generation. They didn't know anyone gay. They were just worried about me and what my life would look like. And even though they acted pretty shitty back then, I know it wasn't malicious." She frowned, and it was obvious that she was thinking deeply about her next choice of words. "I think my parents needed to reject it in order to process it. Does that make sense?"

She didn't give me much time to think, though I couldn't deny my initial reaction was to disagree. A parent's rejection, for whatever reason, was always cruel in my eyes.

"After all, I was their miracle baby who was dropping this huge bomb on them and expecting them to just be fine about it." She didn't appear to be harbouring any real regret or disappointment, which was really more of a testament to her as a person.

I got the feeling it took a lot for her to turn her back on the people she loved. It was her compassion and ability to put herself in other people's shoes that would always surprise me. My parents had always been open and progressive, which meant Nathan and I had grown up knowing we'd be loved and accepted no matter what. I forgot sometimes that not all families were as great as mine. Dani's ability to forgive her parents, despite their rejection, was something I found incredibly admirable.

I wondered if I'd have been as forgiving. "Still, it must have been hard."

"Yeah, but it actually worked out for the best. Because when they kicked me out, I got to go live with my brother. And being Irish, twenty-one, and gay in Boston was the best." It seemed she would forever keep me guessing.

I wondered how she could always maintain such compassion and positivity. She considered her parents practically disowning her as a blessing because she'd gotten to live with her brother in America. It was most likely that compassionate streak that made her co-parenting relationship with Catriona so successful. "Living in the States would be pretty cool."

"It definitely was. And by the time I came home again, my parents had come to their senses. They're great and absolutely adore Jonah," she said between bites. "Not too fond of Catriona, though."

"Well, I can *certainly* understand that." It came out more disgruntled than I had planned.

"Wow, jealous already?" she said, and I felt my cheeks heating up.

"I am not jealous. I just think…" I stopped myself from ranting about Catriona. There was something about her energy that I didn't like. Perhaps it was her fake chitchat that seemed to be rushed and forced, for appearances alone. Or perhaps it was because I knew she'd cheated on Dani, and my protective nature had me disliking her out of loyalty. I couldn't quite put my finger on it. "She wouldn't be my cup of tea," I finished diplomatically, not wanting to appear petty for bad-mouthing her ex, but it only seemed to rouse an interest in Dani.

She put down the rest of her sandwich and grinned. "You don't like her, do you?"

"I just don't know what you saw in her." I put down my own sandwich, my insides feeling too charged to stomach anything else. Especially not with the way Dani was looking at me.

"She's actually really great when you get to know her," she said, and I didn't miss the uncomfortable clamping in the pit of my stomach that I knew inescapably to be jealousy.

But I'd never give Dani the satisfaction of knowing. "Sure."

"You really hate her." She giggled hysterically.

"I don't hate her, I just—" I cut myself off, getting flustered. Dani's eyes were making me forget how to think. "Look, I'm sorry, but I'm just never going to like anyone who hurt you."

The room stilled, and one of the most beautiful expressions came over her. The humour and teasing glint in her eyes disappeared, and she looked as though what I'd said had touched her on some meaningful level.

It caused my heart rate to accelerate, and I knew I wanted to always evoke this softness from her. I wanted my words to be the ones that moved her like that.

She leaned forward and pressed her lips against mine. I had missed the way my lips tingled from her kiss. She cupped my cheek, and without meaning to, I caressed her thigh. The thin material of her trousers sent my thoughts racing. Her lips on mine, combined with the smooth fabric on her thigh, proved to be an arousing combination. Our kiss intensified as if neither of us had control. As soon as her tongue brushed my lower lip, I sprang into action. I straddled her hips in the desperate need to feel her close to me.

The door crashed open. "Hey, do you have—" The intruder gasped just as I caught a glimpse of blond hair before it was gone. "Sorry," she called after shutting the door again.

"Fuck," Dani muttered, sounding disappointed. She checked her wristwatch. "Yeah, I've a meeting with Heather right now."

"Shit," I breathed against her forehead. She held me close as if reluctant to let my body go. "Okay." I tried to get off her, but she held my hips firmly and kept me in place.

"Where do you think you're going?"

"You have a meeting." I tried to keep my voice even as she grazed the exposed area on my lower back between my T-shirt and jeans. It set a fire across my skin.

"Meetings can always be rescheduled." She pressed a kiss to my neck.

My eyes rolled back, but I couldn't stay here forever. I had to collect Ryan from school soon. "Well, this meeting right here…" I pressed her shoulders and gently pushed her back. "Can be rescheduled."

"But this is more important." She tried to come forward again, but I held firm on her shoulders.

"Look, I can't risk you losing your job because you can't stop kissing me, okay?" I said as a wide smile appeared on her face. "I know I'm irresistible, but you need your job, and I need you to keep wearing these sexy little suits."

She laughed in what could only be described as adorable shyness. I loved the way the tips of her ears turned red first, followed by her cheeks. "You are *very* irresistible." She took her time glancing down my body, and I hoped I would never grow tired of how good it felt.

Having her look at me like that did indescribable things to me. Such want and desire. I had felt sexually invisible for so long, so to have someone like Dani look at me like that felt like the ultimate confidence boost. Though, I wondered if anyone had ever really looked at me like Dani.

"But I guess you're right," she said, allowing me to climb off her and settle my raging arousal.

I pulled her up and off the couch, and she walked me to her office door.

"Thank you for lunch."

"Thank you for whatever that was." I nodded at the couch, and she couldn't seem to hide her glee.

"Anytime. Seriously, anytime."

"I'll see you soon," I said and kissed her softly. We pulled back, and she got the door. Heather was lingering outside, unable to meet my eyes. Seeing her looking so mortified seemed to amuse Dani, which in turn made me see the humour in it too. "I'll see myself out." I glanced back one more time, and Dani threw me another sexy wink.

I walked away, knowing that her eyes were still glued to me. I had a sixth sense for whenever she was stealing glances in my direction.

I couldn't shake my high for the rest of the day. Ryan's homework wasn't a chore but a fun activity. The dreaded laundry had me singing to myself. I even let Ryan choose his dinner, which I never did on a school night. Of course, he chose McDonald's, and I didn't even care that he wasn't getting his veggies. Lunch with Dani had filled me with enough happiness that nothing seemed to get me down.

Not only that, but after tucking Ryan in bed, I couldn't shake my overwhelming boost of inspiration and spiritual energy. To sit on the couch all night watching TV didn't interest me; the adrenaline coursing through my veins led me straight to the garage to work on some new pieces. It was exhilarating and thrilling, like it used to be when I was younger. I could spend hours moulding and perfecting my craft. I felt like a kid again, so much so that I barely registered the time.

The garage door creaked open, and I expected to see Ryan. Maybe he'd woken up from a bad dream. It had felt like I'd only put him to bed half an hour ago. I was surprised to see Matt at the door. I didn't think he would be home until late; after all, it was a Tuesday, my least favourite day of the week because it was the night he "worked" late. Except I'd all but forgotten that it was Tuesday.

"Hey, you're early," I said, my voice coming out a little groggy.

He frowned. "It's eleven thirty."

"It is?" He looked baffled. I wasn't even tired, and I'd been out here for almost four hours. "I must have lost track of time. How was work?" I asked, continuing with the glaze on a mug.

When he remained silent, I looked up and realised why he was so shell-shocked. I hadn't asked him about his day in weeks. I had been so filled with bitterness and devastation that I'd abstained from any form of decency. But I didn't feel that sense of powerlessness right now. I felt the complete opposite. Free.

"It was good," he said with a small smile. "Are you hungry?"

I registered the hollowness lining my stomach. "Yeah. I skipped dinner," I said, but of course, I left out the part about being too full from lunch to eat with Ryan. Matt didn't need to know where I was or who I was with.

"Want a sandwich?" he asked. "With a big mug of tea?"

"Sounds good." I couldn't help but smile, and he threw me one of his cute, goofy grins. The very smile I'd fallen in love with. The one that used to brighten my days and though it still created a wave of nostalgia, it didn't have that same breathless effect anymore.

"It'll be ready in five minutes." He disappeared, closing the door behind him.

I cleaned up the workstation and put my pieces in their cooling box; that way, the clay would remain workable until tomorrow. I gave my hands and forearms a good wash in the sink before switching off the lights and making my way back into the house.

Any inkling of conversation would have normally died the second I set foot in the kitchen. It usually did when it was just me and Matt in a room. But I was relieved when it started again. We talked. For the first time in weeks, Matt and I talked. And it wasn't about anything real or important. We talked about the weather and other nonsense. He made me a grilled cheese sandwich with mayo on the outside slice, perfect for frying, and that led to us reminiscing about university. He used to make us these kinds of sandwiches late at night after coming home from the bar.

Laughing with Matt again felt light and effortless. Foreign but familiar at the same time. Like it used to be when we were students. Back when we were friends. I hadn't realised just how much I'd missed him. Missed his friendship. Missed talking and laughing with him about nothing and everything. In recent months, it had become too painful to bear. Too difficult to bring myself to be lighthearted with him when all I could fixate on was *her*.

Sitting across the kitchen island from him while he cooked didn't leave me with any animosity. I didn't feel bitter about her or rather, his relationship with her. I wasn't even thinking about it, despite knowing he had been with her all evening. For the first time in what felt like forever, I could enjoy his company. And on a Tuesday, of all days.

I wasn't entirely sure why I wasn't feeling that sense of powerlessness and betrayal. Maybe it was because my feelings for Dani had sated my resentment, or maybe it was because I didn't feel like I was sharing Matt anymore. As if on some level, deep down, I'd let him go.

CHAPTER THIRTEEN

Dani Raye

I hugged my folder a little closer to my chest as I reached the entrance of Turlough Enterprises. The company had an impressive setup, with the facility and outbuildings occupying several acres of land. Quite remarkable, considering they were situated not far from city centre. On closer inspection, the facility was likely a repurposed factory, but its proximity to the docks implied that it could have been used for manufacturing shipyard materials back in the day.

Harry was nervously blabbing away. I'd tuned him out on the car ride, as his chitchat was not only too quick to follow but also completely unproductive. His nervousness was his Achilles' heel. The conversation jumped from client to client sporadically whilst mingling with current affairs. It ended up being too much for my brain to keep up with, and I stopped replying altogether. He talked regardless. However, I knew as soon as Harry set foot in front of the client, his nervousness would dissipate. He was a trained professional, and while my boss was chaotic around his colleagues, when he was pitching new business, something in control came over him. It was miraculous to bear witness to. It fuelled me with confidence, which was always important when trying to impress a potential new client.

Harry reached the front door before I did and opened it for me. At reception, we requested to meet with Patrick Turlough, the CEO. We waited for a couple of minutes before we were escorted to the meeting room upstairs. Turlough Enterprises was a building and construction company. So as expected, a few of the staff members looked a little unkempt. A cloud of dust practically followed them. I expected nothing less from this sort of company, but what I most definitely didn't expect was who faced me on the other side of the boardroom door.

Matt stood at Patrick's side.

Harry moved straight ahead to start the introductions and held out his hand. "Patrick, how are you keeping? And this must be your son, Matthew." He turned and reached out to Matt.

"Dani?" Surprise was written on Matt's face. I was sure I looked as pale as a ghost. "What are the chances?" Matt patted his dad on the shoulder and pointed. "Dani was at Ryan's party on Saturday."

Patrick seemed to recognise me. Though we'd smiled politely at each other at the party, I'd never actually spoken to him. Panic fuelled my insides, but I had to stomach it bravely. Harry would kill me if my lesbian drama ruined this deal.

"Small world," fell from my lips, and I just about forced a smile.

Harry glanced at me excitedly as Patrick and Matt took a seat. Perhaps he thought this was a slam dunk since our children were friends, but he couldn't have known just how volatile this deal really was.

Miraculously, I shut off my emotions and delivered my presentation like a pro. I was good at my job, but even I was impressed with my ability to separate my own inner turmoil from the job at hand. Harry looked mesmerized for most of the pitch, while Matt appeared to be getting increasingly enthused. I must have been saying all the right things.

Matt seemed far more engaged than Patrick. That was to be expected. The younger people always seemed a bit more clued in on the benefits of marketing and online presence. The plans we had to upgrade and completely reconfigure their website seemed to be all Matt needed to hear to want to sign a contract.

However, Patrick remained quiet. He would be the harder sale. I could already tell he was counting the pennies and worrying about how much this partnership would cost. But that was why Harry was here. My role was to get the strategic forward-thinker on board while Harry was there to persuade the conservative client afraid of change. That was how we usually divided and conquered. But this wasn't just a normal client.

"I can't believe I never put two and two together," Matt said as he led me out of the boardroom.

After my presentation, Harry had proposed we take a breather. It was entirely so he could work his magic on Patrick. Harry had also suggested Matt give me a tour of the facility. I could have throttled him, even though Harry couldn't possibly have picked up on my reluctance, especially when I was burying it so deep.

"I know. I actually thought your last name was Matthews, not Turlough." I said, recalling Ryan's surname but realising my own mistake right after.

"Matt Mathews? My parents aren't that cruel," he teased. "No, Lucy's surname is Matthews, and seeing as Lucy and I weren't together officially when Ryan was born, he took her last name." I nodded and squashed my discomfort at even talking about Lucy in his company. "Besides, everyone in work calls me Matthew. It's just Lucy who calls me Matt. She's been calling me Matt since I was twelve. But you can call me Matt."

I offered a tight-lipped smile and tried to steer the conversation away from his family. "What's your goal for the next five years? Do you envision Turlough Enterprises expanding?"

"That's what we're preparing for," he said as we moved down the corridor. "My old man is on the verge of retiring and giving the reins to me, but he doesn't let go easy."

I cracked a smile. "They never do."

We emerged into the manufacturing wing. It opened into an

atrium, allowing a wealth of sunlight to light up the work space. I was thankful we were on the third floor because on the ground, it was loud and chaotic. The upper walkway allowed me to lean over the railing and look down.

Matt came up alongside me but didn't say anything as I took in the scale of production. It was hypnotic. Workers welded and soldered pieces of metal while others painted machinery and other equipment. It was a full-blown operation with everyone appearing to work in unison.

"Quite the operation you have here," I said, still unable to tear my eyes away.

"It could be a lot better," he remarked optimistically. "But my dad is reluctant to change. I actually have my eyes set on another site somewhere in and around Enniskillen. When Dad retires, I plan on moving ahead with expansion. Lucy and I grew up around Enniskillen, and I always imagined Ryan growing up in the country."

I nodded, though my throat felt like it was closing over. The guilt swirled and sloshed in my tummy to the point that I thought it might surge up my throat. Hearing Matt talk about his family life sounded whimsical and far from what I'd imagined someone who was having troubles to sound like. Then, I thought about the possibility of Lucy moving so far away from the city. That disappointment lingered in my chest, but I wouldn't let it distract me from the pitch.

"Sure." I redirected conversation in an effort to ignore what was happening inside. "In that case, you might want to think about a cloud-based platform where your entire team can interact from both sites. That is something we can help with. We can outsource to another partner, and they can provide the launch and upkeep of the platform."

"That sounds fantastic. Our memory drive is completely outdated. I'm surprised it hasn't had a serious outage yet," he said before leading me into the canteen. "Do you want a coffee?"

he asked, but my anxiety levels were already through the roof.

I worried that a cup of coffee might actually cause my heart to explode. "I'm okay, thanks."

He went about preparing himself a cup. The canteen was quiet, but it was the afternoon. I would imagine few were still eating their lunch.

When silence settled around us, I quickly skimmed through my file and retrieved some marketing brochures to help seal the deal. "Well, I really think Skylar Marketing is well positioned to help you achieve your goals and maximise Turlough Enterprises—"

"You don't need to sell yourself to me, Dani. I was already sold the second you walked into the boardroom."

"You were?"

"Of course. I knew you were going to be amazing. Lucy showed me the Instagram page you helped set up for her pottery. It was incredible, and you're obviously more than qualified." He smiled brightly over his shoulder before going back to focusing on his coffee.

I felt rubbish again. Actually, worse than rubbish. Like the crusty leftovers glued to the bottom of the bin after collection day. His praise was flattering but also guilt inducing. If he only knew what else I'd been doing with Lucy. I hated this. I felt like a cheater, someone I had sworn I would never become.

A woman moved into the kitchen. Her blond hair was in perfect waves and bounced with each step. She smiled in my direction, and I couldn't help but notice her beautiful smile. I glanced at her outfit. She certainly knew how to dress for her curves. Her eyes barely held contact with mine. With each step, she stared intently at Matt.

He looked up. "Hi, Shannon."

My heart stopped as she came to a stop next to him. It was *her*. The other woman. My throat ran dry, and the blood felt like it was draining from my face. I tried to keep my cool and focused on the brochures despite the heart palpitations. I was too afraid of what my face might reveal if I looked up. I did what anyone else in my situation would do, I eavesdropped.

"Hey, I didn't see you at lunch," she said before reaching for a mug.

"Yeah, I had a meeting. Did I miss anything good?"

"Just Jimmy boasting about this so-called model he's dating."

"As if."

She began preparing herself a hot drink as they talked. It was all very innocent, even though I was scrutinising the interaction to see if they slipped up.

"I know." She laughed as she lightly grazed his shoulder with one hand. "I knew if you'd been there, you would have taken the piss."

"I'm sorry I missed it," he said and looked at her.

That was when I saw it. The familiarity. It was brief and over in the blink of an eye. It looked like happiness, though. That made me furious. My thoughts went straight to Lucy and the turmoil he'd put her through. The destruction this fling was causing to their family. But I had to check myself. After all, I was doing the exact same thing.

"I'll talk to you later," she said before turning and leaving again with her cup.

Matt watched her leave. It wasn't leering or creepy. More of a thoughtful gaze. Once again, it was brief. Perhaps he was nervous I would see something I shouldn't. "Dani, let's talk fees," he said, turning back to me.

We made our way to the boardroom as we talked. By the time we made it back to Patrick and Harry, the deal was done. Harry had closed it perfectly, just like I knew he would.

We left Turlough Enterprises seemingly feeling two very different emotions. Harry was already elated about the new deal, while I was feeling the dread and fear of working more closely with Matt.

CHAPTER FOURTEEN

Dani Raye

"I can't believe this," Lucy whispered into her hands, covering her face.

We sat on the bench looking out at the park. I kept a close eye on the boys to make sure they didn't see her distress. They were climbing on the playground and too enthralled in each other's company to pay us any sort of attention.

It was a crisp afternoon. Probably one of the coldest days of the season yet. Summer was now feeling like a very distant memory. We had decided to take the boys to the park after school. It was something we had done a few times during my weeks with Jonah. On the days when I didn't have him, we would meet for a walk in the evening or make out in my car. Or in my office like last week. It was all very aboveboard and almost juvenile, but I was okay with that. Progressing our relationship, or whatever this was, still felt a little too committal. I guessed it was, considering she was still playing at being in a relationship with Matt.

Besides, I kind of liked the air of secrecy. It was a bit of a turn-on, even if we hadn't done the deed yet. Our make-out sessions had still gotten steamy. Very steamy, on occasion, but we always broke apart before we crossed into that territory. Sex was too messy. I knew it, and she knew it. Not to mention, it was very difficult to plan a romantic evening when we couldn't exactly be "out," even to Matt. Since their relationship was open now, he probably wouldn't mind, but I respected Lucy's decision to keep us a secret. And after Jonah catching us, I didn't want to chance it. I was reluctant to have Lucy over to the house when he was home. In fact, I was apprehensive about Lucy coming over, full stop. My neighbours across the street were good friends with Maeve, and I couldn't risk anything related to Lucy getting back to Catriona. No sex also meant that we hadn't crossed the line of this almost "high school teenage romance" into a full-blown "affair." At least, that was what I told myself to ease the guilt.

We had been seeing each other a few times a week for almost five weeks. It was still new, but something was bubbling between us. I could feel myself getting more content with her. I was sharing more of myself, and the openness in our communication was so simple. Our morals and the way we approached things carefully always seemed to be on the same wavelength. There weren't any games with Lucy, and considering my time on dating apps, that was quite refreshing.

I liked how mature she was, especially for her age. I didn't make a habit of hanging around people younger than me. I'd always dated older, and my friends were older too. It likely stemmed from the fact that I'd grown up with an older sibling, and my parents had little time for kiddie things. At least, that was what Catriona had psychoanalysed once. Despite Lucy being six years younger, I didn't feel the age difference so much.

"Do you have to manage Matt's contract?" Lucy asked, pulling me back into the conversation. "Maybe someone else can handle it."

"I won the pitch," I explained and watched her features grow even more defeated. "I'm expected to put in the work. It's my job. Besides, if I did take myself off the account, how suspicious would that look?" She breathed out a sigh of frustration. "Look, I can be professional." I tried to lift her spirits, though it looked to be in vain. "I am very good at seeming cool when I'm not okay. The week after I found out Catriona had cheated on me, I landed Skylar's biggest client ever," I said smugly. "I can keep us a secret around Matt, don't worry." My shoulder collided teasingly with hers, but it didn't calm her.

"I don't want that, Dani. I just—" She sighed desperately. "This isn't fair."

I rubbed her forearm soothingly, and though it was over her coat, it seemed to provide her with some comfort. But when an elderly couple walked past, I had to quickly recant. I couldn't risk anyone spotting us.

That seemed to only heighten her frustration. "I hate all this sneaking around." She was practically seething, shaking her head.

I couldn't quite figure out where her frustrations were directed. Her irritation seemed to be splitting off in every direction. Even when I met her after school, she wasn't herself. Her prickly edge had emerged constantly this afternoon, and I wasn't a fan. She was behaving unpredictably, and it seemed quite out of character. "What is the matter with you today?"

"Aren't you sick of it?" Her voice rose, and she turned to me, showing just how frustrated she was.

"Sick of what?"

"This bullshit," she blurted. "I'm sick of hiding my phone when you text or walking to the corner of the street to meet you at night." She frowned at the elderly couple, who'd sat at the far bench. "I hate that I can't hold your hand when we're out in public."

I had no idea she felt so strongly about me. About wanting to be out with me. I figured, like me, she was okay with sneaking around. At least in the short term, until we figured out what was going on between us. I had to be honest, her words were so raw and full of truth that they warmed the insides of my hopelessly romantic heart. I couldn't help a smile, but she seemed too angry to take note of it.

"I hate pretending to be with Matt." She scowled. "It's forced, and neither of us is happy. And I *really* hate that you're going to have to work with him and that you have to lie every time you see him. I hate all of this. I'm so sick of hiding when all I want to do is be with you." She was still staring straight ahead with her hands clenched into fists. Our emotions seemed polar opposites, and her declaration only seemed to make her furious, while the same declaration left me feeling tingly all over.

"You've never said that to me," I whispered, and she finally turned back. My expression appeared to melt away her anger. "You want to be with me?" I asked seriously, and Lucy's features showed a glimpse of nervousness.

"Well, I mean…" She licked her lips. "Yes." A beat passed, but I was too blissful to speak. "But if you don't want that—"

"No, I do," I reassured her before lowering my voice and checking to make sure no one could overhear. A lopsided smile appeared on her face. But sadly, I had to crush it. "But we can't."

"Why not?"

"Uh, your husband?" I jumped in before she could argue. "And I know you're not married, but you've been together for five years. In the gay world, you're practically married."

"But, Dani…" She sighed, looking out at the park. She was watching Ryan, and the most heartbreaking look came over her. "I don't want to be with him anymore." Staring at the dirt seemed to shift her entire energy to that of a lost and hopeless woman. "My house is loveless. I mean, we love Ryan, but there's so little between us. I can't do it anymore. I just want to be free of it all."

I couldn't quite pin down my feelings. A part of me loved her spontaneity. I admired her for making the decision to leave Matt, and I was more than delighted that she wanted to be with me. But another side of my head was conflicted. The decision felt too impulsive. After all, this was the first time she'd made me aware of any of this. I wondered if maybe she'd had a couple of off days with Matt and was stuck in a "grass is always greener" ideology. It led me to be very cautious. Lucy had to be sure before putting out this kind of declaration into the universe. There was too much at stake to be flippant, especially for such an early relationship.

"Okay, look, maybe you need to think some more on this," I said calmly. Her face scrunched up in annoyance, and it prompted me to lower my voice in an effort to reason with her. "There's a lot going on right now, and this is not a decision you should make lightly. This isn't like ripping a bandage off, you know?"

"I know—"

"The end of your relationship with Ryan's father is something that will affect the rest of his life." Lucy looked confused and a little hurt. "I just want to make sure you're thinking clearly."

"What are you doing right now?" she asked hotly. "Why are you pushing me toward Matt?"

"I'm not. I just want to make sure you're doing this for the right reasons."

"And what exactly are the right reasons?" Agitation was clearly written across her expression.

"I don't want you to regret this six months down the line." She frowned, looking more lost than ever. I had to be blunt, even if it hurt. "Lucy, you're just so young, and this is all very new to you. We've never even slept together. How do you know you're going to like it?"

Her eyes expanded in what could only be described as unshakable outrage. Her mouth fell open, and I could practically see the steam coming off her. I knew then that this wasn't going to end well. "First of all, it's very bold of you to assume I've never slept with a woman before," she said sharply.

I was grappling for any kind of response. I thought I was the first woman she'd been attracted to.

"Secondly, I'm not ending things with Matt because of you. Have you been listening to me? I'm doing it for me. And finally, Dani, if this is ever going to go anywhere, you need to get the fuck over my age. It's getting really old."

"I'm sorry, I didn't mean to—"

"Just forget it." She cut me off before rising and turning back to me in disappointment. "You know, I really expected a little more support from you."

"Lucy," I tried, but she was already off in search of Ryan.

She reached for his hand, even though I'd never seen him so reluctant. He wasn't ready to go, and the cries I could hear from the bench were evidence of that. She walked him off the playground and into her car. Jonah looked to me in concern, obviously troubled by seeing his friend having to leave abruptly. I drove us home but thought of nothing else.

Lucy had gone from saying she wanted to be with me to telling me to leave it. Upon reflection, I realised how patronising I'd been. This wasn't the first time I'd thrown a jab at her age, and it would seem I'd pushed it too far. She had been vulnerable and honest, telling me she wanted to give it a go, and my response had been to tell her to think on it some more? Was I putting what I thought were her needs ahead of my own, or was I trying to prolong these fucked-up make-out sessions that turned me on so much?

It only came to me later in bed, when the house was still and silent. My mind had been replaying the events of the day, and finally, I had some clarity. While I didn't want to admit it at first, I realised that, on some level, I had been enjoying the secrecy of being with Lucy, the thing I'd sworn I wouldn't get involved in. Perhaps, deep down, I wanted to know what it felt like to be in on the secret rather than being the victim of it. Lucy was sexy and young, and I enjoyed that attention. And honestly, it was all the more appealing because she wasn't single. That, in itself, was fucked-up. All of it was wrong.

I had no idea that seeing a "taken" woman would have this sort of effect on me. I was a little ashamed of the person I'd become. But I hoped that not all was lost. If Lucy ended things with Matt, I wouldn't have a reason to feel guilty anymore, but another question had plagued my mind all evening…would I still want her when she was available?

CHAPTER FIFTEEN

Dani Raye

I answered the door to Lucy. Her hard features suggested she still hadn't quite forgiven me. It had been over a week since our talk in the park. Initially, I'd thought I would give her a day or two to stew, but when it rolled into three days, I shifted pretty sharply into panic mode. I'd extended an olive branch, but she remained cold and slow to respond. If I hadn't been persistent, or rather, borderline clingy, I wasn't even sure she would be standing at my front door.

"Is Jonah home?" she asked hesitantly, glancing upstairs.

"No, he's with Catriona until tomorrow."

"Good," she said sharply. I was *really* in trouble.

She stormed past me and moved into the kitchen. I thought about escaping out the front door, but that really wouldn't help my case. Honestly, I didn't think she would still be hurt by our conversation. All I'd said was for her to think twice before leaving the person she'd been with since she was a teenager. I'd wished someone had whispered that into my ear when Catriona and I were first separating. Maybe I wouldn't have been so heartless in ripping Jonah from Catriona's arms and refusing her contact.

"First things first," she said from behind my kitchen island. She gripped the countertop while she focused on me. "Why on earth were you talking to Matt about me?"

The heat in the room skyrocketed, and I could feel the blood rushing around my body. It was a bit like my thoughts, rushing with nowhere to go. Now I knew why she was so angry. Her impatient head tilt didn't help matters.

"Okay, that probably wasn't my finest moment."

"You think?" she shot back.

When I hadn't heard from her for a few days, I'd started to get worried. I hadn't had Jonah this week, so there'd been no need for me to go by school and strategically run into her. I'd had a moment of weakness during my meeting with Matt yesterday:

Matt's office was small and pokey, with just one small window. It wasn't a very nice view, but it seemed to fit well with the rest of the construction facility. After all, it had been a factory at one point. There would have been very little need for extravagant offices or scenic views. Matt's desk was old and rickety, the plastic veneer chipping off the side. When I set down my laptop, I worried it might cause the whole structure to crumble. The dated emerald carpets looked more like charcoal at this stage, and the filing cabinets looked like they might have been left behind from the Troubles.

He must have caught me surveying the space. "I plan on renovating," he said. "My dad still holds the purse strings. I'm limited in what I can do."

"When is your dad retiring?"

Matt shrugged, revealing his frustration. "That's the real question. I don't know what he's waiting on. I think he's afraid I'll run the business into the ground. Maybe he doesn't think I'm mature enough." His head dropped, and I had to feel sorry for him.

I tried to bring him up, but he seemed more lost than ever. "You look to be doing all right from where I'm sitting."

"I think I've just become a good faker, is all." I couldn't help but home in on the darker underlining of his tone. "Pretending that everything is fine." His voice softened as he stared off into the distance. "Do you ever feel like that? So trapped that you even start to fool yourself?" He wasn't talking about work anymore because his eyes shifted to the photo on his desk. I had already peeked at it: Lucy and Ryan. My heart ached for him because I'd seen that same regret on Lucy's face.

"Maybe you should try telling him how you feel," I suggested, and thankfully, he didn't seem to pick up that I wasn't talking about his father anymore.

"Talking never helped before. Maybe too much talking is why I'm in this mess." A sad, glassy look appeared in his eyes. A second later, he broke out of his trance and shook himself. "Sorry, Dani." He laughed it off. "I must have thought this was a therapy session."

"It's okay," I said, and though Matt looked to be about to move on, my gut instinct made me want to stay on topic. "Is everything okay?"

He was silent for a moment, perhaps debating whether to divulge. "Not really," he said, squaring his jaw almost painfully. "We're going through a bit of a hard time." I thought he would keep it vague; we had done until this point. "Lucy and I." I felt my shoulders tense as I shifted back in my seat and away from him, the guilt no doubt causing my avoidance. "I'm sorry, I shouldn't be bringing you into it. I know you two are friends."

"Yeah..." I trailed off awkwardly. "Well, kind of."

"Kind of?"

I couldn't take control of what came flying out of my mouth in panic. "I just mean, we're new friends. You know, I mean, I haven't talked to her in ages." I wasn't even fully aware of what I was trying to say, and by the look on Matt's face, he wasn't either. "Uh, you know, I don't know what's been going on between you two...not that I would pry or anything. I just...she's not talking to me right now."

"Did you fall out?"

Now I was in dangerous territory. "No." I tried to play it cool as best I could with my fast heart rate. "I think she's just busy, is all." I shrugged it off, but he seemed even more intrigued. "I'm busy too." I tried a different direction to try to ease his unwavering interest in every word I was saying. "We barely hang out—"

"I thought you two were together yesterday." That left me shocked. She'd told him she was with me, but she hadn't spoken to me in almost a week. I couldn't be sure what came over my face, but it was likely something very telling. "Wait, you haven't seen her, have you?"

I could have lied, but his mind seemed to already be racing. "Matt, I really don't want to get anyone in trouble."

"You're not, Dani. You're just being honest." My insides churned under the weight of his misconception. "Lucy said she was with you yesterday, but I can see now that was a lie."

I didn't know what to say, and it would seem my silence told him everything. I couldn't help but feel a little betrayed as well. Lucy had gone cold with me too. Sure, she wasn't lying to my face, but that was only because she wasn't telling me anything at all, fact or fiction. What was worse, why was she using me as a cover story for her boyfriend? Perhaps she had already moved on to someone else, leaving me and Matt in the lurch. I told myself that was my own internal insecurities playing on my mind.

"You're a good friend, Dani," he said with conviction. It could not have been more misplaced. *"And don't worry, none of this will make it back to Lucy."*

It seemed like that couldn't have been more incorrect, either.

"Well?" Lucy pressed when I couldn't conjure up a response.

"I have to work with him," I stated slowly and calmly. "We talk about stuff, and unfortunately, you came up in conversation."

"Next time, change the topic," she said angrily, but her accusation only resulted in shortening my temper.

"That way, we don't *both* catch you in a lie?"

It shocked her into silence. The tension in the kitchen was deafening. "What are you talking about?" she said after a beat.

"Matt seemed to think we hang out all the time. Even as recent as Thursday because that's what you told him."

Her eyes bounced around the room. I could see her mind at work. I could tell there was guilt and something else hiding there. "My question is, why are you using me to lie to your boyfriend when I don't even know where you've been?"

"What is *that* supposed to mean?" Her anger returned in seconds. When I said nothing, she asked, "Now you think I'm cheating on you?" in disbelief. She was talking so fast, it was hard to get a word in. "You think I'm cheating on Matt with you, and I'm also cheating on you? Why stop there? Don't you know I've ten different affairs on the go? You clearly think I'm this insatiable whore who just can't get enough—"

"I don't know what to think. Put yourself in my shoes. What am I supposed to think?"

"You're supposed to trust me."

"Where were you that you couldn't tell Matt? Or me?"

"I was at a market," she said, seeming a little ashamed, as if maybe she wasn't ready to tell me. "There. Satisfied?" I didn't know what to think or feel. When I didn't say anything, she continued, "Last weekend, a craft market organiser reached out to me on Instagram. She loved my work and invited me along to set up my own stand."

I could feel the disappointment in myself brewing uncontrollably. I was letting past experiences make me untrusting. I was annoyed at myself for being so accusatory.

"That's where I was. I was at my first market. I have the organisers' phone number. You can call her, and she will tell you."

"No, I don't need to call them," I said weakly, more ashamed than ever. I'd never wanted to be paranoid and untrusting, and I'd hoped Catriona's cheating hadn't compromised my ability to trust people. But clearly, it had. The fact that my relationship with Lucy wasn't exactly ethical was also likely contributing to my mistrust.

"I wasn't ready to tell Matt that I was trying to make a living for myself." Her voice was low and full of truth. "And he knows we hang out, so I pretended that was where I was going. It was just easier. And I didn't tell you because I was still mad at you from last week. I'm trying really hard to stand on my own two feet so I don't need to rely on anyone to provide for myself and Ryan." She breathed out desperately. "For the first time since Ryan was born, I'm earning my own money. I mean, it's not much. I only sold a couple of pieces at the market and a few things online, but we would get by. I don't need to stay with Matt, and he doesn't need to take care of us anymore."

I watched her helplessly, feeling smaller than a speck of dirt. "I'm sorry," I said in a voice that didn't even sound like my own. "I didn't know."

"Dani." She sighed and reached to find my hand. Her expression didn't show anger. More of a hopefulness, which was more than I deserved after what I'd suggested. "You're the first person I wanted to tell when I found out I'd be at my first craft market. I was so nervous on Thursday that I almost called you to come help me."

"You should have—"

"No," she cut me off sadly. "My whole life, there's always been someone there to shield me. My parents and Matt. I don't want to replace him with you." She let those words sink in for a beat. "You helped me get my work out there, but I needed to be able to do this on my own. To go and stand at a fair by myself and be scared. And I was terrified. So afraid of the rejection and judgement." She smiled, seeming proud of herself. "But I did it. I really did it." She let out a shaky breath, and I couldn't have been prouder. "And it was fun. I sold that mug set you like."

"The blue ones?" My voice rose excitedly.

"Yeah, and someone bought two white bowls and a serving dish to match." She smiled. "And someone even haggled with me."

"No!" I couldn't hide my smile.

"Yeah," she said, hopeful. "The organiser invited me back next month."

"Of course they did. You're amazing," I murmured and

squeezed her hand softly. "I'm sorry that I didn't trust you, and I'm really, *really* sorry that we fought last week." I tried to keep my voice as heartfelt as possible. I wanted her to know just how much I'd regretted all of it. "I don't know why I was trying to talk you out of leaving Matt." I shrugged. "I think part of me was scared. That if you left him for me, you would regret it. Or maybe you'd resent me."

"I would never."

"But another part of me liked sneaking around," I said honestly and didn't turn away from the look of uncertainty on her face. "A part of me liked that it wasn't serious between us. That it was just a bit of fooling around."

"Is that what you want?" I heard the disappointment in her tone.

"I thought I did. That casual was all I needed. I've a career and a child and an ex-wife," I rattled it off. "I figured, sneaking around might be nice. Might be better than anything real." She looked sad, but as I went on, her expression warmed. "But when I didn't hear from you for over a week, I missed you. I couldn't believe just how much I missed being around you. I knew then that it wasn't just a bit of fooling around. You are quickly becoming someone I want to have around, Lucy." A small smile played on her lips, making her look beautiful, and the warmth in my chest caused me to declare more. "I want this. I want you to leave him. Be with me."

She rounded the island, and her hands breezed up my arms, causing a ripple of goose bumps in their trail. Her lips found mine in a powerful, searing kiss, one that knocked the air from my lungs and propelled me close. We started off slow and exploratory. I could taste sweetness on her lips and tongue when she deepened the kiss. Her hands were smooth, and while they'd been a little cold earlier, I was pleased to report that they were heating up each time they ran up my back and into my hair.

Our kiss turned hungry. Our panting provided the only disturbance to the silence in my kitchen. Her hands roamed my body and rested on my hips. She found the sliver of skin between my jeans and T-shirt. She caressed delicately along my pelvis before moving to my hips. It was sensual and tantalising, and before I could grow impatient with the teasing, she was tugging at the hem of my shirt and pulling it over my head. Her jacket went next, and her top quickly followed. Feeling her skin against mine seemed to ramp every urge to another level.

She cupped my breasts while I eagerly unbuttoned her jeans. Our movements were hurried and restless. This was the furthest we'd reached in the past, and I didn't want it to stop. Not this time. Not with so much raw chemistry swirling between us. I desperately wanted to feel her body on mine, and the thought of it alone was enough to have my legs quaking.

I pulled back breathlessly. Her eyes revealed a yearning that I'd not seen to this degree. She looked unbelievably gorgeous.

"Do you want to go upstairs?" I watched her every move for hesitation or reluctance. I needed complete consent before we went any further, but she didn't need to think on it.

"Yes," she whispered in a frenzy.

She grabbed my hand, and I practically ran out of the kitchen, pulling her with me. We were climbing the stairs at record pace, and I made the mistake of glancing back. Lucy's eyes were dark, and her hair was unruly. It left me breathless, and she took the break in my stride as an opportunity to kiss me again. She pushed me up against the banister. It hurt my back, but I didn't care. I loved her eagerness.

I would have let her take me there, but her tugging on my jeans resulted in me losing my balance. I was falling toward the landing at literally the last step from the top. We both slipped, but Lucy placed her hand on my lower back and supported my weight to ease the fall. Landing on top of me, she giggled between kisses, and I could barely stop laughing.

"Come on," she murmured against my lips and pulled me up with her.

I couldn't tear my lips from hers as I walked us backward to my bedroom. My back hit the door, and Lucy pressed her entire body against me, making it hard for me to find the handle.

She pulled back with amusement. "Need a hand?" she asked just as I managed to open the door.

"I need your hand elsewhere."

I tugged lightly on the nape of her neck and pulled her into my lips again. She was charged, unstoppable, and moving clumsily across my torso. She undid my bra and had removed hers before I even knew what was happening. As soon as the back of my legs reached the bed, I sat and began pulling down her jeans.

She straddled my hips and kissed me feverishly. Her warm breasts pressed against my chest, heating up the space between us. Her kissing slowed as she seemed to get caught up in her own need. Her thighs tightened around my hips, and I found myself in the best position imaginable. Her hooded eyes couldn't seem to focus as she lazily wrapped her arms around my shoulders, holding herself upright and ensuring she didn't fall off the bed.

Her forehead rested against mine as I moved my hand between our bodies and her legs. She gasped, and her fingernails dug into the back of my neck and shoulder. I maintained a continuous rhythm below while I explored her breast with my mouth.

Having her grinding against me in ecstasy made the ache between my legs intensify.

"Oh God," she panted into my ear.

Her legs were tightening, her grip on my shoulders was bone-crushing, and her breathing was raging. I could feel her getting close. I picked up the pace, and within seconds, she was starting to shake. Her grip on my shoulders would cause bruises tomorrow, but I didn't care. She yanked me away from her breast and pulled me back to her lips.

It didn't take long before she reached her climax. She pulled back, and the sexiest moan filled my entire bedroom. Her movements slowed, and her breathing was drawn out. Her eyes were still squeezed shut as her forehead rested against mine. I removed my hand, and she spasmed one last time. Sighs of contentment surrounded us, and I watched her mouth slide into a very lazy smile.

"You're so fucking beautiful," I whispered without thinking.

She pressed a light and sweet kiss to my lips. "And you," she croaked and proceeded to clear her throat, "are very, *very* good at that." I let out a small laugh against her lips, but she was still too spent to move anywhere fast.

"I hope that's not you all done."

"I'm just catching my breath," she replied cockily, though her voice revealed an exhaustion.

"Here." I tried to shift her off me, but she moaned in disapproval. "Come lie down."

We moved farther up the bed and climbed underneath the covers. They were cooling against my heated body, but Lucy actually shivered at the contact.

"Come closer. I'll heat you up." I gestured for her to move into my side.

I expected her to snuggle up alongside me and perhaps fall asleep. But she surprised me by pulling me in for a kiss. She raised herself up on an elbow and deepened our kiss with me struggling to keep up.

"Aren't you tired?" I pulled back. Just looking at her revealed no signs of laziness. In fact, she appeared fully alert and charged up.

"Tired?" she repeated as if it was a crazy notion. "I have thought of *nothing* else but going down on you for weeks," she said with such confidence that it turned me into a mess underneath her.

I couldn't form words, and instead, she was on the move, kissing down my stomach. I disappeared into a haze of pleasure and hoped that I would never be disturbed again. Embarrassingly, I lasted barely a couple of minutes before she had me coming undone.

Afterward, she moved back up again and cuddled against me. My breathing was short and still recovering. She rested her head on my chest and draped an arm over my stomach, then broke the silence smugly, "Still think I haven't slept with a woman before?"

"Nope," I breathed out, still in awe, making her giggle. "No, it's pretty clear you've done that before."

"Yeah, it was cute that you thought I hadn't, though."

"When..." I asked breathlessly, kissing her forehead. "Did you get so much practice?"

"At uni."

"Such a cliche," I teased, and she nipped at my side.

"I didn't hear you complaining during that entire thirty seconds."

"It was more than thirty seconds. Right?"

"Barely." She chuckled. "I take it as a compliment."

"You must have had a lot of practice."

"Not really," she replied thoughtfully as her index finger traced patterns on my stomach. "At least, not with a girlfriend per se. No one was really serious apart from Matt. And, well, now you."

"I'm serious?"

"I think so," she said, and when I paused too long, she looked up at me, a little unsure.

I kissed her lips reassuringly. "I think so too."

It had turned dark outside, and I was perfectly content listening to the rain beat on the roof. Having her beside me felt like a dream and yet was grounded in reality. As if this was where she'd belonged all along.

"I could stay here forever," she mumbled, snuggling that bit closer.

"I wish you could too."

We stayed like that for a while. And we kissed. Of course, our kissing led to a lot more exploration. I was glad that I got to return the sexual favours. Again. And again.

Chapter Sixteen

Dani Raye

Loud knocking at the front door downstairs caused my eyes to spring open. The fast exposure to light led to a sharp pain behind my eyes, but that was the least of my worries. Lucy propelled herself upright beside me. We turned to each other in a beat of blind panic. It was morning, when did that happen?

"Fuck," she whispered as she bounced out of bed and hurriedly searched for her clothes.

I grabbed a pair of jeans and sweater on my way to the bedroom window. Because of the angle, I couldn't see who was knocking at the door. But parked in the driveway behind Lucy's car was Catriona's car. It caused my heart rate to spike through the roof. "It's Catriona."

Lucy slapped a hand across her mouth. "Fuck."

"She's early." The clock revealed it had just turned ten a.m. "Really early." I wasn't supposed to collect Jonah until dinnertime.

"What do I do?" she asked, clasping her bra.

"Just stay here. I'll come get you when she's gone."

She nodded, and I left my bedroom, closing the door shut behind me. I stopped briefly halfway down the stairs to check myself in the mirror. I was glad I did because my hair was all over the place. I tucked it behind my ear and moved swiftly down the stairs.

When I opened the door, Jonah launched himself at me. "Hey, little man." I returned the hug. "You're early. I wasn't expecting you until four." There was a low tone directed at Catriona.

Her brow furrowed. "I texted you last night. Maeve has a match today, but Jonah wants to watch the football on TV." I stared at her blankly, causing her to arch a brow suspiciously. "I texted you twice."

"I must have missed it." I shrugged it off. "I went to bed early."

"I texted you at seven thirty." Her sceptical tone lingered.

When I met her again, I noticed she had craned her neck around me. It looked like she was trying to see if there was someone else inside. I knew I had to be quick.

"This is great. We're going to have so much fun, Jonah," I said in the most enthusiastic voice I could muster and held out my hand to accept his bags. Catriona handed them over but showed no signs of leaving when Jonah disappeared into the house. "Thanks for bringing him back." I tried to be blunt, hoping she would take the hint and leave. "Tell Maeve I said good luck."

"Okay, now I definitely know something is up." She crossed her arms. "Since when do you care about Maeve's games? And who owns the flash car?"

I followed her gesture to the driveway as if I didn't already know there was an unfamiliar car there. In fairness, Lucy's Jeep was really nice. I'd admired it before because it wasn't the type of vehicle someone would miss easily. The shade of blue almost seemed custom, while the black alloys added an element of cool. I knew it was only a matter of time before Catriona drew attention to it.

"Oh, it's my neighbour's," I replied, nonchalant. "She was having a party last night and asked if she could park in my driveway. She wanted to avoid any of her guests getting a ticket. You know what it's like on this street."

Catriona appeared to buy it, and even I was impressed with how believable it was.

Until there was a loud thud from above us.

I tried not to react in the hope that she'd missed it. I was thankful that she didn't say anything.

"What was that?" Jonah asked, having come into the hall again.

He looked at the ceiling above the threshold of the front door. Catriona's ears perked up. After all, she used to live here and knew exactly where my bedroom was. Her eyes followed Jonah's.

"Nothing, love," I said to Jonah and quickly turned back to her. "See you later."

She still looked suspicious, but I had already closed the door on her. It was practically an admission of guilt, but any more questions, and I would have tripped up in my own messy web of lies. I saw her retreating form in the translucent glass and breathed a sigh of relief that she was gone. For now, at least.

I knelt in front of Jonah. "Hey, why don't you go put on the TV?"

He scampered off, and I was upstairs again in seconds. When I reached my bedroom, Lucy was fully dressed and seated on my bed. She was wearing one of my T-shirts. Her jacket and top were still downstairs on my kitchen floor.

"I'm so sorry, my phone fell off the bed."

"It's fine, she doesn't suspect anything," I said, making my way to the window and feeling my shoulders ease when I could no longer see Catriona's car.

"What about Jonah?"

"He's watching TV." I moved closer to her. "It takes a lot to tear his eyes away from the screen." Lucy cracked a smile as I sat next to her. "My top looks good on you."

"Thanks, I had to borrow something. Mine is downstairs." She shifted around so that she was facing me. "About last night…"

My heart rate picked up, afraid that perhaps she might have regrets, but when I shifted to look more fully into her eyes, I knew there was no cause for concern. She looked just as content as I felt. Her eyes were warm, and a bashful smile tugged at her cheeks adorably. Her hand found its way into mine, a little cold, as always, and I revelled in the way her touch made me feel.

"Yeah, it was, uh…" I paused and licked my lips. It only seemed to cause an excitement to brew between us. "Pretty good."

"Just pretty good?" she teased, narrowing her eyes. Her other hand crept up my thigh boldly.

"Quite good? Average?" I teased some more.

"Average?" She gasped in amused outrage. "I'm going to have to do much better next time," she flirted before leaning forward and planting a soft kiss on my lips.

The moment was perfect. The air around us was perfect. It was exciting but somehow still calming and serene. Her eyes held mine, and I could practically feel myself falling for her. And the whimsical smile that appeared on her face when she scooped some of my hair behind my ear told me she felt the same. The glow emanating from her was breathtaking. I wondered if she would look this effortlessly beautiful every morning.

"I should probably get going." She sighed before finding her feet. "What will you say to Jonah? About why I'm here."

"The football is on." I shook my head. "He won't notice a thing. What about Matt?" My question caused a frown. Dread replaced my joy at the thought of forcing her to admit our relationship to him before she was ready. Everything would be simpler if he knew, but at the same time, I didn't want to be the reason someone's relationship ended. It was too much of a reminder of my own failed marriage. The sooner their relationship was over, the better, just as long as I wasn't held accountable. "Won't he wonder why you didn't come home last night?"

"Probably." She hummed to herself, getting lost in what seemed like the implications of that.

A feeling of disappointment lurched in my tummy. The feeling didn't sit well with me, and the thought of looking Matt in the eye at our next meeting certainly didn't settle the tension.

"I guess I will tell him."

"About us?" It came as more of a gasp.

"No. But that I'm seeing someone." She nodded a few times as if thinking carefully. "He should know I'm moving on too, and maybe it will speed things up."

"Speed things up?"

"Our relationship is ending, and I don't want to draw it out any longer. Not after..." She glanced at the bed, and I couldn't ignore the confliction in my gut.

I was grappling with guilt and elation. The end of her relationship was unfortunate, but at the same time, the prospects of their separation had me rejoicing. And by the soft smile on her face, perhaps she was just as happy about that as I was.

And that was how we left things.

Later that night, I still couldn't stop thinking about Lucy. Our night together was wonderful, and the ache in my muscles was a blissful reminder. More importantly, though, I couldn't stop wondering about how her conversation with Matt went. I imagined he would have been suspicious when she'd arrived home in the morning. He must have had some questions about where she was last night. She would have had to tell him something, right? I was driving myself insane with the possibilities but was even more surprised when I didn't hear from her all day. I figured she would have been excited to tell me how it went. It was a big deal, her admitting that she wanted their relationship to end.

Once I'd gotten Jonah into bed and tucked in, I decided to give Lucy a call. I was pacing in my bedroom just thinking about the possibilities when she picked up.

"Hi." Her voice was low and gravelly, and it was clear she didn't want to be overheard.

"Hey, how'd it go today?" I launched straight in, too anxious to make pleasantries. I was dying to know how he'd reacted. I could hear her walking, with doors opening and closing; perhaps she was going somewhere quieter.

"Okay," she said, but it was more like a sigh. Her voice

sounded cold and lacking in that energy I was used to. That made me worried. "How was your day?"

Her question threw me. It was as if we were having two very different conversations. "No, I mean…" I said, hoping she would follow along, but when it became clear we weren't on the same page, I was forced to be blunt. "Did you tell him?"

"Oh no," she said in a tone that sounded blasé. As if she'd somehow forgotten about what we'd talked about this morning. "It wasn't a good time." That left a pit of disappointment in my stomach, a hollowness that caused me to actually stop pacing and slump onto the bed. "I was going to but…" She trailed off, unfazed. Like it was no big deal. Like she could just get to it tomorrow. And that hurt.

When she'd left my house this morning, she'd assured me that she would tell Matt where she'd been. That her "new romance" could be the start of a bigger conversation about separation. I had thought that was what she had wanted too, but I guess I was wrong. That left me feeling deflated and disappointed.

"I get it," I said. "If you're not ready, I understand."

"It's just really complicated, Dani." That certainly wasn't the first time I'd heard that. My doubts began to settle in and around my chest. Perhaps Lucy was never going to leave Matt. "I wish I could tell him, but I just can't." *Can't or won't?* was all I could repeat in my mind. I wanted to give her the benefit of the doubt. I knew that I should. "Look, I can't really talk," she said hurriedly. "I'm going to have to go. I'll call tomorrow."

I didn't even get a chance to say good-bye before she was gone. Silence surrounded me in my bedroom as I looked around and recalled what had happened here last night. The excitement and energy that had swirled around us all night long, but now, I'd been subjected to a one-minute conversation several hours later. It made me feel a little used.

Chapter Seventeen

Lucy Matthews

I drove home thinking about Dani. Replaying last night in my mind caused a jolt of excitement down my thighs. I couldn't wipe the smile off my face. She was incredible. The extra flutter in my heartbeat was all thanks to her. I wanted to be with her all the time. Blissful thoughts of her surrounded me as I parked the car and moved up the walkway to the front door.

I moved into my house as quietly as possible, not wanting to draw too much attention to my late arrival. I could hear faint sounds coming from the kitchen: the clattering of cutlery against a bowl and kettle coming to a boil. I removed my jacket and shoes, leaving them in the closet before making my presence known to the rest of the house. I was nervous. Petrified to see Matt. He would no doubt be curious about where I had been, but that would just give me the opportunity to ask for a separation. Honestly, I would have rather had that conversation before Dani and I had slept together, but sometimes, things didn't play out the way I wanted them to. And I was past beating myself up for the way I felt. I'd spent far too long suppressing my emotions in my relationship with Matt to do it all over again with Dani.

"Morning," I said to Ryan, though he barely tore his eyes from the iPad.

"Coffee?" Matt asked.

"Uh, sure." I moved cautiously toward him.

I'd imagined he would have quite a few questions for me. I

used to tell him if I wasn't coming home. Staying overnight with my parents was a rarity; therefore, my absence had definitely been noted. It was only a matter of time before he launched into a round of questioning. But I was okay with that. In fact, I was waiting for it. Although, when the conversation did turn that direction, I would have to insist we leave the room. We would need to figure out the logistics before sitting Ryan down. There was an excitement brewing in my stomach, and I couldn't squash it. Finally, it was all coming to an end. Soon enough, I'd be free to be whoever I wanted and to be with whoever I wanted.

Matt placed a coffee in front of me at the kitchen island. I cupped the hot drink and stared at it, waiting for him to ask. This was my opening. The moment I'd been waiting for, an out.

"I'm sorry about last night," he said before taking a bite of toast. That was most definitely unexpected. What did he have to apologise for? I was the one who'd slept with someone else. "Time just got away from us, and my dad…well, he wanted us to stay for dinner. One beer led to two beers, and that led to wine and…" He sighed hopelessly, as if something sad was getting him down. "You know how persuasive my folks are at making us stay the night."

The penny dropped.

They weren't here last night. Which meant they didn't know I wasn't here, either. I couldn't help but feel mild relief, coupled with disappointment. Relieved that I wasn't coming home to an angry boyfriend with lots of questions, but at the same time, I was *so* ready to tell him. To have it all out in the open and to be free from hiding how unbelievably happy I was with Dani. I had planned it all out in my head, and now I was going to have to broach the topic differently. And when Ryan wasn't around.

"It's okay," I said and took a sip. "How're your folks?"

"Okay," he said, but there was an unsure edge to his voice, and it had me worrying.

At Ryan's birthday, Matt's mother had told us that she was due another scan in a couple of weeks. That the consultant wasn't entirely confident they'd gotten all the cancer. I hadn't asked him much about it because we weren't really talking lately, but perhaps I should have. He was an only child, and he shouldn't have had to go through that alone. The guilt made me want to dig a little further.

"And your mum?" I said quietly. His eyes snapped to mine, revealing almost fear. It shifted to sadness, on the verge of losing it. "What happened?"

"It's not good," he said in a low and shaky tone.

"I'm so sorry, Matt." I kept my voice equally low.

The distress was written across his expression, even though he struggled to hold eye contact. He didn't say anything but shook his head in what looked like a total loss of faith. I thought the worst. His hand found mine on the island, and he gripped it desperately. It made me feel a world of pain, heartbroken to see him so upset and even worse when I imagined how Patrick must be feeling. His grip loosened, and he ducked his head as the dining chair scraped back along the floor tiles. I could hear Ryan's footsteps coming closer, and I took it upon myself to distract him. Matt wouldn't want Ryan to see him upset. After all, Ryan still didn't know his grandmother was sick.

"How about we get you into some fresh clothes, huh?" I ushered Ryan out of the kitchen, and though he protested, I kept him walking. I was too afraid of what state he would find his father in if he went back.

The rest of the day, Matt seemed on the edge of tears. He told me that Audrey's cancer had spread to her lungs, and though I was no doctor, even I knew that wasn't good. He had this vacant look all day long, and it was heart-wrenching. Even during dinner, he struggled to find anything to talk about. He was not the silent type, but that was just an indication of how much Audrey's diagnosis had devastated him.

I was cleaning up dishes when my phone started to buzz on the countertop. It was Dani. "Hi," I whispered before moving out of the kitchen and into the garden for some privacy.

"Hey, how'd it go today?"

"Okay," I said after unlocking the garage door and moving inside. It had felt like such a long hard day, and the cold in the garage was making me feel even more miserable. "How was your day?"

"No, I mean…" Dani sighed. "Did you tell him?"

It clicked what she'd been referring to. "Oh no. It wasn't a good time." Silence engulfed the other end of the phone, and though I couldn't see Dani, I knew she was disappointed. Perhaps worried that I'd chickened out when in actual fact, I hadn't had the mental capacity to even think about it. "I was going to but…"

"I get it," she said, and I could hear the disbelief like a foghorn. "If you're not ready, I understand."

"It's just really complicated, Dani. I wish I could tell him, but I just can't." Something caught my eye outside of the window: Matt, sitting at the kitchen table with his head in his hands. His shoulders were shaking as if vibrating, and it was clear he was crying. My heart broke for him. "Look, I can't really talk," I said, my eyes still glued to him. I switched off the garage lights and locked the door behind me. "I'm going to have to go," I said, moving toward the house. "I'll call tomorrow."

Once inside the kitchen, he looked at me with tears streaming down his face. I moved to his side, and he wrapped an arm around my waist, pulling me close. He cried into my sweater, and I rubbed the back of his head. It was as if I could feel every ounce of his pain. It was horrible to listen to his sobbing. It felt like it was never going to end and that he would be this heartbroken forever. There was nothing I could say to make it better. I just held him close, wishing there was something I could do.

CHAPTER EIGHTEEN

Dani Raye

A few days passed before I heard from Lucy. She'd called last night to apologise for how we'd left things at the weekend. After hearing about Matt's mother, I felt incredibly disappointed in myself. I hadn't exactly been the kindest on the phone, and I should have been more understanding. Lucy seemed to be quite distressed as well. I imagined it was because she'd known Audrey most of her life, even if they didn't have the most amazing relationship.

Lucy was also worried that Matt's despair was filtering down to Ryan again. She had to meet with the principal yesterday as Ryan had broken down crying in the middle of class. Lucy had said he didn't know about Audrey, but something must have been bothering him. Perhaps it was just the worrisome energy. In an effort to get Ryan out of the house and into a better headspace, she'd invited Jonah and me to the cinema after school. With any luck, it would help uplift Ryan's spirits.

I had just pulled up at the school and hopped out of my car, already seeing Lucy waiting in her usual spot. The spring in my step brought me all the way to her side, and I didn't miss the way her smile became radiant when she locked eyes with me. "Hey."

"Hey, yourself."

"How was your meeting with the principal?" I asked tentatively.

That smile faltered. I knew it would. It was a touchy subject. "Don't remind me." She sighed. "At least he wasn't fighting. Still, it wasn't easy on him, and Mr. Simmons is now building quite the record against him."

"The old man needs to lighten up."

"He's just so sensitive to any changes in the house," Lucy said, more like fretted.

"I know." I thought about Lucy and Matt's future breakup and what effect it would have on Ryan. It concerned me, but I didn't bring it up. Lucy had enough on her mind. "Give it some time, and Matt will be okay. Ryan will see that," I said, even though I didn't quite believe my own words.

"I really hope so."

She got lost in her thoughts, and I tried to change the topic to something lighter. "Did you get your clay delivery?"

"Nope," she said, exasperated. "It sucks because I can't do anything else until that's in."

"From your Instagram, it looks like you've been making lots. I loved the dinner set you posted last night," I said excitedly, and I loved seeing her mirror my enthusiasm. "That grey colour is so pretty. It reminded me of pebbles on a beach."

"Well, that was my inspiration."

"And did you see how many likes you got?" She nodded. "And did you see that one comment about someone asking how much it costs? And that other comment saying they wanted to buy the whole set." Something thoughtful softened her features, and it made me slightly self-conscious. "What?"

"You're really cute." I felt my cheeks reddening. My face was growing so hot that I had to drop my eyes. "I love it. I love how supportive you are of my work."

The look on her face made me want to lean in and kiss her, but I knew that wasn't possible. It was only when I broke away and glanced back toward the school that I panicked. "Oh shit."

"What?" Lucy said from beside me, but there was no time to explain when Catriona was right in front of us.

"What are *you* doing here?" she asked me, failing to even acknowledge Lucy.

Lucy looked positively enraged that someone would speak to me in that tone. That was just Catriona.

"I'm picking up our son from school."

"I told you last week, I would pick him up."

"You did?" I tried to think back, but it failed to register.

"I texted you twice on Saturday night," she said with an eye roll. "I told you I had to drop him off early on Sunday, which I did, but that I would pick him up from school on Friday to make up for it."

It partially rang a bell. But I had barely glanced at those text messages last Saturday night. I had a slim window to check my phone while Lucy was in the bathroom. I didn't fully digest the information because as soon as Lucy had come out of the bathroom again, she was on top of me.

"Oh," was all I could conjure up. "Sorry, I forgot."

"Jesus, Dani." She grunted, and I had to admit her belittling tone had me a little embarrassed. Especially in front of Lucy.

"I said I'm sorry, Catriona. But you know, you could have called me or maybe told me in person—"

"I would have, but you closed the door in my face," she shot back with a lift of her brows. She kinda had me there. I was too busy trying to get her to fuck off last week so she didn't catch Lucy in my bed.

"Don't mind me," Lucy said with a snarky edge to her voice. Perhaps she was trying to defuse the tension.

That was my cue for introductions. "Uh, Catriona, this is Lucy, Ryan's mum." I gestured accordingly. "And Lucy, this is my ex-wife, Catriona."

"Yes, I think we've met before." Catriona mustered a smile.

"Right." Lucy returned a barely passable "polite" smile.

It was awkward. I was glad when Catriona perked up again, addressing me. "Anyway, I can pick him up today, and we can call round for his things later."

"Well, actually," I started and rubbed the back of my neck, feeling the heat of having both sets of eyes on me. "We promised the boys a trip to the cinema after school."

Catriona's face fell. "Perfect." It wasn't passive-aggressive; she looked more disappointed. "I booked the rest of the afternoon off so that Jonah and I could do something together. Well, what are you going to see?"

"The new *Star Wars*," Lucy replied, and I wished she hadn't.

"Oh, I've been wanting to see that," she said excitedly. I knew Catriona loved *Star Wars*. She loved anything to do with space, and just like that, there was no way out of it. "Would you mind if I tagged along?"

"Of course not," I said, and I could hear Lucy's sigh.

"Are you sure?" Catriona asked sweetly. "I don't want to impose." She glanced between us. When I took a second too long to respond, I could practically see the cogs in her brain turning.

"The more the merrier," I said.

I wasn't sure when the school bell rang, but soon enough, the boys were standing in front of us. I drove like a madman all the way through town. I wanted to make it to the cinema before Catriona. I was glad that Lucy pulled up behind us in the carpark.

"I am so sorry," I said while we were moving in the direction of the entrance. Ryan and Jonah had already run on ahead.

Lucy's face showed her discomfort, but she also showed an amusement that I was thankful for. "Come on, it's kinda funny."

"Is it?"

"Your ex-wife is on a date with us." She cracked a smile before her features hardened. "But what was up with the way she was talking to you?"

"What do you mean?"

"She was so fucking rude."

"That's just Catriona."

"Does she always speak to you that way?" Lucy asked, and I had to bring her temper to a simmer as we approached the entrance.

"Okay, the jealousy thing is cute and all, but you need to chill. Catriona can't know anything is going on."

"I'm serious, Dani. Why do you let her talk to you like that?"

"She's just a very direct person. That's the way she talks to everyone."

"And she's supposed to be a therapist?" Lucy's green side reappeared. "She needs to work on her fucking attitude."

I found her irritation with Catriona entertaining more than anything else. "Or what are you gonna do?" I teased. "Beat her up for me?"

She smirked, clearly unamused that I was teasing her, but she seemed to swallow it when something in the distance caught her eye. "Here comes the she-devil."

"Be nice." I lowered my tone. "She's not that bad."

She threw me an unconvinced look before opting to queue up with Ryan and Jonah. Once Catriona was inside, we joined the queue as well. While I would have liked to have paid for everyone, it would have raised too many questions. Lucy paid for herself and Ryan, while Catriona got in ahead of me and paid for the three of us. The power move wasn't missed by Lucy, and her frostiness for Catriona only seemed to grow from then on.

"What would you like, Jonah?" Catriona asked as we approached the confectionary counter. "The kid's box?" she offered, already knowing him too well. He got it every time we came to the cinema. It consisted of a soft drink, a small box of popcorn, and some sweets in a pouch. Ryan had just gotten it in front of us. "Do you still like sweet popcorn?" Catriona asked me as Lucy watched me carefully.

"Yep," I replied.

"Ok, I'll get half-sweet and half-salted." Catriona placed the order to the person behind the counter. She turned back to Lucy as her hand gently rested on my shoulder. "Dani likes sweet popcorn, but I prefer salted. We could never agree on it, could we, D?"

I really struggled to hide my discomfort. It was an innocent conversation, and the gesture didn't seem to be premediated, but that probably wasn't how it looked to Lucy. I didn't want her learning things about me through my ex. Not to mention, Catriona's comfort levels around me, especially when it came to physical contact, were coming across as too familiar, and I could see a disgruntled expression on Lucy' face. And if I could see it, Catriona would too. I hoped Lucy would get her emotions under control a little better before Catriona figured it out.

"Did you even want popcorn?" Lucy asked me, but it was her way of pointing out the fact that Catriona hadn't bothered to ask.

"We always get popcorn when we go to the cinema," Catriona returned matter-of-factly.

I didn't have the nerve to point out it had been years since Catriona and I had been to the cinema together. It felt like it would only add more fuel to the fire between these two. It didn't matter what Catriona said; everything just seemed to rub Lucy the wrong way.

"And two medium Diet Cokes," Catriona said to the cashier before turning back to me. "You're still on that no-sugar kick, right?"

"Yeah."

"What no-sugar kick?" Lucy asked me, confused.

"Oh, it's nothing," I tried to play it down, but Catriona stepped in.

"It's hardly nothing. Diabetes runs in Dani's family. She's always watching her sugar intake. That's why we're so careful with what Jonah eats too."

Thankfully, Catriona was paying, so she didn't catch the look of betrayal on Lucy's face. She looked so hurt that she hadn't known that information, and I felt terrible for not disclosing it in the first place. It truly was something I rarely thought about, but it was just another thing Catriona knew about me that Lucy didn't. Catriona turned back to us again and snuck a few pieces of popcorn into her mouth as we moved toward the screening room.

"Oh!" Catriona latched on to my arm in excitement. "You have to try some of the popcorn, Dani." She handed me the box. "I've really missed sweet and salty popcorn. Maeve likes salted too, so I never get it anymore. This is a real treat."

Knowing her the way I did, I knew it was completely innocent, but by the sour look on Lucy's face, I knew she took it to be more flirtatious than it was. There was absolutely nothing between me and Catriona, but to onlookers, our friendly banter could be mistaken for affection.

We moved into the cinema and found our seats. The boys sat next to each other while Lucy sat next to Ryan. I was seated next to Lucy, with Catriona on my other side. I was closed in by two women who had seen me naked, and it was about as uncomfortable as I could have imagined. The trailers were playing as Catriona excused herself to use the washroom, and once she was gone, Lucy was whispering in my ear:

"Why didn't you tell me about the sugar thing?"

"It never came up. Besides, Catriona worries about it more than I do—"

"I gave Jonah two pieces of cake at Ryan's birthday," she returned sharply, and now I realised what she was really upset about. "You should have told me."

"Oh, don't worry—"

"I could have made him really sick."

"No." I shook my head, trying to ease her guilt. "He's not actually diabetic." She wasn't listening. "Look, I promise, you didn't do anything wrong. Catriona is just being cautious, okay?" I reached for her arm in the dark. "Hey, I'm sorry."

Lucy bit her lip, but I could tell she was still a little hurt. "She just knows you better." Now we were getting to the crux of the problem.

"Yeah, she does." Her eyes met mine. "We were together for

a long time, Lucy. But if it helps, I'm really excited that you're getting to know me."

"Really?"

"Yes. And I want to know you more. Like, are you allergic to anything?"

"Just penicillin."

"That's something I should totally know," I said and she gave me a double take. "I was actually going to cook you penicillin pasta the other night." That caused a pout to appear, no doubt in order to hide a grin. "I'm so glad I changed the menu last minute."

"You're an idiot," she whispered sweetly. Thankfully, Catriona arrived back at that moment; otherwise, I might have done something silly like kiss her.

The rest of the movie went by without a hitch. The boys were out of the cinema first, and we emerged into the darkening night. Jonah and Ryan were play fighting with imaginary lightsabers while singing the theme song. Badly.

"Well, that was a success." Catriona perked up as we all walked back to the carpark. "It still wasn't as good as the original."

"I haven't actually seen the others," Lucy said.

"Well, they're probably a bit before your time," Catriona said.

I could feel the tension rising instantly, and so I spoke up. "Not everyone is into *Star Wars*, Catriona."

She looked indifferent and like she might say something else that would no doubt rile up Lucy, but thankfully, we had reached Lucy's car.

"Bye, Ryan," Jonah said as he took my hand. "See you at school next week." Ryan waved good-bye, and Lucy pressed the button on her keys and unlocked the car.

"Wait," Catriona said, almost like a revelation. All eyes turned to her. "This is *your* car."

It was at that moment that the atmosphere turned cold.

Catriona's eyes narrowed at Lucy's Jeep, and then she looked to me. The custom blue colour was too rare to pawn it off as someone else's; add on the flashy black alloys, and it was unmistakably the car Catriona had seen in my driveway on Sunday morning. I couldn't hide my panic, and neither, it seemed, could Lucy. With one look, I knew Catriona knew. She'd pieced it together. The "friend" I'd kissed who Jonah saw. The new relationship I wasn't ready to talk about. I felt vulnerable and naked. As if she could see right through me. I couldn't control my expression, and I knew it must have been an admission of guilt.

"It's a very unique colour," Catriona said to Lucy with what sounded like a double meaning. "Unforgettable, you might say."

"Thanks for coming, Lucy." I blanked Catriona, unable to stare directly at that much energy and focused on Lucy. "Safe home."

"Yeah," she muttered. "See you later." She put Ryan in the back seat and quickly climbed into the car. The speed with which she left made it look like she was fleeing the scene of a crime.

"I'll drop him round to you this evening," I said to Catriona but didn't look at her. I was afraid of what I would see. "I just have to pack up his things first." I was already lifting Jonah into the back seat while Catriona hovered somewhere behind me.

"I'll follow you back home."

"No, that's okay. I can just—"

"I insist," she said sternly from behind me. It caused me to jump slightly, and all I could do was nod.

To say the entire drive home was stressful would be underselling it. I could barely focus on Jonah's chitchat. I tried to come up with a game plan. Play innocent, act a fool, or go straight to recognising the errors of my ways? I knew Catriona would have a lot of opinions. Lucy wasn't exactly single, and she was the mother of Jonah's best friend. If something went wrong, their friendship would be ruined. I knew how bad this was, and now I was going to have to listen to how bad Catriona thought it was. I could practically hear the tone of judgement in my head. I planned on lying about the entire thing, but as soon as she came upstairs and into Jonah's room, I knew there was no escape.

"I can pack his things by myself," I said trying to sound self-assured.

Jonah was downstairs on his iPad, so thankfully, he wasn't about to hear all hell break lose. She closed the door behind us, essentially trapping me. "What were you thinking?" she said accusingly. Gathering his things was an easy distraction from her. "Dani?"

"What are you talking about?"

"Do you think I'm blind?" Her voice rose to extreme highs, and I finally had to look to her.

"Lower your voice."

"How long has this been going on? I can't believe you're sleeping with a married woman. A straight married woman. A straight married woman who also happens to be Jonah's best friend's mum. What were you thinking?"

"She's not married," I said, somehow finding the strength to make up an excuse for myself. "And she's not straight."

"Oh, come on, Dani." She rolled her eyes. "Is that what she told you?"

"Look, Lucy is separating from her boyfriend."

"Please tell me you're not that stupid."

"Fuck you, Catriona."

"No, fuck you, Dani," she shot back, then adjusted her voice. "Jonah doesn't make friends easily." Her stern yet desperate expression caused the guilt to slosh around in the pit of my belly. She was right. Ryan was basically Jonah's only friend. "And now you've gone and fucked up that friendship for him. How could you be so bloody selfish?"

"We like each other, okay?"

Catriona returned a horrified expression. "Tell me you're not falling for her." When I didn't respond, her face seemed to contort into disbelief. "Please tell me you're smarter than that,

Dani." I turned away from her again and packed more of Jonah's belongings. The sooner Catriona left my house, the better. "She's just a kid. She's got to be, like, ten years younger than you."

"No, she's not. She's twenty-six. And let's not forget, there was an eight-year gap in our relationship, Catriona."

"And look how that turned out," she spat back. "God, you really haven't thought this through at all."

"She's going to separate from him." I tried to grasp at anything to fight my case. To make it not as terrible as it sounded, but I knew it was a sinking ship, and the guilt consuming my insides was only making me feel more attacked. "He's seeing someone else too."

"They're in an open relationship?"

"Yes. For now—"

"And you think she's going to leave her perfect little hetero lifestyle for you? Especially when she can have her cake and eat it too?"

"Why are you being so—"

"How did you think I would react?"

"Are you jealous?" I slung back at her. "Is that it? You can't stand that I've moved on. That I might actually be happy." I had more to say, but she cut me off.

"You call 'being the other woman' happy?"

I saw red. Fury rushed to the surface. "I am not the other woman! I'm not Maeve, okay?" She looked enraged, furious, in fact, but I couldn't stop myself. "Lucy's relationship is ending. It's completely different than the hell you put us through. We were happily married when that bitch hooked her fangs into you. You were fucking her while I was at home taking care of our baby." I was baring my teeth, the venom pulsing through my veins. "I am not the other woman. I am nothing like you and Maeve."

Catriona looked shocked and disturbed. My ragged breaths were the only sounds keeping us from deathly silence. Then, regret flooded in. I wished I could have taken back my choice of words, but at the same time, my pride wouldn't allow me to apologise.

She took two steps toward me. "Give me his bag," she said in an eerily calm voice.

I wasn't even sure I had properly packed everything, but the anger behind her eyes told me not to hesitate in giving it over. Once the bag was in her hands, she left his room. I let out a shaky breath and replayed the entire conversation. Regrets, guilt, and shame filled my insides. I hated confrontation, especially with Catriona. I always felt like, after the number of arguments and disagreements we'd had, that we should have maxed out on how many times we'd screamed at each other.

I wanted to hide in Jonah's bedroom forever, but I knew I couldn't let him leave without a good-bye. He was too observant. I didn't want him to know something was wrong. I came downstairs just as they reached the front door.

"Bye, Mum." He was just going to wave, but I knelt and hugged him.

I held on a little tighter, not ready to be alone for the week. When I stood again, Catriona didn't even bother to look at me. With his hand in hers, they disappeared into the night and down the footpath.

I spent the rest of the night slowly sinking further into shame. I knew I shouldn't have spoken to Catriona that way. It had been one of our worst fights, and that was including during our divorce. Upon reflection, my reactions had been nasty, and I couldn't handle being challenged on my feelings for Lucy because deep down, I was ashamed of how things had started between us. But it was like a car crash that I couldn't look away from. Except, I was in the passenger seat, and Lucy was driving us straight over a cliff. I felt like I had no control in a situation that was beginning to feel uncomfortably like the end of my own marriage.

I needed to take back control, and maybe I could hold my head up high again when the time came to apologise to Catriona.

The hurt in her eyes kept replaying in my mind, and I wished more than anything that I could go back. But in order to make things right, I had to face Lucy head-on and end whatever this was. At least, until she was officially single. Which thankfully, shouldn't have been too long a wait.

Chapter Nineteen

Lucy Matthews

"Will Catriona tell anyone?" I asked Dani as I clasped my hands. "She obviously thinks I'm no good," I added bitterly, not appreciating the things Catriona had said about me.

"I don't know. I haven't spoken to her yet. It only happened a couple of days ago. I felt so bad, I couldn't even face work today," she said as her head fell into her hands hopelessly.

We were seated in my living room on the couch. It was Monday morning, and I was surprised when Dani had insisted on meeting. Ryan was at school, and Matt was at work. We were always more partial to an evening rendezvous, or at the very least, an afternoon playdate with the boys. She was tense; there was no denying the effect a fight with her ex-wife had taken on her. I had never seen her quite this distressed before.

At times, I was in awe of her relationship with Catriona, even if I was a little jealous. Putting aside my own dislike for Catriona as a person, I couldn't deny her commitment to Jonah and Dani. Though I knew there was nothing between them anymore, the fact remained that Catriona knew Dani in a way I could only daydream about. Then, there were the progressive parenting roles they'd adopted. No one would know Jonah was a child of divorce.

Perhaps that was just Dani's confident and positive persona. She was the kind of woman who usually intimidated me. Strong, brilliantly smart, and put together. Gorgeous, of course, but also sweet. I was usually attracted to those sorts of attributes, but at the end of the day, sexual attraction could be stifled if I tried hard enough. But for me, Dani's personality had won me over. Because for some reason, she could see me. Even when I didn't know myself, Dani seemed to pull the best parts of me to the surface.

"Well, I'm glad you're here." I tried to ease her worries by touching her hand. But her eyes went somewhere else, and the energy between us shifted. "Is everything okay?"

She took a long inhale. "I'm not just here to tell you about Catriona," she said in an ominous tone that had me panicking. "I don't think we should do this anymore."

My heartbeat was sounding loudly in my ears, and I was already rubbing my thighs, perhaps to offer some distraction from the pressure tightening around my heart. "Why?" My voice sounded small.

Her expression softened. "Just until your separation is final." Her optimistic, lopsided smile didn't ease my concerns.

"But my separation could take weeks, maybe even months. I can't just leave him, not when Audrey's sick," I tried. "Why should we stop seeing each other when it's practically over, anyway?"

"Don't you feel bad?" Her change in tone took me by surprise. "Lying to his face about where you've been? Who you've been seeing?"

"He doesn't ask." That didn't help my case. It just made Dani look even more unsure. "We don't talk when Ryan isn't in the room. We don't hug or be intimate in any way with each other anymore." My tone was emotionless because that was what my relationship had come to. Of course, I had warmed up to Matt in the last week, but that was only because of his devastation with Audrey. "But, Dani…" I laced our hands and stared at them. "It's you I think about when things are rough here. You keep me strong. You're keeping me sane while all of this horrible tension is floating around this big house." I rested my forehead against hers. "I can't lose you too."

A second later, I felt her lips graze mine. They were soft and delicate. The kiss intensified, and though I think it took her off guard for a beat, her hands crept into my hair. She pulled me closer, and I gladly took charge. I rested a hand on her thigh, revelling in the warmth, while my other found her waist. I was glad that the tension in the room had lifted and turned to something more desirable. She seemed to need this just as much as I did. She repositioned herself and lay back onto my couch, pulling me on top of her, never breaking her lips from mine. In our new position, she pulled me impossibly close while grinding against my front. I was enjoying the contact too much to slow down for even a breath.

My top and bra were discarded somewhere on the floor. Her movements were desperate and seemed fuelled by unsatiable desire. It wasn't the time or place for foreplay. I unbuttoned her jeans, evoking a gasp of delight. She arched as soon as I touched where she needed me most. I watched the crease form on her forehead and enjoyed every moan that left her lips.

I hovered above her, taking it all in. She clawed at my back as I built up speed, drawing pleasure from her. Touching her was almost more arousing than being touched. Her frown in ecstasy, coupled with shallow breathing, caused heat to grow between my legs. She pulled me down and kissed me desperately. I knew she was getting close to the edge.

"Lucy?"

I yanked away from her and saw Matt standing in the doorway, looking in on us. I jumped off Dani in panic and grabbed my shirt. "Matt," I started with no idea what to say next.

"You two are…are…" He couldn't finish, but I knew it was hard to deny what he'd just walked in on.

Dani had buttoned her jeans but remained in a rigid position on the couch. She avoided eye contact. Once my chest was covered, I took a few steps toward Matt as I took in his heavy breathing and what could only be described as a disgusted expression.

"What the hell, Lucy?" he said angrily. "You're cheating on me." Dani's head snapped up to me, but I couldn't face her. "And you were fucking in on it?" He pointed to Dani.

"I'm sorry—" she tried, but he cut her off.

"I've been pouring my heart out to you when you've been sleeping with my girlfriend!"

"Don't blame Dani," I said as my need to protect her took control. "*You* did this."

"How could I have done this?" he asked, outraged. "I'm not the one cheating, Lucy."

The room submerged into silence.

"What?" Dani rose to her feet, looking betrayed. "What is he talking about?" She stared at me like I was a stranger, and it caused my chest to tighten. She glanced in Matt's direction before she seemed to get a grasp on her voice again. "You said you two were separating. You told me you were in an open relationship—"

"Separating?" Matt cut in, looking to me for answers. "That's the first I heard of it."

I was stunned into silence. He had the audacity to make out like I was the one who'd been cheating when he'd been doing the exact same thing for much longer. The two people I loved most watched me in disbelief, and it caused my limbs to shake. My breathing felt out of control. A thousand thoughts were running through my head, and I couldn't make heads or tails of who to comfort first.

"I'm sorry," Dani said to Matt. "She lied to me. Catriona was right about you." Hearing those words, coupled with Dani's devastated expression, caused me to jump to attention.

"No," I tried, but Dani was already moving toward the door. "Dani, wait." I ran after her, leaving Matt behind.

In the hallway, she pulled at the front door, but I got there in time to grab her arm. She yanked it violently from my grasp. "Don't, just don't. I can't believe I was so stupid to get involved with you," she said angrily. "I never wanted to break up your relationship. I never wanted any of this." She looked at me with disgust. "It's over."

It felt like I'd been kicked in the gut, and a thousand pieces of my heart were thrown up in the air, landing upon broken glass.

"Don't do this." I could hear the desperation in my voice. "It's you I want to be with. Please." My heart felt like it was breaking in two.

"You lied. And you made me lie." Unshed tears of fury lingered in her eyes, and I hated myself for being the cause of her pain. "All this time, I thought it was over between you two. That you *were* separating." I tried to cut in, argue my defence that he was lying, but she refused to let me. "I actually believed you, and I let you make me into a person I never *ever* wanted to be." Her eyes were fixated behind me on my living room door, and I knew then exactly how I'd hurt her the most. "You made me into the other woman."

Seeing her so distraught had a physical reaction on me. I couldn't form words through my own crying. Heartbreak was clouding her features, but her anger seemed to keep it from breaking through.

"He's lying. I can explain," I whispered, my voice too fragile to reach any volume. "Please, let me make things right." She shook her head and shuffled back from me like I was dangerous. "I'm sorry, Dani—"

"I don't like who I am with you." Those words caused a tidal wave of emotion, and her bottom lip quivered. It was clear at that moment what I'd done to her. And I knew I'd broken us beyond repair. "It's over."

She walked down the footpath, and I couldn't hold back the tears any longer. I watched her leave me without looking back, and it felt like she was tearing my heart apart with each step.

My chest ached, and my limbs felt like lead. It pulled me

down. Somehow, I closed the door just in time for my legs to give up. I slid down the wall until my bottom hit the tiled floor with a thud. I wept into my hands, feeling utterly broken inside. Like I might never breathe properly again through the agony in my chest. Like I would never be able to take a full breath again without causing a thousand papercuts to my bruised heart.

"You and her." Matt's voice pulled me back into reality. It wasn't a question.

I wasn't even sure what he was asking, but I pried my hands from my face and looked up at him. He was crying as he stared at me from the opening of the living room. I didn't know how long he'd stood there. Perhaps he'd seen it all, or maybe he was just seeing the aftermath in my broken body.

"Yes," I whispered. The feeling of hopelessness was replaced with fury. "But you ruined it."

His eyes snapped to mine before his jaw squared. "Good." He walked away and into the kitchen.

My breathing turned angry and shallow. My tears dried up, and I could feel my teeth grinding. I hadn't felt this kind of rage for him in weeks, ever since Dani and I had started seeing each other, and just like that, it returned with a vengeance. Heat spread into my arms and legs, making me feel hot and frantic. I felt uncontrollably livid, and every morsel of hurt and pain I felt for Dani transformed into rage. It powered my legs like fuel in a car, and before I knew it, I was on my feet and moving with purpose into the kitchen.

"You just couldn't let me be happy, could you?" I spat at him in the kitchen. He had his back to me, but I could see his hands gripping the countertop. I could practically see the hairs rising on the back of his neck. He spun to face me, showing me just how riled up he was. "You're with Shannon, why do you care who I sleep with anymore? Why did you make it out like *I'm* the cheater? You made Dani think I've been lying to her. Like we haven't been discussing separating."

"We haven't talked about separating in weeks. I thought we were doing better. I thought we were happy."

"Happy people don't sleep in separate bedrooms. They have sex, Matt."

"Well, now I know why you're not interested in sex with me."

"Fuck off."

"I always knew you were a lesbian."

"Don't you dare," I shouted, but he barely seemed to register how much he'd upset me. He knew I'd always been open about my fluid sexuality.

"God, Lucy, you're such a fucking hypocrite."

I breathed out in disbelief. "*I'm* the hypocrite."

"For months, you punished me. I came to you lost and scared, looking for help. When I told you I had feelings for Shannon, you treated me like scum," he said, slamming his hands on the countertop. "You iced me out. You turned Ryan against me—"

"What did you expect?" I shouted. "You told me you wanted to fuck someone else!"

"I needed support. I came to you, afraid that my feelings for Shannon would end our relationship. I thought if I told you about it, we could work through it together, but you destroyed us."

"You're so full of shit," I returned, feeling a serious lack of empathy. "You and Shannon ruined this relationship."

"You told me I could explore things with her."

"Because you were fucking miserable. What was I supposed to do? Now you get mad at me for sleeping with someone else? Double standards much?"

"We agreed to be open and honest. You never told me you were seeing someone else." I opened my mouth, but nothing came out. "You never told me about her. You never gave me that same decency." He was right. There was no escape from that gruelling truth, and just like that, it felt like I'd been submerged in icy waters, and I was treading desperately to stay afloat. His features shifted from anger to hurt, and I realised my mistake.

Perhaps I hadn't wanted him to feel the helpless betrayal I'd felt. The knowledge that his partner yearned for someone else, and there was nothing he could do about it. That he wasn't enough for me like I wasn't for him. Learning that Matt had feelings for Shannon had caused an open wound in our relationship, and as the months had rolled on, we'd drifted further apart. It was as if that gash just kept getting yanked apart until eventually, we were split down the middle. But maybe I'd never told Matt about Dani because I didn't want to be the one at fault. I didn't want my attraction for someone else to be the reason we fell apart. It was easier to let his indiscretion be the blame for our failed relationship.

"I know, and for that, I'm sorry," I whispered, unable to hide my shame. "I should have told you." His temper seemed to ease. "But, Matt, we were already over."

"Were we?"

I stared at him in disbelief. "Did you think this was working? Really?"

"I know we have problems, but so does everyone."

"Did you honestly think we could continue on like this?" He looked to be getting lost in his thoughts. "You don't kiss me anymore."

His eyes collided with mine helplessly. "I didn't think you wanted me to."

"We don't laugh like we used to." His frown deepened. "We don't say good night to each other or kiss good-bye." My words looked to finally be sinking in. "I don't want to settle for whatever half-assed relationship this is."

"Lucy, I still love you." His small voice broke my heart.

"And I love you." I breathed out and allowed myself to really feel the rush of emotions inside. "I do." His face saddened as he watched me from a safe distance. "But I'm not in love with you anymore."

"Are you in love with her?"

Our words settled around us, and I thought deeply for a moment. I didn't know why it took losing her to realise how strongly I felt. I met his eyes and nodded. He rubbed his forehead desperately, as if trying to make sense of it. I moved to the kitchen table and took a seat as my legs had reached peak exhaustion.

"I'm not ready to give up on us," he said with determination before taking a seat at the table opposite me. He lowered his head to meet my eyes. "Maybe now that we've both explored other options, we can be together." His hand reached out and landed on mine on the table. "Just us."

"Will you give her up?" I asked him. "Can you even give her up?"

"I will, for our family."

I didn't know fully what response I was looking for, but I wasn't expecting that. If he'd have said that two months ago, things would have been different, but a lot had changed. I'd changed. It left me speechless and made me look inward.

I recalled our eight years together. Actually, my mind recalled our entire lives together. Other than my immediate family, I'd never known anyone as long as I'd known Matt. Friends to lovers. It was the fairy tale that any high school crush wished for. Matt wasn't a bad guy. He loved me, and I trusted him when he said he would give up Shannon for me. Because that was how much our family meant to him.

But the reality was that we could never come back from this. At least, I couldn't. I couldn't get past his feelings for someone else. Someone who he saw every day at work. I couldn't trust he wouldn't slip up, especially when I'd witnessed firsthand just how indescribably happy he'd been. Every time he left for work, he was excited, and I knew it was because of her. His Tuesday late night "meetings," which used to leave him drained and wanting to cuddle when he got home, led to him looking refreshed and energised. That was all her. I hated sharing him, but more than that, I hated that he only had enough affection for one of us. And despite what he said, he had chosen Shannon.

He'd meant well by declaring he would give her up for me. And I knew he would have tried, but he would be miserable again, or worse, it would only be a matter of time before he found someone else to direct his affection toward. He had always been like this. When we were younger, I used to joke that he was polyamorous because he could never commit to one person. Maybe I should have taken my own observation more seriously.

Though, when I really considered my feelings for him, I knew I couldn't go back to the way things were. I'd had a glimpse of what my life could look like without him, and I wanted it. I wanted a different future. A future that I hoped included Dani.

"Why are you fighting for us? For this?" I asked.

"We've been through so much. Nothing has ever broken us, remember?" he tried, but it wasn't a good enough reason. Not anymore.

"You don't want to admit defeat?" He frowned. "That's why you're holding on so tight to something we didn't even want in the first place?"

"That's not true," he said defiantly.

"Would we even be together if it weren't for Ryan?" That stunned him, but it was only because it was the brutal truth. A truth we'd never had the courage to admit. "Would we have lasted this long?" The answer was no, and his inability to say otherwise was a declaration in itself. Ryan was the glue holding us together, but there was a limit to what Super Glue could fix. "I know you don't want him to come from a broken family," I said, recalling his despair from months ago when he'd told me about Shannon. He hadn't wanted us to break up because of the effect it would have on Ryan, and at the time, that had also been a fear of mine. It was the whole reason we'd entered into an open relationship all those months ago. But now, I feared that our unhappiness with each other would inevitably be much more detrimental to Ryan. It was already affecting him. "But, Matt, this has to be worse. Ryan can see we're not happy."

"I can do more—"

"You don't want me," I said, and though he shook his head, I knew it was true. I'd known it for some time. "You're just too decent to admit it."

"What about Ryan? I don't want to lose him."

"You'll never lose him." I took his hand, and relief washed over his features. "Even though we won't live under the same roof, he will always have us both."

Silence settled between us. It was as if Matt had needed that reassurance. Perhaps losing Ryan had been a major fear of his in recent months. I could imagine why. I'd been quite dismissive of him after he'd told me of Shannon. Perhaps he feared that if he said he wanted a separation, I would take Ryan away from him. It was like my reassurance had lifted a weight off him.

"Okay," he said, showing a mix of emotions. "That's it, then." The strength in his voice was gone, and he looked broken.

"I think so."

He was no longer trying to hide the fact that he was crying. He covered his eyes, and his shoulders started to shake. I rubbed his shoulder and swiped at my own tears, wishing things hadn't come to this in order for us to accept we weren't right for each other.

My devastation shifted to Dani.

I pulled back from comforting him, remembering what devastation he'd caused. For leading Dani to believe that I had been anything but honest with her. I could forgive him a lot of things, but I didn't know if I could ever forgive him for destroying what I had with Dani.

I left him at the table and went to the garage to be alone. Even my safe space seemed to remind me of her. My inspiration and creativity had left my soul, along with my heart, and I feared none of it would ever return again. I sat at my painting station and let myself go. I cried thinking about her last words, knowing that I had lost Dani before she was even mine.

CHAPTER TWENTY

Dani Raye

To say it had been a rough few days would have been a serious understatement. Being alone made it all the more difficult. Jonah wouldn't be with me for days, and I was practically counting the minutes until I could have him home. I needed a distraction from the heartache. From the constant feeling of betrayal and hopelessness.

I had so many feelings and emotions to sift through that I didn't know where to start. I would never forget the look in Matt's eyes when he'd caught us. His heartbreak and betrayal. I'd never wanted to hurt him. He'd never deserved to find out that way. It had been careless and cruel. In his own home, nonetheless. At least Catriona had had the decency to cheat on me out of the house. Sadly, I couldn't afford the same luxury. It made me feel wretched just thinking about it. To imagine what Matt was going through right now.

And then I would think of Lucy, and every single time, my eyes would start to sting, and my chest would expand, searching for breath. It still felt like a kick in the gut when I thought of how she'd lied to me.

"I'm not the one cheating, Lucy."

Matt's voice echoed in my mind, revealing his betrayal and disgust. His voice had been raw and angry but also somehow lost. It repeated in my mind constantly, driving me further into shame. How could she have lied to me for so long? Were there signs of her deceit, and should I have been smarter? I was annoyed that I had allowed myself to become someone I had spent years detesting. A cheater. The other woman.

It seemed that Lucy had made it all up: Matt's cheating and his indiscretions. All of it, lies? Was he even involved with Shannon? Part of me felt like an idiot for believing her, and another part of me struggled to believe that she would have lied about it all. The raw emotion and devastation that first time we'd met. Was it all a ruse? I didn't know what to believe anymore, and that made me feel like even more of a fool.

I was playing with fire when I'd met Lucy, but her allure had had me in a trance. Her creativity and openness were like a breath of fresh air. I could have breathed her in forever. But now, I screened her calls. It had been days. Countless phone calls, several voice mails that I refused to listen to, and what seemed like a million texts. I had read the first. It was so long, I'd had to download it. I got about halfway through her apology that was dripping with more lies, and I couldn't take it. I'd deleted it. Hearing from her caused too much agony. My soul couldn't bear it.

Lucy had come over unannounced last night. It had started with a knock at the front door. I'd moved to answer it like with any other visitor, but I'd stopped. Though the glass in the front door was translucent, I could tell it was her. Her silhouette was unforgettable, and I had memorised it after the first time she'd come to my house. My silence prompted her to call my name. She'd begged me to answer the door. Talking through the door in a desperate plea. It had almost been enough to break me. But then it had gone silent. She'd given up.

I was filled with dread and regret. The mere thought of seeing her at school pickup left me riddled with anxiety. I wanted to run away and hide from the mess I'd made. The worst part of all was that Catriona was right. She had preempted a horrible breakup that would leave me wanting to cut Lucy, and inherently Ryan, out of my life. The idea of a playdate with Ryan was terrifying, and I knew Jonah would be asking for one eventually. Who would I rather have chaperoning alongside me, Lucy or Matt? Both seemed impossibly awkward, not to mention painful.

These were the thoughts filling my head as I sat in my car outside my ex-wife's house. It was time to rotate Jonah once again. I moved up the footpath that weaved through the garden. My movements were sheepish, and I couldn't even muster enough strength to hold my head high.

Catriona would no doubt be ready to give me a piece of her mind. After how I'd spoken to her, I wouldn't be surprised if she never spoke to me again. Even if she did somehow manage to muster the energy to look me in the eyes, I knew I would have to face her gloating. She would take pleasure in telling me what an idiot I was for falling for a taken woman.

I knocked, and a tiny part of me actually hoped no one was home. Like perhaps she'd just forgotten I was collecting our son today. We hadn't spoken since our argument. She hadn't texted or called, not even to talk about Jonah. I worried what would face me inside.

Maeve answered the door. I watched her face go through a series of emotions. From awkward to pleasant to a little standoffish. It put me on edge before she'd even said a word. "Dani." She said my name as if it was a greeting. "They're just playing in the garden." She smiled, though it was tight-lipped and fleeting.

I nodded several times, accepting the cold shoulder. I deserved it.

Maeve took a step back and gestured for me to come through. It would be rude to refuse, even though all I wanted was an extremely quick and easy handover. I moved through their house with Maeve awkwardly following. We didn't make small talk. Though we never usually did.

The back door was open, and I emerged into the sunlight. Jonah's eyes lit up when they landed on mine, and for the first time in a week, I felt warmth in my blood. Like I wasn't barren of happiness. I felt like my skin could finally absorb the sunlight, and all it took was the look on my son's face. I knelt to meet him as his body collided with mine in a thud. A thud that seemed to restart my aching heart. It was a couple of seconds of bliss because as he pulled away, I caught a glimpse of Catriona over his shoulder.

She looked at us thoughtfully, but she was staring at Jonah. Her eyes couldn't meet mine. "Maeve," Catriona said, "could you take Jonah upstairs to get his things? I need to speak with Dani."

My stomach lurched, and dread filled my insides again. The contents of my belly swirled like lava that might erupt at any moment.

She met my eyes once we were alone. "I think we need to clear the air," she said calmly. "For Jonah's sake." It was like the calm before the storm, and I kept myself on guard just in case she turned on me. She had every right to after how I'd spoken to her. "I'm sorry." My head snapped up in surprise. "I should have never spoken to you that way," she continued calmly and heartfeltly. "My reactions were coming from a place of concern for you and Jonah but—"

"Wait," I cut in, unable to believe *I* was getting the apology.

"No, please let me finish," she asked kindly, making me feel even worse. "I feel terrible for how I reacted. My words were accusing and hurtful and—"

"Catriona, you really don't need…" I tried, but despair had taken over my voice. I couldn't meet her eyes as a stinging sensation made it difficult to focus.

"Dani, we have always put our differences aside for Jonah, and I can't stand you being angry with me. I should have trusted you when you said you knew what you were doing with Lucy." Hearing her name caused a lump to form in my throat. "And I want you to know I'm happy for you and—"

"Stop it, just stop," I said, my voice cracking. It took

Catriona aback. "You were right." My voice was small and desperate. "You were right about her." I looked up, and her entire expression softened instantly. "I can't believe how stupid—"

"Dani, I'm so sorry." She pulled me into a hug. The embrace caused a release, and before I knew it, the tears had escaped. "I didn't want this."

"She lied," I whispered. "She was never going to leave him." Catriona pulled back but kept a hand on my arm for comfort. "It's over."

"Do you want to talk about it?"

"I can't." My reply was weak, but I was thankful it didn't seem to disappoint her. She nodded and squeezed my arm in solidarity.

"I'm here," she said, but I could already hear Jonah's voice approaching, and so I wiped at my eyes to hide all signs of heartbreak. He didn't need to be worried about me. "I can keep him for longer if you need time."

"No," I said clearing my throat. "He's exactly what I need." Then the dread of school set in. "Though it means I have to face her tomorrow."

"Why don't I take him to school tomorrow?"

"You can't do school pickup forever."

"But I can do it tomorrow." She tilted her head. "I've a late meeting anyway. I can swing by and drive him from yours."

I'd never felt more relief. "Thank you," I just about got out, feeling more sobs en route.

"You're going to be okay." Catriona offered a small smile before she was moving behind me and meeting Jonah, giving me another moment to compose myself.

"All ready to go?" I heard her asking and leading him back inside.

I followed soon after, and we said our good-byes to Catriona and Maeve. Though I felt relief at having told Catriona about my breakup with Lucy, I also had to shoulder the shame of being burnt by someone who wasn't available. Truly, I blamed myself for being so naive. I should have known better than to get involved, but now the question remained, how would I cope when seeing Lucy later this week at school pickup or at any time in the future?

CHAPTER TWENTY-ONE

Lucy Matthews

It had been an entire week since I'd spoken to Dani. My calls didn't go through anymore, and there was little indication that she was reading my texts. I even showed up at her house, ready to pour my heart out, but she wouldn't come to the door. I knew then that there was very little hope for us. And while that devastated me beyond words, I couldn't fall apart. I had to rebuild my life.

"Can I come see the house too?" Ryan asked from the passenger seat.

"No, honey. You gotta go to school."

"But after school."

"The woman showing the house can only do this morning," I explained and watched his face drop. "But I will take lots of pictures."

"Okay," he grumbled. "Take a video of my new room."

"I promise." I couldn't contain my head shake.

He was handling all of this incredibly, considering his parents were separating. He'd had his fears and concerns initially. We'd told him this day, last week. We didn't see the point in dragging it out. It had already been dragged out to the point of destruction. I was expecting the worst, tears or an outburst. That he would need a couple days off school to process, but it wasn't necessary. He was in school the next day.

At first, he had some questions when I'd explained that I was moving out. I think he was afraid that I would leave him behind, but when I explained that he would do one week with me and one week with Matt, he couldn't have been more excited. He was going to have two houses, which meant two bedrooms, just like his best friend, Jonah. I had to give credit to Jonah because he really had "sold" coming from a divorced family. Ryan had explained these so-called perks that Jonah got, including two birthdays, two summer holiday trips, Christmas twice, and sometimes, he even got dessert twice. I still hadn't figured out the dessert part, but these benefits seemed to outweigh most of the downfalls of our separation. He had sounded okay about the situation, though I was hesitant to believe that would last forever. It would be an evolving roller coaster of emotions for him. For all of us. There would be good days and bad days, but for now, I could take solace in the good days.

Matt and I had agreed to leave out the part about Shannon and Dani when talking to him. It didn't seem important because ultimately, Matt's and my problems had been there long before. We told the truth and explained that we'd fallen out of love with each other. I felt better about being honest. We could have made something up, but we'd already kept Ryan in the dark for far too long. He deserved to know, and though I couldn't be sure, perhaps he was even a little relieved. He had always been a brilliantly sympathetic little boy, and I think he had been picking up on the bad vibes between us for long enough.

"Is it the house with a garden?" Ryan perked up.

"Yes. And a garage."

He and I had been looking at pictures online of a few properties for rent. I was viewing the top contender after school drop-off. He liked the look of this one and so did I. My budget wasn't exactly huge, and the little terrace house off Stranmillis seemed to tick all our boxes. It wasn't far from school, and Matt was no more than a five-minute drive away. He had insisted I didn't have to move out until I was ready, but looking up places to live had never felt better. I was more than ready to go out on my own.

Mum had offered to let me move in with them, but that felt like a ginormous step backward. I had no interest in moving back to Fermanagh; my life was in Belfast. At least, that was the life I wanted to build. True, the properties I was viewing weren't amazing, but they would help me get back on my feet again. I had to hold on to some kind of motivation in and around all the heartbreak. Besides, I didn't want to be shipping Ryan almost two hours up and down the country every time I wanted to see him. If I'd learned anything from Dani's example, it was to keep his life as routine as possible, even if that meant slumming it in student accommodation for a little while.

We pulled up outside the school, and I walked him to the front entrance. On my way back to the car, I scanned the carpark, hoping to catch a glimpse of Dani, though I had no idea what I would even say to her. I couldn't be sure I wouldn't just burst into tears. And how pathetic would that make me look? I was just nearing my car when I spotted someone waiting for me.

"We need to talk," Catriona said, freezing me on the spot.

I was still about six feet from my car, and she decided to close in on me. I couldn't move or contain my rapid breathing or the way it felt like I was going to vomit.

"You need to stay away from her."

I couldn't meet her eyes out of shame. I wasn't expecting her to know what had happened.

"When you see her at school, don't look at her, don't speak to her—"

"Don't breathe near her?"

"God, you're so immature." That ignited an anger in me. "I'm so glad she's through with you."

"Go to hell."

"Excuse me?" She took a step closer.

"You heard me," I said, somehow finding my voice, even though Catriona intimidated me no end. "You know, I don't give a shit what you think about me. Dani is the only person I care about—"

"Funny way of showing it. Go home to your boyfriend." That hurt more than she would ever know.

She turned away, but I couldn't stand her thinking so little of me. "I left him." My voice stopped her, and she turned back. "I love her."

I felt vulnerable revealing that to someone who I didn't really care much for, but she was important to Dani and Jonah. Her expression remained stern, but something in her eyes softened. Perhaps it was because of how desperate I must have looked. It was clear she didn't know whether or not she could believe me.

"You really hurt her."

"I know. I'm trying to make things right."

"Try harder or just stop. Because I'm sorry, but Dani deserves better." Catriona left, and I knew in my gut she was right. Dani deserved so much better.

While that worthless feeling stayed with me for some time, I made myself shake it off. I would make something of myself, and I wasn't ready to just let Dani go. People like Dani didn't come around often, and I was never going to give up without a fight. I just had to get my life together first.

CHAPTER TWENTY-TWO

Dani Raye

Though I'd gotten out of drop-off and pickup duties on Monday, I knew Catriona couldn't do it forever. On Tuesday, I was a barrel of nerves pulling up to school. I couldn't see her car in the carpark, and I was relieved when I'd made it to the entrance and waved bye to Jonah without seeing her. It had felt like a small win, though it was clouded in sadness.

Later that afternoon, at school pickup, I wasn't so lucky. I'd seen her standing in her usual spot, though it turned out she had enough sense not to approach me. The rain meant I could at least hide under an umbrella, but I knew she had spotted me. She stood at one end of the school entrance, and I stood at the other. It was as if we didn't know each other, though the pain in my chest was a constant reminder of just how deeply I knew her.

By Thursday's pickup, I was getting very good at ignoring her. And I had very mixed emotions about that. I wanted to feel relief that she wasn't speaking to me, but at the same time, I couldn't deny a small element of disappointment that she hadn't tried to get my attention. That wasn't the only thing that left me feeling a little sorry for her. As each day passed, she seemed to look a little more dishevelled. Her hair was unkempt, and I could swear she looked thinner too. Her skin had also deteriorated, from what I could see from a short distance away. She had broken out in spots, which she had once told me only happened when she was stressed.

I wondered about her homelife now. I couldn't quite piece together what had happened between her and Matt when I'd left their house that day. After we'd gotten caught. Though it was something I thought about often. Especially during a slow day at the office. A bit like today.

It was Friday, and I had somehow successfully made it to the weekend. I was already mentally preparing myself to see Lucy again at pickup when the ringing from my desk phone pierced the office space.

"Hi, Dani," the receptionist from downstairs said. "I have a Matthew Turlough here to see you."

Panic erupted from my core and ran through every inch of my body.

I couldn't understand why he was here. He had no business being at Skylar Marketing. Not anymore. Not after he'd told his father about me and Lucy, and that had resulted in Patrick Turlough bursting into one of our senior team meetings and successfully destroying my reputation:

Harry was leading the room through projects upcoming. I was still finding my focus a little rocky after what had happened a couple of days previous. Lucy had been texting me every day, and I found it exhausting screening her. I couldn't bear to speak to her after all the deceit.

"Dani?" Harry interrupted my thoughts. "Are you still with us?" he joked and a couple of the other senior team members chuckled.

I glanced around the table, not realising I'd been mentally absent. Heather watched me sadly from across the table. She was the only person who knew the turmoil I was dealing with. "Sorry, what were you saying?"

"I asked, how are we progressing with the Morgan pitch—"

Loud shouting from outside the conference room distracted him. The entire table's eyes were on the door as the shouting got louder. Harry was on his feet, moving to find out what the commotion was all about. He didn't make it to the door before Patrick Turlough, Matt's father, burst through. My heart rate spiked as his eyes homed in on me.

"You fucking home-wrecker!" He pointed in my direction, and everyone's eyes landed on me.

"Excuse me, Patrick." Harry stepped in front of him. "This is quite inappropriate."

"She destroyed my family," he shouted. "My son's family has been ripped apart because of that bitch."

His face was angry and red, and I could feel my own cheeks heating up out of embarrassment and shame. Harry looked to me for an explanation, but I was frozen in my chair. Everyone looked to me for some kind of response, forcing me out of the daze.

"Patrick, I—" I started, but my voice shaking made it difficult for me to string an apology together. "Can we speak in private?"

"Why? So your coworkers won't know you're sleeping with my daughter-in-law?" The gasps around the table caused me to shudder. I was speechless and reeling. "You're done." He pointed at me and turned to Harry. "Cancel the deal. I'm not working with a company that employs a lowlife like her."

"Get out," Harry shouted. Patrick looked shocked and equally offended. "You heard me, get the hell out of my company."

Patrick puffed out his chest and threw me one more glare before leaving. The conference room turned cold and tense. No one knew where to look.

Harry rubbed his forehead, seeming a little lost for words. "All right." He sighed. "That's enough for today. Everyone, get back to work." Chairs had never moved so fast across the floor as everyone disappeared from the room.

"Are you okay?" Heather rounded the table and placed a hand on my back.

"I can't believe that just happened." It came out as a whisper. I tried to gather up my things, but his voice stopped me.

"Not you," Harry said before he looked to Heather. "We need a minute."

She squeezed my shoulder one last time before she left the room as well. Harry moved to the door and closed it, filling the room with silence.

I sat back in my chair. My head was heavy, and I couldn't quite find the strength to make eye contact. I had never felt so humiliated in my life. People on the team who I rarely worked with now knew my deepest shame. The rumour mill would be churning out speculation by lunchtime. I couldn't cope with any more. Harry moved slowly toward his chair. He seemed stunned into silence, which I didn't even think was possible for a man like him.

He broke the silence what felt like an eternity later. "I don't need to know what happened, Dani," he said carefully but with compassion I didn't deserve. "Though, I can probably make a decent guess."

"I'm sorry." I met his confused eyes from across the table. "I've always prided myself on keeping my personal life separate from business." I could barely keep myself together. "I'm sorry this happened. I'm sorry I lost the account—"

"I don't care about that," he interrupted, seeming almost annoyed. "I care about you."

My chest tightened, and my eyes stung. "I really fucked up," I said hopelessly, never feeling quite as low in all my life.

He got up and took the chair next to me. For the first time, I didn't see him run from a crying person. He embraced me and listened with very little judgement. *He would never know what that meant to me.*

I truly thought that would be my, and Skylar Marketing's, last interaction with Turlough Enterprises. I was wrong.

"Send him up," I said down the phone before shifting back in my seat.

I knew I had a minute or two while Matt made his way upstairs. I couldn't believe he was here, and I wondered if maybe he was here to humiliate me some more. Perhaps Patrick's visit last week just hadn't been enough. Dread filled my insides, and it made me feel stodgy and nauseated. A knock at the door had me rising from my chair, but I stayed safely behind the desk, creating some barrier between us.

"Come in," I said in my bravest voice.

There was a lag—perhaps he also needed a moment—and the door opened cautiously. Matt entered the office seeming unsure of himself. He seemed rigid and on guard, looking around the space, taking it in. His awkwardness wasn't really a surprise, considering the last time he'd seen me.

"Hi," I said.

"Hey," he replied.

"What can I do for you?" I kept it polite, though it was undoubtably awkward.

"I...well, I called Harry yesterday to see about changing account managers." He threw me a tired shrug. "I figured that it would be easier to work with someone else." He cleared his throat. "But Harry told me my dad was here last week. Created quite a scene, I hear."

"Yep." I tightly folded my arms. "Thanks for filling him in, by the way," I added sarcastically, unable to hide the bite in my voice. "Now my entire workplace knows."

"Well, you ruined my relationship," he bit back, plunging the office back into silence.

"What are you doing here, Matt?" I said, unable to drown my emotions any longer. "Are you here to have another go at me? Because there's nothing you could say that would make me feel any worse about—"

"I'm not." He cut me off, looking ashamed. "That's not why I'm..." He sighed and rubbed his jaw tiredly. "I'm sorry." It was genuine, and it surprised me. "I want to talk."

He looked almost as terrible as Lucy. Heavy stubble, his tie barely done, and a crinkled jacket. It made me wonder what was going on between the two of them that could leave them both looking so beaten and exhausted.

"Okay," I said, trying to at least appear civil. "Do you want to sit?" I gestured to the armchair in front of my desk.

I would have offered the sofa, but memories of her on that seat circulated in my mind against my will. It made me feel like a wretched cheater again. He accepted and took a seat opposite me. He blew out a breath as he stared at the carpet, perhaps avoiding me.

"Why are you here, Matt?" I asked in the kindest tone I could muster. "Surely, you could have just met with Harry? He would have facilitated your request."

"I wanted to speak to you." His lost eyes locked with mine, no doubt searching for something that made me feel vulnerable. His eyes revealed his pain, and while it hurt to keep eye contact with someone I'd betrayed, it was the least I could do. "But now that I'm here...I can't really remember why." He looked heartbroken and small.

It made me feel awful. "I'm sorry, Matt," I said gingerly. He waited with an openness that prompted me to continue, "I thought you two were separating, I swear." He tensed. "That's what she told me. I would have never started anything with Lucy if I thought—"

"We were," he cut me off guiltily. "We *are* separated."

I digested the new information, feeling an ocean of emotions. My heart rate accelerated as I felt something resembling relief. She hadn't lied to me. She'd wanted to be with me. I couldn't believe his words. The relief was euphoric, but it was short-lived.

"And we were splitting up long before she ever met you."

That was a complete one-eighty on what he'd said last week. I was still reeling and trying to piece together the implications of this new information. Was he lying now or before? Had she been telling the truth? "I don't understand. Why did you accuse her of cheating?"

He showed what looked like regret. "I was in shock seeing you two. Together. Like that." His jaw squared, but he didn't seem, angry, more hurt. He squeezed his eyes shut. "When I asked Lucy if I could explore things with someone else, to make our relationship more open, I thought it was just me." He grimaced. "I didn't think Lucy wanted to see someone too. I thought it would just be me who...who liked someone else. Not Lucy."

I found myself judging him for the double standards. After everything he'd put her through, I struggled to give him compassion. There was feeling shocked by a situation, and there was being cruel and manipulative. I couldn't help but feel like Matt's reactions when he'd caught us were leaning more toward the latter. He'd wanted me to hate Lucy, and it had worked. It made me angry that I'd trusted him rather than listening to her.

I felt horribly guilty for not giving her an opportunity to tell her side of the story. Perhaps my silence revealed my lack of empathy.

"It wasn't fair, and I'm not proud of it. I was just so angry when I walked in on—" He was shaking his head. "In my own living room." His eyes collided with mine, and a guilt settled in my tummy, making me feel very uncomfortable. "Were you two just laughing at me?"

"No," I said without hesitation. "Matt, we never set out to hurt you. It wasn't about you at all. I don't even know what happened—" I cut myself off, getting tongue-tied and lost in my own confused feelings. "It all happened so fast and...one day, I don't know. I woke up and it was...I was in love with her." It came out before I could pull it back. I hadn't admitted that to anyone, not even myself, and I was shocked to have voiced it to Matt, of all people.

I thought he would be angry, but instead, he showed this strange, thoughtful look. "That's exactly what Lucy said."

That revelation caused my chest to tighten. She loved me. Something which should have brought me so much joy made my heart ache. I'd thought I was nothing more than an affair, a distraction from her failing relationship, but that wasn't true. We were something real. We could have been something real.

"It's true." I said, noting how empty my voice sounded. Full of regret. "But I'm still sorry."

"She moved out."

The three words caused my heart to skip a beat. I didn't know how to respond or if I should be happy. My insides felt like liquid, and my mind felt like it had been shoved under an ice-cold faucet.

He cracked a brief smile. "You two really aren't speaking, huh?"

"No," I returned solemnly, and he seemed to show a glimpse of regret. It made me curious as to why. "When did she move out?"

"Two days ago."

I got lost in my thoughts. From hopefulness to dread and guilt to shame and back around to feeling hopeful. Wishful thinking was propelling the stream of thoughts. Above all else, I had to give Lucy credit for following through. She'd left an unhappy relationship, just like she'd said she would. I just wished she'd done it sooner; perhaps we would still be together. While I was angry at Lucy for not telling Matt sooner, I should have still trusted that she wasn't lying to me about her feelings. I owed her an apology for that, at least.

"She loves you, you know," he said honestly, no malice. It was like he'd let go of his anger and hurt. Or perhaps he'd just let Lucy go. "And I know that because she's…" He trailed off desperately. "Broken." His voice dipped heartbreakingly. I pictured her from yesterday, looking like a shell of the woman I loved. "I thought it was because of us breaking up initially, but I realised who she was really missing."

His revelations were thrashing my insides around hard, and my heart was picking up the pace in what felt like hope. "Why are you telling me this?" I asked.

He didn't think long on it. "I just figured that I'd hurt her enough already." He sighed. "Maybe I could make things right again, you know." I knew what he was getting at without him having to say it. "I just want her to be happy. And if that can't be with me…" He threw me a challenging look. "Maybe you're not so bad."

I had to laugh. Weakly. It seemed to break the tension a little.

He seemed to find his confidence again. "But I really need a new account manager. So who is as good as you?"

"No one," I joked, and he chuckled. "But we can find you someone who's not so bad." He smiled at that. "But you have to promise, Turlough men will no longer be showing up here unannounced."

He smiled, showing a little bit of shame. "I can certainly promise that. I'm sorry on behalf of my father." He reached out.

It was a gesture of honour and perhaps surrender. I made sure that my grip mirrored his strength, and he shook my hand, offering me a solitary nod. As if allowing us to move on. We got to work on transferring his account to my best colleague. And while I wasn't necessarily ready to start anything up again with Lucy, it was at least comforting to know we had Matt's blessing.

I just had to get her to forgive me first.

Chapter Twenty-Three

Dani Raye

Later that day, after meeting with Matt, I arrived to collect Jonah from school. Lucy was in her usual spot. I didn't know what to say and kept my distance. Though, I didn't stand as far away this time. That was progress. I had no idea what to say to her. Part of me felt terrible for thinking the worst. She had been honest with me throughout all of this, and I should have believed her. I owed her that, but at the same time, I still couldn't shake the feeling of regret in all of it.

Our relationship never should have moved out of the realms of platonic until she'd left him. I had become a person I'd never wanted to be: the Maeve in a relationship. Someone who had caused me so much pain, and now, I was no better. I hated that my feelings for Lucy had made me into someone so heartless. My own feelings of worthlessness, coupled with how things had ended with Lucy, made approaching her all the more complicated.

Thankfully, I didn't have to wait long before the school bell rang, and Jonah came out the front doors alongside Ryan. They moved to where Lucy was standing, which wasn't really much of a surprise. I used to stand there too. Jonah and Ryan were talking excitedly while Lucy appeared to be following along but looking very hesitant. I dreaded the thought of having to be in her company, but I didn't exactly have a choice.

I moved toward them, and with each step, my mouth grew

drier. My hands shook, and I tried to keep the discomfort from my face. The children didn't need to know anything was wrong. I begged that Jonah would turn and see me and was annoyed Lucy hadn't sent him to me in the first place.

My emotions were flipping faster than a fish out of water.

"Jonah," I said from behind him. I remained far enough away that I didn't have to make chitchat.

He turned excitedly. "Hi, Mum, can I go to Ryan's new house?" Panic filled my insides. "He got this new game, and I really want to play it."

"It's a two-player," Ryan interjected. They both talked about a mile a minute, using every feature of the game to persuade me.

"Please," they sang in unison, making me feel even guiltier.

"Today isn't a good day," I said to Jonah.

"Please, Mum, please," he tried again, successfully softening my insides.

I glanced at Lucy. I didn't want to judge her, but I had to be honest, she looked dreadful. Her skin was dotted with acne while her dull eyes searched mine. She must have been really stressed. I could imagine why. Going through a separation, moving to a new house, being heartbroken…

I broke contact with her and met Jonah again. "Not today," I said firmly. "Come on." He didn't budge when I gestured to the car.

"Can I go over tomorrow?" he asked in what sounded like desperation.

"Tomorrow is Saturday."

"Please, Dani," Ryan added sweetly. It was beyond awkward, but I knew I couldn't keep them apart forever.

"Okay," I crumbled, resulting in the boys cheering and talking excitedly with each other. When I looked to Lucy, a small smile appeared on her face. It caused a rumble of frustration in me, prompting me to go off script. "Please go wait in the car, Jonah. I need to speak with Ryan's mum."

Lucy looked startled but gathered herself quickly. She

reached into her coat pocket and clicked the unlock button for the car. "I'll be there in a minute, Ryan."

We watched the boys move in the direction of the cars. The rain gently beat on our umbrellas, creating something to distract from the tension.

"Dani." Lucy's voice was soft and hurried. She took a step closer, and her pleading eyes collided with mine, twisting my insides in knots. "I'm so sorry. I never wanted—"

"No. Please, not here." I scanned the space around us, suddenly feeling vulnerable. As if everyone knew our dirty secret. "Our children are friends." I tried to keep my tone even, though it was difficult because of the pounding in my chest. "They want to spend time together, and I don't want to get in the way of that. I just want to make this as easy as possible on the boys, and I don't want them to be around a hostile environment. They didn't do anything wrong."

"I know," she whispered and took a step back, most likely feeding off my tense energy. "I don't want them to be anywhere near a hostile environment, either. That's why I moved out."

I couldn't work through my emotions. A part of me had wondered if what Matt had said about Lucy moving out was true, but hearing it from her solidified it. I couldn't process what I was thinking or feeling. My wires had been tripped, and I felt vacant.

"Dani, I know I hurt you," she said in the most heartbreaking voice I'd ever heard. "And I know you probably never want to speak to me again but…" Her watery eyes met mine, and it gave me the kick-start I needed.

"We're not doing this here," I said, scanning the parking lot in a frenzy to make sure no one was looking. I'd already been humiliated at work; I wouldn't be humiliated at Jonah's school too. "You can't just bring that stuff up at school pickup, okay?" It was harsh and borderline cruel. I regretted it after seeing the way she had to swallow the hurt.

"I'm sorry. You're right," she said in a monotone voice I barely recognised. "Drop Jonah around tomorrow, anytime after eleven." Her voice cracked, though I could tell she was trying so hard to keep it together.

It made me feel even worse. "Okay." I hated seeing her this distraught and fragile. Seeing her so upset did things to me that I didn't dare unpack. Especially not at Jonah's school.

"I'll text you the address," she said almost mechanically. She turned away from me and was gone.

I dragged my feet, feeling like I'd just kicked someone who was already down. It was just too difficult to be in her presence without cracking.

We were driving for a little bit before Jonah perked up from beside me. "I can't wait to see Ryan's mum's house," he said excitedly, but his voice dropped. "He has two houses just like me."

"His mummy and daddy broke up, huh?"

He nodded but didn't say anything.

"Are you okay?" I asked carefully and watched his reaction. I thought perhaps it might have brought up some PTSD. Perhaps seeing his friend's family split had brought up painful memories of our separation. Catriona had always worried that Jonah could need therapy coming from a family of divorce.

He replied too quickly to be lying. "No."

It caused my shoulders to relax. "Is Ryan okay?" I dug a little deeper, even though I knew I should have stayed out of it.

"He was a little sad last week. But he said that his new house is really cool. And there's a Dominos at the bottom of his street. How cool is that? Lucy is letting him paint his room whatever colour he wants."

"That's good."

"Yeah, it is. Hey, do you think you will get married again? Like Mum and Maeve?"

I thought for a moment, trying to figure out where his mind was jumping to. I gave up and decided to answer truthfully. "Maybe. If the right woman came along."

"You should marry Lucy."

BEFORE SHE WAS MINE

That threw me for a loop. "Why?"

"Because me and Ryan would be brothers."

I laughed at his logic but felt the need to correct his line of thinking on the prospects of marriage. It was too serious a commitment to think of as fleeting. "That would be fun, but you know, you can't just get married to anyone. It's a big deal, and you should only get married to someone who makes you really, really happy."

"You're always really happy when you're around Lucy," he said, revealing just how observant he was. It caused my chest to ache when I remembered just how happy Lucy made me. "And she's really nice and pretty. I think she would be a nice wife."

Though it was completely crazy to even be having this conversation, Jonah had made some valid points. Though he didn't stay on the topic for long, I couldn't say the same for myself.

Chapter Twenty-Four

Dani Raye

The next day, I was on my way to pick up Jonah from his playdate. I'd dropped him off a few hours ago, and though Lucy had invited me inside, I'd politely declined.

I'd regretted that decision all day.

It wasn't like I had done anything interesting. In fact, an afternoon with Lucy and the boys didn't sound so bad. It sounded pretty great, actually.

After meeting with Matt yesterday and talking to Lucy, I had felt my icy exterior thaw. I was finding it incredibly difficult to come up with a reason why we shouldn't be together. There was nothing standing in our way. The hurt and heartache I'd been feeling these last two weeks were just a reminder of my feelings for her. And the knowledge that Lucy had been honest with me throughout all of the confusion made me feel like I should have been the one to apologise. I should have given her the benefit of the doubt. I'd treated her like a pariah, and it wasn't fair.

Her separation from Matt had eased my conscience. Even though I wasn't okay with how it had started between us and I didn't like the person I'd become, it was only to my own detriment to hold it over us forever.

That realisation provided me with some compassion for Maeve.

I felt like I understood her a little better, and perhaps, it could lead me to forgive her—and myself—and move on. I had always thought I'd forgiven Catriona, mainly because we were so amicable with each other, but deep down, I realised I hadn't. The anger I used to feel toward Maeve, and her presence in Catriona and Jonah's life, had faded because I knew what it was like to be in that situation. Perhaps they had tried as hard as we had to stay platonic, but when the connection was that strong, it was impossible.

Sometimes, we didn't get to choose who we fell in love with. I knew that to be true with Lucy, and my gut feeling was telling me that it was likely the same for Catriona and Maeve.

I would never be proud of how Lucy and I had started, but the bottom line was, I missed the way she made me feel. If she forgave me for not trusting her, maybe we could find a way to start again.

I was too wound up to sit at home with my guilt and regrets. I wasn't supposed to be collecting him until six, but that felt like an impossible feat at four. I gripped the steering wheel as I drove to Stranmillis. When I'd left her house this morning, I had been in too much of a panic frenzy from being around her to really take in their new home. It was terrace house, two-up, two-down, in a busy neighbourhood. I hadn't been inside yet, but I could tell it was a step down from her previous middle-class area. Stranmillis was typically regarded as the student area, but there were some other children playing in the street.

The exterior wasn't nearly as glamourous as her home with Matt, but I still couldn't help but admire it. She'd really done it. She'd plucked up the courage to leave a relationship of safety and go out on her own in search of the unknown. To find happiness. It left a warmth in my chest as I remembered the Lucy I'd met for the first time all those months ago in the principal's office. I'd never thought that woman would be here now.

I got out of the car and made the walk to the front door while anxiously cupping the plant. I'd bought her a new one at the supermarket after leaving her house this morning. I had wandered around the supermarket for an hour, just trying to find something. It was the polite thing to do, though now I fretted that it was an overstep, especially after how abrupt I had been with her yesterday at school. I had been trying to set boundaries, and today, I was buying her a new-home gift. And just like that, I was sent into a spiral of overthinking. It must have seemed like I was sending mixed messages; what was she supposed to think?

"Hey." She opened the front door. I was standing halfway up the path, about to turn back to the car to leave off the plant when she'd caught me. "What are you doing?" She tilted her head in the cute way that she did.

"I…was just…" I moved closer. "I got you this." I practically threw the pot at her and hated myself for being so clumsy.

"Thank you. It's lovely," she said, admiring it, but her brows knitted together. She didn't look like she liked it.

Regret set in, and I was doubting the gift all over again. It was basic. I should have done better. "It's silly."

She must have heard the edge of doubt in my voice. "No, I really like it, it's just…" She bit her lip nervously. "I wasn't expecting you until later."

"Shit, I'm sorry." I took a step back. "I'll come back."

"No." She reached forward and touched my arm. I stared at her hand, and she let go. As if I was fire. She was fretting now, and I knew it was my fault. I wished I didn't feel so awkward. I came here wanting to make things right, and everything I was doing just seemed to be putting her more on edge. "No, I mean, it's great that you're here. Come in." She gestured for me to follow her inside, and this time, I accepted.

I moved into the narrow hallway. It had dated carpet, and the staircase looked old and creaky. But the new paint cans by the door revealed vibrant greens and other colours. I knew it wouldn't be long until Lucy put her stamp on this place. That gave me an excited flutter in my stomach.

"It's a bit of a disaster right now," she said anxiously. "I just moved in, so we're still unpacking." She scanned the place, looking a little in doubt.

"It's really great." I hoped she heard the genuineness.

"Come on through." I followed her to the kitchen at the back of the house. She made incessant chitchat as we walked. It was cute because I knew it was coming from a place of nervousness. "I ordered pizza not long ago, so that's who I thought was at the door. You're much better, though," she said candidly, and panic seemed to set in, and she spun to face me. "I'm sorry, I shouldn't have said that."

"It's okay." Just looking at her did things to me. It was overwhelming to the point where I had to look elsewhere.

"Jonah was so excited about the pizza." She spoke up again. "He will be devastated if you leave before it gets here." I nodded along, already accepting that he would be staying for dinner. I was early, after all. "You see, we ordered pizza with this barbeque base—"

I could feel my face scrunching up, and it caused her to giggle softly. It took me by surprise, and she even tried to hide it. She covered her mouth, but she couldn't shield the shaking of her shoulders as she laughed. She looked adorable, and it made my heart race. "What?"

"It's nothing. It's just…" She grinned. "Jonah pulled that exact same face." I was rolling my eyes as she went on. "He said he never had it before."

"Because it sounds bloody terrible."

"Have you ever tried it?"

"Well, no, but—"

"Then how do you know?" she asked, still laughing.

I didn't have a response, and the longer I stayed silent, the more her face started to fall again. It went from playfulness to a tense expression, the way it had been before she'd started giggling. She was back to doubting herself. I already missed her more relaxed energy. "I guess I'll just have to stay for some of this barbeque pizza."

"That would be…nice." The intensity in her eyes returned, and it left me breathless.

I glanced around the kitchen, anything to bring whatever was brewing between us to a simmer. "Is that your garage?" I pointed out the back window.

"Yeah, it was important for me to get one. I need somewhere to work." She shrugged before tilting her head. "Online sales have been really great this week. I'm really considering looking into a studio."

"Really?"

"Yeah, I think it might be kinda cool to have my own place. That way, people could come collect their orders from there rather than the house. Or who knows? Maybe I'll have enough pieces that people can come in off the street and shop." Her confidence in her own work was like a breath of fresh air, and I loved watching it.

"That's great." I had to redirect attention from those eyes before I did something silly like kiss her. "You have a nice garden." I motioned out the window. I was being generous, as it looked like it hadn't been taken care of in a while.

"Thanks, my dad is coming by tomorrow to get rid of the weeds. And Mum is going to help me paint the living room." She moved back so I could see the box-sized space to the left of the kitchen. It was small, with just a little two-seater couch in the corner, surrounded by more boxes. But I couldn't deny just how happy she looked here. "It's all a work in progress."

"Well, if you need any help..." I trailed off. "I can put up some pictures or curtains." She cocked a brow. "I'm actually pretty good with a hammer."

"I bet," she said in a sultry tone that sent a rush from my tummy downward. She was quick to correct herself, "I mean, because you have pictures. On the walls. In your house." It came out sporadically, and I couldn't hold back the awkward laughter.

"Good save."

"You could say I nailed it." She grinned smugly.

A knock at the door led her to excuse herself to get the pizza. When she returned, I helped pour glasses of juice for the four of us and get plates set up. The boys came stampeding down the stairs as soon as they heard pizza had arrived.

"You have to try the barbeque," Ryan said to Jonah, putting a slice on his plate.

Jonah looked to me for reassurance. "I'll try some too," I said as a way of encouraging him.

"There's plain pizza if you don't like it, Jonah," Lucy said as he looked at her from his seated position. She took the seat next to him and soothingly rubbed his back. "It's not for everyone."

I'd always loved watching her interact with Jonah. She had such kindness, and I knew Jonah felt comfortable around her. After all, he'd practically married me off to her yesterday in the car. Jonah took a tiny bite and scrunched up his face in anticipation of hating it. Lucy caught my eye and winked, reminding me once again that Jonah was a mini-me. The table watched until he had swallowed.

"Not bad," he said, resulting in Ryan cheering in success.

Jonah took another bite and seemed to enjoy it even more the second time. He ended up eating three slices of barbeque and none of the plain pizza. It was clear that we now had a new favourite pizza order in our house.

We sat chatting around the table for a little while after everyone had finished. Over the last few months, we'd had lunch or snacks quite a few times, so we had gotten quite comfortable being in each other's company. I'd forgotten how much I enjoyed it and just how much I'd missed it during the last two weeks. The boys went back upstairs again to finish their PlayStation game while I helped Lucy clean up.

"Well, what did you think of the pizza?" she asked, even though she'd caught me going back for a second slice.

"It was okay." I shrugged, and she shook her head, amused.

She bumped her hip with mine before passing me another plate to dry. I took it off her and dried it as we stood shoulder to shoulder, washing up. It was relaxed and domesticated. I thought for sure we would have a thousand things to say to make things right, yet it turned out that returning to our normal selves was all it took.

"Thanks for dinner," I said as the air stilled around us.

"Anytime. Ryan loves having Jonah here. I do too." She turned and looked at me for a moment. "I like having you here too." I didn't miss the way her tone dropped.

I held her gaze and realised just how close we were. Her eyes desperately looked from my eyes to my lips and back up again. It was pure lust, and it caused my stomach muscles to jerk. Her lips looked soft and delicate, just like I remembered, and I had to turn my head away just to stop myself from leaning in. Lucy went back to scrubbing the next plate, but I could hear her heavy breathing, revealing she was just as worked up as I was. But there was something I had to say before I could allow myself to get wrapped up.

"I saw Matt yesterday." I launched straight in, having very little concern for small talk.

Her hands stilled in the soapy water. "Where?"

"He came by my office."

She sighed in frustration as her jaw tightened. "I'm so sorry, Dani. I will talk to him and get him to stop harassing you—"

"Well, actually...he came by to apologise." That seemed to surprise her into some kind of paralysis as her hands stopped moving again. "He said some things."

"What things?" She turned to me again, revealing those piercing eyes that made me breathless every time.

"I'm sorry." She frowned, and a crushing force surrounded my lungs as I remembered just how horrible I'd been to her. "For not trusting you. For believing him over you." Her eyes softened, and she looked a combination of touched and hurt. It pained me to see it. "I'm sorry for cutting you out like that." I touched her forehead lightly, sweeping the fringe to the side. Her eyes closed as if savouring the intimate contact. Without meaning to, I cupped her cheek.

Her breath hitched, and she sucked in her bottom lip.

"Don't," she said in an almost pained voice. Her eyes opened again as I removed my hand. "Not if you don't mean it."

Before I could stop myself, I leaned in and pressed my lips lightly to hers. My body tingled. Her kiss revealed a longing, but it remained modest. I could still taste the barbeque on her lips when I pulled back. "I love you."

Her breathing sped up rapidly. "I love you too," she whispered before her lips collided with mine.

Having her this close again proved to be the only thing that would ease the pain I'd been carrying around for weeks. It was her. Her breathless moans surrounded me as she pulled me closer. My head was swimming while I latched on to her back, waist, and hips. She walked me backward until my back collided with the fridge. A rush erupted, and I couldn't help the gasp that left me. Lucy's arousal was present in the frantic movements of her hands. They dipped below the hem of my shirt and moved up my stomach.

She broke away from my lips and kissed my neck between words. "I. *Really.* Want. You." Her voice was husky and full of need. "But what about the boys?"

"Shit." I let out a breathless laugh. "I forgot we had kids."

"Is that how good I am?" she said before stealing another kiss.

"Keep kissing me like that and…" I didn't need to finish the sentence because her face flushed with undiluted desire.

I kissed her again, and this time, there was reduced levels of raw passion, but that did nothing to detract from its strength. Instead, it was more intimate. She pulled back and rested her forehead against mine. The sweetest and most contented sigh left her, and it resulted in me smiling dopily. She rested her hands on my shoulders.

"What are you doing tomorrow?" I asked her tentatively.

"Nothing."

"Catriona has Jonah. Do you think Matt could take Ryan?"

"If he can't, my parents will." She pressed against me

seductively, perhaps already preempting where this was going. "Why?"

"Do you want to go out with me?"

"Like a date?"

"Are we twelve?" I said, rolling my eyes, and she giggled against my lips. "Yes, like a fucking date."

"Okay." She kissed me before pulling back with raised brows. "But you should know, I don't have sex on the first date."

"That's funny because I seemed to remember at Basement, you would have come back to my place in a heartbeat."

"Well, that's because we were dancing. Did I not tell you dancing makes me slutty?"

"Did I forget to mention our date is at a dance club?" I teased, and her lips were on mine before I could say anymore.

Chapter Twenty-Five

Dani Raye

I arrived at Catriona's a little earlier than expected. I didn't want to be late for my first real date with Lucy. However, because I was going straight to meet Lucy afterward, I was already dressed to impress.

Catriona opened the door, and her eyes expanded, taking me in. They quickly shifted to Jonah. "Hey, baby." She kissed his forehead. "Emily is in the kitchen with Maeve."

Jonah's expression grew excitedly, and he disappeared into the house. Most likely to see Maeve's niece. They were around the same age, and he always had a great time when Emily came to visit.

"Is Emily staying overnight?" I asked.

"Yeah, we have tickets for the ice hockey game later." She glanced back over her shoulder as if to make sure no one was listening. "I haven't told Jonah yet."

"He's going to love that."

Her eyes proceeded to travel down the length of me fleetingly. I didn't think I was wearing anything too outrageous to warrant this kind of attention from my ex-wife, but in hindsight, I usually dropped Jonah off in a pair of old jeans and a haggard hoodie. My tight, low-cut blouse did reveal a little more skin than usual. It was probably the heeled boots adding to the ensemble, giving my legs the extra boost of length and a toned appearance. I'd felt good when I left the house, but her nod of approval was also giving my confidence a boost. I just hoped Lucy would approve.

"Where are you going tonight?" Her tone revealed her intrigue.

I thought about downplaying it, but I was too excited to hide it. "I have a date."

"You move on quick," she said in surprise. I guess it did seem like a fast turnaround, considering the last time she saw me, I was sobbing over my breakup with Lucy. "With who?"

"Actually, with Lucy." I couldn't contain my smile. It seemed to relax her, though distrust peppered her brow. "It's okay," I added. "She and Matt are separated. Lucy even moved out so..." I trailed off, expecting to have to explain my rationale more.

"That's great, Dani." Her eyes softened before she glanced back inside the house. "Does Jonah know?"

"He knows something's going on." I rolled my eyes, and Catriona cocked her head, showing her curiosity. "There's no hiding anything from him."

Yesterday at Lucy's house, we hadn't realised that the boys had come downstairs and were eavesdropping in the hall while we were flirting. It was a fairly innocent conversation, but when I got into the car again, Jonah had started the inquisition. Apparently, Ryan was all over Lucy as well. Though we'd agreed to wait to tell the children until things were a little more serious, Jonah couldn't have been more supportive. He really was incredibly fond of Lucy.

Ryan might have needed a little more reassurance, given that his parents had just separated, but that was expected. It was precisely why we would be taking things slow. When the time was right, we would officially come out to the kids, though I got the feeling they already knew more than they were letting on.

"He's so nosy," Catriona teased, but something softer appeared on her face. "You look happy, D. And that makes me happy."

"Thanks, Catriona. I know you weren't thrilled about me and Lucy."

"Not at first but it's obvious you love her." She sighed in exasperation "And it's clear she loves you too." It was genuine, and that felt good. "Maybe you could even take her to the wedding."

I half expected her to be joking, but she looked serious. "Don't you think that would be weird?"

"The fact that you're coming to my wedding at all is already a huge deal. Especially for Jonah," she said in what sounded like appreciation. Though we'd never talked about it explicitly when I'd agreed to go to her and Maeve's wedding, she was right in thinking the only reason I was attending was for Jonah's sake. "You should bring the woman who makes you happy."

"Thanks, Catriona."

She raised her shoulders, perhaps to hide her blush. "Now, go see your girl." She waved me off. "Don't waste that outfit on me."

❖

An excited pit kept expanding in my tummy as I drove to Lucy's house. I'd never been quite so nervous to see her before. I wondered what she would say or think when she saw me. I'd never been this dressed up for her before. I imagined what she might be wearing, and well, that took my mind into the gutter. Especially because I started to fantasise about what she would be wearing underneath her clothes.

After being unable to think of anything else for most of the drive, by the time I was getting out of the car, my skinny jeans felt tighter than ever. I wished I could be cool. It wasn't like Lucy and I hadn't already slept together. But the air felt different tonight. It would be our first time in public together where it didn't matter who saw us.

The door swung open before I had a chance to knock. I was surprised to be greeted by Denise. Her hair was decorated in a colourful scarf, with several beads hanging around her neck. Her smile enlarged when she glanced down my front and back up again. "Hey, Dani, you look hot," she said with a wink.

"Thanks," I muttered awkwardly as she let me in past her.

"Seriously, you look…" She shook her head as if lost for words but seemed to check herself. "Great. But don't tell Lucy I was flirting with her date." She laughed, and I found myself taken aback that Lucy had told her parents about us.

"I won't say a word."

"Hey, did I ever tell you about the time I was a lesbian?" Denise started as she led me into the kitchen. Lucy's dad was sipping a cup of tea at the kitchen table. His clothes had grass stains up and down them, and he looked exhausted, but from the glimpse I had in the garden, I could see a world of difference in the backyard.

"Denise, she doesn't want to hear about the time you snogged a woman," he interjected. "We were all a little gay in the eighties." I couldn't contain my laughter as the two started bickering.

"I've slept with more women than you have."

"That's because I only had eyes for you," he said sweetly.

Footsteps came down the stairs, simmering the bickering. While I was expecting Lucy, it was Ryan who had appeared. He paid close attention to my outfit, and a mischievous grin appeared on his face. "Hi, Dani."

"Hi, Ryan," I replied in the same playful tone. "What are you up to?"

"Helping Mummy get ready."

"Does she look nice?" Denise asked, and Ryan nodded bashfully.

"Are you doing anything fun tomorrow?" I asked him. It was a bank holiday tomorrow, and the schools were closed. I already knew that Lucy was planning on taking him bowling, but I wanted to hear how excited he was.

"We're going bowling. Can you and Jonah come too?"

"I'm sorry, Ryan. Jonah is with his other mum tomorrow."

"Oh." He looked disappointed for a moment. "That's okay. Do you want to come?"

I was surprised he extended the invite to me. It was thoughtful, and I couldn't contain my smile. He waited for my answer as I glanced toward Denise, who shared a proud look with her husband. "I'd love to."

"Good, because Mum is really bad at bowling. She needs all the help she can get."

Lucy's dad chuckled to himself before climbing from his seat. "Those weeds aren't gonna collect themselves," he said. "Ryan, can you help me?" Ryan followed his grandfather out back.

There was a bang from above.

Loud steps, most likely a pair of heels, travelled across the ceiling before they descended the staircase. "Mum, please don't answer the door to Dani," Lucy said, still coming down. "I don't want you embarrassing me when I'm nervous enough as it is. This dress is so fucking tight, I don't know what I—" She rounded the stairs and saw me standing in the kitchen. "Shit."

I couldn't tear my eyes away from her outfit. Her bare, toned legs caused my mouth to grow dry. The dress was stunningly gorgeous and hugged her body. Her strappy heels clicked along the carpet as she moved sheepishly into the kitchen. The natural light in the kitchen radiated off her, and her skin looked bright and clear again. Her hair was curled in light waves with her fringe perfectly framing her face.

"Hi," I just about croaked out. "You look beautiful," I said, causing a crimson blush to flush her cheeks.

"You too." She practically gulped and turned her attention to Denise. "We're going to go, okay?" She was in a rush to get me out of her parents' company, or perhaps she just wanted me alone. "Bedtime is at eight," she said over her shoulder to Denise, who was following us to the front door.

"I know, I know."

"And don't let Ryan eat too much sweets. And not too much time on the PlayStation," Lucy continued once we had stepped outside into the evening light.

"Got it," Denise said from the doorway. "You two have fun now." Her eyes fell on me cheekily. "And don't worry, we brought an overnight bag. Just in case you don't bring her home tonight."

I was speechless at the insinuation, and Lucy was completely mortified. "Mum!"

"Well, honey, come on. Look at her," Denise said.

"You're so embarrassing," Lucy mumbled, and I had to laugh.

Denise closed the door as Lucy breathed out in what appeared to be humiliation. I took her hand, revelling in how good it felt to have her hand in mine. "Your mum is anything but subtle."

"I can't believe her nerve."

"I can't believe you told her about us."

"Of course," she said like it was a no-brainer. "She was actually really happy for me. Besides, I think my mum has a weird crush on you."

"It's kind of obvious," I joked as we got in my car. "But at least she's resourceful."

Lucy side-eyed me from the passenger seat. I wrapped my hand around the back of her head and pulled her lips toward mine in a searing kiss. "Because there's no way I'm letting you go home alone tonight," I whispered and watched her eyes expand excitedly as a smile played on her lips. I drove off and enjoyed what would most definitely not be my last date with Lucy Matthews.

Finally, she was mine.

About the Author

Emma L McGeown is an Irish writer who lives in Northern Ireland with her wife, daughter, and dog. Previous work includes Golden Crown Literary Society Debut Finalist *Aurora* and *Sugar Girl*.

Books Available From Bold Strokes Books

Before She Was Mine by Emma L McGeown. When Dani and Lucy are thrust together to sort out their children's playground squabble, sparks fly, leaving both of them willing to risk it all for each other. (978-1-63679-315-3)

Chasing Cypress by Ana Hartnett Reichardt. Maggie Hyde wants to find a partner to settle down with and help her run the family farm, but instead she ends up chasing Cypress. Olivia Cypress. (978-1-63679-323-8)

Dark Truths by Sandra Barett. When Jade's ex-girlfriend and vampire maker barges back into her life, can Jade satisfy her ex's demands, keep Beth safe, and keep everyone's secrets…secret? (978-1-63679-369-6)

Desires Unleashed by Renee Roman. Kell Murphy and Taylor Simpson didn't go looking for love, but as they explore their desires unleashed, their hearts lead them on an unexpected journey. (978-1-63679-327-6)

Here For You by D. Jackson Leigh. A horse trainer must make a difficult business decision that could save her father's ranch from foreclosure but destroy her chance to win the heart of a feisty barrel racer vying for a spot in the National Rodeo Finals. (978-1-63679-299-6)

Maybe, Probably by Amanda Radley. Set against the backdrop of a viral pandemic, Gina and Eleanor are about to discover that loving another person is complicated when you're desperately searching for yourself. (978-1-63679-284-2)

The One by C.A. Popovich. Jody Acosta doesn't know what makes her more furious, that the wealthy Bergeron family refuses to be held accountable for her father's wrongful death, or that she can't ignore her knee-weakening attraction to Nicole Bergeron. (978-1-63679-318-4)

Tides of Love by Kimberly Cooper Griffin. Falling in love is the last thing on either of their minds, but when Mikayla and Gem meet, sparks of possibility begin to shine, revealing a future neither expected. (978-1-63679-319-1)

Catch by Kris Bryant. Convincing the wife of the star quarterback to walk away from her family was never in offensive coordinator Sutton McCoy's game plan. But standing on the sidelines when a second chance at true love comes her way proves all but impossible. (978-1-63679-276-7)

Hearts in the Wind by MJ Williamz. Beth and Evelyn seem destined to remain mortal enemies but are about to discover that in matters of the heart, sometimes you must cast your fortunes to the wind. (978-1-63679-288-0)

Hero Complex by Jesse J. Thoma. Bronte, Athena, and their unlikely friends must work together to defeat Bronte's archnemesis. The fate of love, humanity, and the world might depend on it. No pressure. (978-1-63679-280-4)

Hotel Fantasy by Piper Jordan. Molly Taylor has a fantasy in mind that only Lexi can fulfill. However, convincing her to participate could prove challenging. (978-1-63679-207-1)

Last New Beginning by Krystina Rivers. Can commercial broker Skye Kohl and contractor Bailey Kaczmarek overcome their pride and work together while the tension between them boils over into a love that could soothe both of their hearts? (978-1-63679-261-3)

Love and Lattes by Karis Walsh. Cat café owner Bonnie and wedding planner Taryn join forces to get rescue cats into forever homes— discovering their own forever along the way. (978-1-63679-290-3)

Repatriate by Jaime Maddox. Ally Hamilton's new job as a home health aide takes an unexpected twist when she discovers a fortune in stolen artwork and must repatriate the masterpieces and avoid the wrath of the violent man who stole them. (978-1-63679-303-0)

The Hues of Me and You by Morgan Lee Miller. Arlette Adair and Brooke Dawson almost fell in love in college. Years later, they unexpectedly run into each other and come face-to-face with their unresolved past. (978-1-63679-229-3)